# CASSANDRA'S WAR

DAVID BRUNS

CHRIS POURTEAU

SEVERN RIVER PUBLISHING

# ALSO BY BRUNS AND POURTEAU

**The SynCorp Saga**

The Lazarus Protocol

Cassandra's War

Hostile Takeover

Valhalla Station

Masada's Gate

Serpent's Fury

Never miss a new release! Sign up to receive exclusive updates from authors Bruns and Pourteau!

severnriverbooks.com/series/the-syncorp-saga

*For our children*
*Alex, Byron, and Cate*

# 1

## ANTHONY TAULKE • ADX FLORENCE, COLORADO

Packed snow crunched under Anthony Taulke's prison-issued work boots.

*Forty-eight, forty-nine, fifty ... turn.*

The repetition appealed to his engineer's brain. Measuring the dimensions of his captivity brought an ironic sense of comfort to a man who controlled nothing about his present life.

He faced due east, eighteen feet of shining steel fencing mere inches from the shoulder of his orange prison jumpsuit. Rolls of close-packed, serrated razor wire gleamed on the fence top above him. The prison yard was blanketed with knee-high, pristine snow. Anthony stepped forward.

*One, two, three...*

This was his twenty-sixth circuit today. He had no way to tell time accurately—the guards had deactivated his "rich man's implant" and laughed when he'd asked for a set of data glasses.

But he had the sun. And he had his feet.

*Forty-eight, forty-nine, fifty ... turn.*

Anthony faced due north and continued his pacing.

By his reckoning, it was around two p.m. on his seventy-fourth day of incarceration in ADX Florence, the Alcatraz of the Rockies. His prison was famous, like its richest inmate. His incarceration had proven a popular story on the YourVoice network for days until displaced by the latest weather disaster.

An aircar swept through the secure traffic corridor in the western sky. He watched it disappear behind the concrete bulk of the massive prison complex. Corporate model, seven-seater Cadillac, probably had a built-in bar and buttery-soft leather seats. He closed his eyes, imagining himself inside the Cadillac wearing the latest fashion instead of this dirty jumpsuit. Sipping a drink while scanning the newsfeeds on his retinal display.

Seventy-four days. Long enough for Teller to get reelected President of the United States. Anthony had seen that bit of news on the sole WorldNet screen in the cafeteria. Somehow, the bastard had even silenced the clamor of UN voices calling for his head. Prosecuted as a war criminal? Hell, they hadn't even bothered to censure Teller. And here Anthony was, paying Teller's check for him, hour after agonizing hour.

He focused on the subtle crunch-squeak of his soles in the snow.

The UN had bigger problems to solve, more immediate problems. Anthony had caught snippets of climate news from the WorldNet during meals. Beijing was one giant sand dune, millions of its residents buried alive. A section of the Mexican peninsula had been scalped by a hurricane, tens of thousands missing. The Congo was flooding. Paris was like a greenhouse, but Scotland was having its worst winter in recorded history as bomb cyclones hammered the Highlands.

No rhyme, no reason—just freakish, extreme weather events that had some commentators proselytizing like street corner evangelists, claiming Mother Earth was settling the score for centuries of abuse at the hands of mankind.

Yet in the United States, all was calm. Normal, even moderate weather prevailed in the lower forty-eight. Whoever was behind the weather changes—and it was a someone, the same someone who'd stolen Viktor Erkennen's cryptokey from his lunar laboratory—their plan was obviously to isolate the United States from the United Nations. Whoever it was knew about politics and how to manage power dynamics. They knew if they just applied enough pressure, the UN collective would fracture into a world of separate nations, all fighting amongst themselves, each striving to protect its own people.

A world in political chaos. Who would benefit from that?

"Inmate!" The guard's flat bark echoed in the prison yard. "Time's up."

Anthony gazed toward the sun like a lover. Another twenty-three hours before he could be with her again.

"Inmate! Now."

He stamped his feet on the doorstep and walked inside. The heavy steel door slammed behind him as the guard muttered his status into his head-set. After an hour in the fresh air, the smell of the corridor was stale and industrial: part hospital, part machine shop. He stayed the regulation three paces ahead of the guard as he walked to his cell. Metal tumblers slid aside. Once Anthony was inside, the magnetic lock engaged with a loud *shuck*.

How he missed his penthouse apartment in downtown San Francisco with its sweeping view of the Pacific and the inner calm it brought him. Here, the view was more ... utilitarian. A narrow bed, steel toilet, sink, and small space of painted gray floor. If he stretched his arms, Anthony could almost touch the walls on either side of the cell.

Thinking about it only made it worse. Routine was the friend who helped him pass the time. He dropped to the floor for his daily push-ups.

*One, two, three...*

Finally, his arms quivering, Anthony stood and stripped off his jump-suit. The water in the sink was frigid. He soaked a scrap of washcloth and scrubbed his skin, starting at the top of his body. He shivered with cold, but at least it was a genuine feeling. Somewhere along the way, simply washing his skin had become an emotional experience all its own.

*Clack-clack.*

Two raps of a nightstick, the signal the guards used to warn him the door was about to open. Anthony hastily stood with his back against the far wall of the cell, hands in the open.

"For God's sake, put on your clothes," the guard said. "No one wants to see that."

Anthony pulled his jumpsuit on, his mind racing. Why was the guard here? It wasn't dinnertime yet. By his count, the return walk to the cell, push-ups, and a sponge bath should only take him halfway to dinner. This was unexpected, bordering on exciting.

"Approach and present," the guard said.

Anthony shuffled forward, his forearms extended. The man clapped handcuffs on him, then stepped aside.

Anthony exited the cell. A female guard he hadn't met before waited. The woman had sharp eyes and thick, linebacker shoulders. Her nightstick was out.

"Inmate," she said, pointing her baton to the left. "Come with me."

Anthony complied, his pulse hammering. He'd never gone left before. From the day he'd arrived in the facility, he'd only ever entered and exited his cell from the corridor to the right. He felt a tiny thrill of excitement at the change, followed by a sense of self-pity at how his life had become so excruciatingly boring that simply turning left instead of right was enough to pique his interest.

"Straight," she said at the first intersection.

The gray paint of the concrete floor dead-ended at a steel door. The woman flashed a badge and the magnetic lock clicked.

"Open it," she ordered.

On the other side of the door, the hallway was carpeted. That reminder of luxury came unexpectedly, and Anthony had to fight the impulse to kneel down and stroke the softness.

"Straight."

Where was she taking him, and why? Counting his steps helped calm his nerves.

*One, two, three…*

They passed doors with blue and white labels reading Interview Room followed by a number. The guard told him to stop at the fourth door.

"You got thirty minutes, inmate. Make 'em count."

Anthony put his hand on the doorknob—a normal, round, metal doorknob!—and turned.

A woman stood inside the room, her back to him. Over her shoulder, she said, "Surveillance is off, correct? This is a private meeting between Mr. Taulke and his lawyer."

The guard nodded. "Yes, ma'am. Per orders." She prodded Anthony forward, then closed the door, leaving them alone.

Anthony gasped as his memory of the woman's voice clicked.

"Adriana?"

The head of the Rabh Conglomerate, the largest money management firm in the world, turned to face him. Anthony drank in the sight of a friendly face, the first tangible link to his old life he'd seen for seventy-four days.

"Anthony, so good to see you again," she said. She kissed his shocked face on both cheeks. "I'm getting you out of here."

Anthony blinked. "Wha...?" was all he managed to say.

Adriana peered into his eyes. "What have they done to you? Drugs?"

He shook his head slowly like a man drunk. He'd never realized Adriana's eyes were such a rich, deep brown before, a shade of dark caramel with little gold flecks...

She drew a hand back and slapped Anthony's cheek. Hard. The sharp sting filled his cheek with heat. "Ow!"

Adriana used her nails to dig into the loose material on the front of his jumpsuit. "Wake the fuck up, Anthony. I'm here to get you out, but you have to work with me."

"We're short on time, Ms. Rabh," said a voice behind her.

A man dressed in a business suit stepped forward. He placed a briefcase on the table in the center of the room and snapped it open.

"Anthony, meet Justin." Adriana busied herself with the contents of the case.

"Who?"

"Don't file his name away in long-term memory. He's you, from now on," Adriana replied. "He came in as your lawyer, and you're leaving as him."

Justin removed his glasses, and his features immediately began to change. His jaw squared up, his temples lengthened. Lines accentuated his cheeks. The crow's-feet around his eyes deepened.

Before his very eyes, this man had become Anthony's twin.

"It's the glasses," Justin said. "They can alter your features for a short time. The glasses will make you look like I did when I walked in here. It'll last long enough for you to get out."

Anthony moved forward to touch the man's cheek.

Adriana knocked his hand away. "You can play with yourself later,

Anthony. We've got work to do." She positioned Justin next to Anthony and inspected them side by side.

"The plastic surgeon did a pretty good job," she muttered, sizing up Justin.

"You had him altered—to look like me?" Anthony asked.

Adriana sighed. "Do I need to slap you again? Yes, it was necessary for him to pass as you for longer than a few minutes, so he had plastic surgery. He was paid very well for his part in our little masquerade."

"My family can afford to move inland now, and live in style to boot," Justin said. "Put these on."

Adriana ran her fingers through Anthony's hair, then drew them back in disgust, rubbing the grease between her fingertips. "You've gone gray, Anthony." She selected a thin wand from the briefcase and painted Justin's hair with streaks matching Anthony's graying temples. After making an adjustment, she reversed the process with Anthony's hair, darkening it. "Here," she said to Justin, handing him a small bottle from the briefcase, "oil yourself up. You have to sell it."

She stepped back and pursed her lips, comparing the two. "Good." She snapped her fingers. "Now, swap clothes."

He was out of his orange jumpsuit and prison-issued boxers before Justin had taken his pants off. Anthony slipped on Justin's silk underwear, then his charcoal-gray trousers and cream-colored shirt. He pushed his arms through the lined sleeves of the suit jacket. The suit molded to his body like clothes were supposed to, instead of flapping against his naked skin like the jumpsuit.

Anthony met Justin's eyes and extended his hand. "Thank you."

The man taking his place gripped his hand. Anthony felt a sudden impulse to tell him all about his routine, the fifty steps in the prison yard, the push-ups, but Adriana interrupted by handing him the glasses.

"Now for the finishing touch," she said.

He weighed them in his hand. They were heavy.

"The latest in face-skinning tech," Adriana explained. "It gets the job done, but very uncomfortable to wear for more than a few minutes."

"Hurts like hell." Justin tapped his temple. "Massive headache." The guy even sounded like Anthony. How many YourVoice videos of Taulke

Industries events must Justin have watched to get his voice down so well? He felt a faint stirring of hope in his gut. This could work.

"It takes about three minutes to map your existing features and then develop the composite projection," Adriana said. "So chop-chop. We're on the clock, Anthony."

He slipped the glasses on. An intense light pierced his pupils. He felt Justin grip his arm. "Don't fight it," his own voice told him. "It'll just hurt more."

Anthony forced his eyelids open and stared at the light. Where the glasses touched his temples, he felt a tingling, then pain as his skin began reshaping itself. His stomach queased. It felt like worms crawling under his skin.

"It's working," Adriana said in a tone like cool water. "The glasses stimulate your facial muscles, then fill in any gaps with holo-tech."

Painful minutes passed before she spoke again.

"The process is settling down. How do you feel?"

The skin on Anthony's face ached, and his vision was veiled in a thin red haze. A headache was creeping up from the base of his skull.

"I'm good."

"All right, then. Let's move." She pressed the button on the table, and the female guard appeared at the door. Justin stepped out of the room, turned, and was gone.

The hope in Anthony's belly blossomed.

"We're not done yet." Adriana took his arm and steered him to the door on the opposite wall. They passed a security station and walked through a wide flagstone lobby, Adriana's red-lacquered nails gripping Anthony's bicep.

Then, for the second time that day, Anthony tasted the sweetness of fresh air. The imposing concrete bulk of the Alcatraz of the Rockies loomed behind him. Through the thin soles of Justin's leather loafers, he could feel every ice crystal in the snow-packed parking lot.

He was walking away.

When they reached Adriana's Cadillac, she paused at the open door. Through the red veil of the face-skinning glasses, Anthony could see the invitingly soft seat cushions. The air wafting out of the cabin smelled like home.

"You ride up front, dear," Adriana purred. "You're the help now, remember?"

Anthony circled around the aircar and slid into the passenger's seat. The driver nodded at him. "You can take them off now," she said.

He yanked off the glasses and massaged his temples. The aircar's drive spun up.

"They work well enough, but the side effects suck," the driver said. "Hydration helps." She handed him a pouch of water and Anthony drank it down. Real water, refined water. He hadn't known he was so thirsty.

"Thank you." Behind closed eyes, purple-green blooms, remnants of the face-skinning tech, persisted in his vision.

"No worries."

Anthony froze, finally placing the driver's voice. He forced himself to open his eyes and look at her.

Helena Telemachus, the woman who'd escorted him to the ADX Florence hellhole as Teller's representative, grinned back at him. Her green eyes gleamed, and her elfin-sharp ears poked through her mop of dark hair.

"H," he managed to say. The warm hope in his gut dimmed. "What are you doing here?"

She hissed out a sharp breath of derision. "You don't think the queen back there put all this together on her own, do you?"

Anthony gritted his teeth, trying to reconcile the pain from the face-skinning glasses, his joy at being free, and the desire to strangle the gallingly confident young woman sitting next to him.

She draped a limp hand over the top of the steering wheel as the Cadillac climbed to its cruising altitude and leveled off.

"You're welcome for your freedom, Anthony. President Teller has a message for you: get your ass back to work and fix this weather shitstorm you created."

# 2

## MING QINLAO • LUNA CITY, THE MOON

Ming Qinlao twisted her lithe frame in the narrow maintenance access tunnel and heaved on the wrench, leveraging her full body weight. The fitting turned another few degrees.

"That's good, Mary!" came the muffled voice of Alvin Rue, her supervisor, from the maintenance bay.

Ming let the light Moon gravity slide her down the access tube. Accepting Alvin's hand at the bottom, she stood up straight and stretched, feeling the vertebrae in her back pop in relief. The front of her jumpsuit was covered in a slimy substance Ming preferred to think of as *unidentified* until she could take a shower. Just a normal day working on the waste reclamation system in LUNa City, the United Nations' first sustainable community on the Moon.

Alvin was already packing the tools into the scooter they used to transit the vast sublunar maintenance bays.

"Mary," he said, using Ming's assumed name. "I just don't know what I'd do without you. That section has been a pain in my ass for the last six months." She braced herself for the inevitable next sentence. "Those damned topside engineers couldn't design their way out of an airlock with the instructions written on the inside of the door. Well, I'm ready for a drink!"

Ming nodded, glad Alvin's thirst for vodka had cut his storytelling short for once. He'd come to the Moon in his sixties to make a second career, living and working in the so-called Underworld beneath LUNa City that no one but maintenance crews ever visited. A vast honeycomb of caves and bays carved out of raw rock kept the growing lunar colony supplied with the essentials of existence: waste reclamation, water, air, power, and data. Few people wanted to work in the Underworld. What the techs called the "back alleys" were rough-hewn, dirty, smelly, and isolated.

And that suited "Mary Wu" just fine. The best place to hide out was the place where no one else wanted to go looking for you.

Alvin engaged the scooter, which lifted off the rocky, uneven tunnel floor. As the vehicle picked up speed, Alvin began an anecdote that only required the occasional grunt of acknowledgment from Ming.

Less than a year ago, Ming had been one of those "damned topside engineers" Alvin so enjoyed taking to task. She had roamed the topside halls proudly, unafraid of who she was. Every day after lunch, she would venture onto the lunar surface to inspect the LUNa City dome—the greatest architectural achievement in mankind's history, in her opinion.

Now, Ming Qinlao was Mary Wu, Underworld technician and woman on the run.

The Moon had proven a good place to hide. LUNa City contained more than eight thousand souls and, between the mining camps and the contract workers, consisted of a heavily transient population. Work was plentiful, the pay was decent, and recruiters were skilled at sensing—and avoiding— questions their clients didn't want to answer. A perfect place to hide.

Ming's rational side liked to believe she had taken all those benefits into consideration when she fled to the Moon with her fourteen-year-old half-brother Ruben—now Rodney Wu—but the truth was, if she had done those calculations at all, it was subconsciously.

Lily was here, that was the real reason. Ming had come home, plain and simple. She'd needed refuge and Lily had provided it.

Rational Ming knew she might be placing Lily in real danger. Her Auntie Xi wanted the reins of power for Qinlao Manufacturing, and she'd stop at nothing to take them from Ming. Ming had seen on the YourVoice network how Xi had taken over QM following the disappearance of Ming, its rightful CEO. But the old bat couldn't make it permanent unless Ming could be either physically brought before the board and voted out or declared dead with an official death certificate. Yes, anyone who stood between Xi and power was definitely in danger.

So Ming grew her hair long, wore baggy jumpsuits, and avoided any places where she might possibly run into someone she knew from her prior life as a damn topside engineer.

"Mary? You listening to me?" Alvin's bushy gray eyebrows jutted out above his frown. "Girl, you zoned out. You taking drugs or something?"

Ming rolled her eyes. "No, I'm not taking drugs, Alvin." But it was an attractive idea—banishing her dark thoughts for even a little while. She'd probably even get away with it. Drugs, gambling, prostitution—all of it was legal so long as no one got hurt. Injury meant reduced construction efficiency, and the marshals, the local arm of UN enforcement, took a dim view of crimes against efficiency.

"Do you want to pick up another shift?" The scooter jostled them both. "We can get a head start on that sorter at the recycling plant—"

"Sorry, boss," she replied, shifting in the seat. "Gotta pick up my brother from school."

Alvin was silent for a moment. She could tell he was disappointed. He seemed to enjoy her company—or maybe he just enjoyed talking. "Okay, well, I'll drop you at the stairs then."

Ming watched the tunnels fly by. Occasionally, she saw the dim glow of another maintenance crew at work, but the vast network of the Underworld was mostly empty. In contrast to the living quarters above, with their well-mapped geometries, these tunnels were dug on an as-needed basis, resulting in a rabbit's warren of alcoves and winding passages. The perfect hiding place, if she ever needed one. As long as she had food and water, she could live down here for weeks, months, maybe forever.

The scooter rolled to a stop next to the main staircase leading up to the habitat levels. Ming swung lightly to the ground and looked up at the forty levels between the alleys and proper society.

Alvin nodded at her, his good humor returned. "Just think, Mary. We get do this all again tomorrow."

"And they even pay us for it," Ming said, finishing their common farewell. "Have a drink for me."

"I'll have two!" The old man's laugh echoed in his wake.

---

Ming took the stairs three at a time to the upper levels. She loved the freedom of low-gee, how strong it made her feel. The flip side of that sensation was her constant struggle to maintain muscle tone after months on the Moon. In her previous life as a LUNa City engineer, she'd been a regular at gravity rehab labs, but now the chance of meeting someone there who might recognize her was too great. Her daily work kept her arms and upper body in shape, but maintaining muscle tone in her legs required conscious effort.

Lily had come up with the idea of teaching Ruben self-defense skills as a way for both him and Ming to work out. Four days a week, after she picked him up from school, they headed to one of the communal gyms for weight training and light sparring.

Ming bounded up the steps, but her mind refused to let her body simply enjoy its exercise. Her revived relationship with Lily was severely strained, but—to her surprise—not broken. Lily had not taken another partner after Ming's rejection. Whenever Lily probed about Ming's romantic status, Ming stayed silent or changed the subject. She had no desire to hurt Lily and even less to sully the image of Sying in her own memories.

A young couple, newly minted engineers by the sound of their banter, made way for Ming, who leaped past them on the stairs. Their easy familiarity tugged at her conscience, and she pumped her legs harder.

She needed Lily. Pretending to be Mary Wu, a nobody technician, was hard, a prick at her family pride. Every time she assumed Mary's persona, Ming felt like a little bit of her own personality was leaching away.

Lily stopped that bleeding. When she was with Lily, Ming felt like she was back to a simpler time in her life, a place where she was not a CEO and had no desire to know her estranged father. In that existence, there had been only two people in her life: Lily and herself. A perfectly balanced dyad of love and trust.

She and Lily were sleeping together again, but it was a move of convenience more than intimacy. There was one double bed and one sofa in the apartment, and Ruben had claimed the sofa so he could fall asleep playing vidgames on weekends.

Sometimes, after he was sound asleep on school nights, Lily reached across the small chasm afforded by the double bed to touch her back. Sometimes, Ming responded to her touch.

Was it wrong? Lily always seemed to want to go back to the way they were, and Ming needed to feel alive again, so they both got what they wanted—if only for a while. They gave to each other and they took, and that was how they existed. For now.

The data glasses hummed in her pocket, indicating an incoming call. Ming topped the landing and stopped to catch her breath. She cast her eyes down at twenty-eight flights of metal stairs climbed. Her thighs throbbed, her calves burned.

The glasses vibrated again. Ming put them on and saw Lily was calling. She had to eye-scan the toggle on the cheap device twice before Lily's face appeared.

"Hey, sweetie," Ming said in her cheeriest voice. "I'm on my way—"

But Lily's eyes were wide with panic and tears streaked her cheeks. She fiddled with a lock of blonde hair behind her right ear, a clear sign of agitation for her.

"What's the matter?"

"Rodney—" Lily's eyes cut to the right, letting Ming know there was someone else listening in on the call. "Rodney got picked up by security. He hurt another kid." She lowered her voice. "They have him in lockup."

Ming cursed, a slew of fear rushing through her mind. If they scanned his biometrics into the legal system and uploaded them through an Earth-based connection ... no doubt Auntie Xi had bots trolling every data stream in the known universe. ...

"You're his legal guardian, Mi—Mary. They won't release him to me."

Ignoring her aching legs, Ming began taking the stairs four, five steps at a time. "I'm on my way. Stay there."

When she reached the neighborhood levels, she had to muscle her way through the crowds coming off the freight elevators. Shift change.

Ming reached the level 16 security station and took a moment to catch her breath. Sweaty, dirty, her hair a bird's nest of tangles, she didn't exactly present the picture of a responsible guardian, but she had to get her brother free before they scanned him into the system.

This far down in the colony, the station was no more than a two-man outpost: one marshal on local patrol, another on desk duty. The station itself was one room with a desk and a single chair, the back half partitioned off by a transparent plastic wall. Lily occupied the chair, the officer the desk. Ruben slumped against the back wall of the cell. He avoided Ming's piercing glare.

Lily jumped up and seized Ming's hand, dragging her forward until Ming's thighs touched the front of the desk. "This is Marshal Timmer, Mary. He picked up Rodney for fighting."

Ming offered the marshal her hand and the exasperated expression of an adult long past the limit of her patience.

Timmer's gaze took in her dirty hand and dirtier jumpsuit before giving her a perfunctory shake using only the tips of his fingers. He was young, only a few years older than Ruben, and his eyes kept flitting to Lily.

"You're the boy's guardian?" he asked, frowning.

"I am," Ming said, adding a touch of regret to her tone. "Can I see my brother?"

"He put another boy in the infirmary with a broken nose, ma'am. That's a serious offense. If the boy had been of working age—"

"He was being bullied, Marshal," Lily offered. Ming did her best to hide her surprise at Lily's tone. That was her girlfriend's—ex-girlfriend's, she reminded herself—seduction voice. Lily leaned over the desk.

The disgusted expression on Timmer's face gave way to appreciation. He licked his lips.

"That other boy has bullied my friend's brother at school. Every day. Terrible things, racist stuff." Lily settled one buttock on the desk. She glanced down at the 3-D nameplate. "I heard the other officer call you Nate. Can I call you Nate?"

Timmer cleared his throat. "Um ... sure."

Ming backed away from the desk, letting Lily take over.

"Look, Nate, Rodney is a good kid. He won't do this again. Do you think maybe you could talk to the boy's mother about not being such a racist? This is a UN city, after all." Lily flipped her blonde hair behind her ear.

Ming tried not to gape. Lily was hair-flipping this guy?

"Rodney's had a tough time. Not a lot of good role models"—Lily slewed her eyes toward Ming's dirty jumpsuit—"especially *male* role models. And it's hard when people call you names like that. Mary and I will make sure he knows that violence is not a proper response to name-calling. I'll keep you updated on his progress. Personally."

Nate busied his hands rearranging the items on his desk. "Well, it's a first offense, and he is a minor, and no workers were taken offline as a result of the injury." He squared his shoulders. "But he broke the other kid's nose. His parents are—"

Lily put her hand on Nate's bicep. "I'll talk to them. I'll be honest—I plan to give them a piece of my mind about the name-calling. I'll let you know how it goes, okay?"

Ming watched the gears whirring in the marshal's head, though his eyes were focused on Lily's cleavage. She couldn't remember the last time she'd seen this side of Lily.

Marshal Timmer pressed a button on his desk, and the clear steel of the cell door slid aside. Ruben stepped out, head down. Ming seized his arm, pulling him toward the door. "You and I need to have a talk." When she looked back, Lily was leaning across the narrow desk typing her net address into Timmer's tablet, her head practically touching the marshal's.

Ming paused in the doorway, looking back into the security station. When she was that close, Lily smelled like jasmine and musk, a scent that still made Ming quiver. Lily's low laugh, throaty and suggestive, wafted toward them. Ming tightened her grip on Ruben's arm.

"Hey! Ow! I'm sorry, okay?"

Rational Ming knew Lily had just helped them out of a jam that could have been a whole lot worse. More to the point, the woman Ming had loved —then discarded, then come back to looking for safe harbor—had just pimped herself out to save Ming and her half-brother, whom Lily had known for all of a few months.

An emotion Ming hadn't felt in a long time rushed through her.

"Stop!" Ruben was trying to pry his arm free. Ming released him.

Lily extracted herself from Timmer's attentions and turned toward the door. Her face was flushed as her eyes found Ming's.

Ming stepped into the crowded hallway outside the station, breathing deeply. She finally put a name to the feeling slithering around inside her.

Jealousy.

# 3

## WILLIAM GRAVES • HAVEN 6, BLUE EARTH, MINNESOTA

As the aircar pulled through the 'lock on Haven 6, Colonel William Graves blinked at the bright sunlight flooding the windows. His vehicle rose swiftly into the cloudless sky above Blue Earth, Minnesota. Beyond the half-kilometer security perimeter circling the dome, people dotted the landscape as far as he could see. The full spectrum of humanity—from rich to poor, from young to old, from every culture and ethnicity—spread out across the expanse of the empty prairie. They'd arrived in everything from expensive aircars to ancient gasoline-powered automobiles. Some slept in campers, some in tents, and some on the frozen ground—wherever they could find a warm, dry place to lay their heads. Not easy to do in December in Minnesota.

They all wanted one thing: to get inside the dome.

Haven 6 receded until the massive structure was no more than a shiny blister on the prairie.

"How many of those people you think will get in, sir?" Captain Jansen asked. She looked as tired as he felt, and her dark skin had an ashen undertone. They'd both barely averaged four hours of sleep a night for the last few months. Probably less for her, since whenever he woke up and entered the command center, she always seemed to be there already.

"Not enough," he replied. As commanding officer of the US Army

Disaster Mitigation Corps, there was one part of the job he was never able to get away from. Whether it was drought in Phoenix, wildfires in California, a hurricane in Miami, or whatever the hell he was doing in Blue Earth, there was always one common denominator: he was never able to help enough people.

"Not your call, sir," Jansen said quietly.

He knew she was right, but that didn't help. He had control over the crew, not the civilians. There was an entirely separate admissions division, operating under their own set of rules that seemed focused on a person's genetics. The mission of the Havens was to act as a vehicle for the preservation of humanity. Volunteers from all counties and ethnicities, known as Pioneers, needed to be willing to cut all ties with their past and live inside a self-sustaining silo for the next century. When the siloes opened again, there would be a new generation to pick up the pieces.

When he'd first heard of the idea, Graves had dismissed it as science fiction. Now, with Earth's climate in full crisis, he wasn't so sure.

He slipped off his data glasses and pinched the bridge of his nose. Unsolicited, Jansen handed him a stim tablet. He accepted it, too tired to even say thank you. She knew he had a briefing to read before they arrived in Washington, DC.

"How's your family, Jansen? They okay in all this?"

*All this that I've caused* was what he wanted to say. The world-saving bio-seeding technology that he'd released across Mother Earth had backfired spectacularly. Graves had given the order to launch the missiles that deployed those billions of tiny nanites now manipulating the world's atmosphere. The power of those man-made mites was still unfathomable to him: entire cities buried under sand, storms wiping out entire population centers with near-surgical precision, polar vortexes putting areas in deep freeze...

"There's only my brother left now, sir," Jansen said, bringing him back to the moment. "Parents passed a few years ago. We don't talk much. He lives in Georgia—inland, of course."

"Is he a candidate for a Haven? There's one in Arkansas he could apply for. I could look into it."

Jansen shook her head. "Don't think so, sir. He says he's not going to hide in a dome. If the world ends, he says, so be it. He's just going to meet it head on."

Graves turned back to the window. Not a bad headline philosophy, but shortsighted. When that time came, those thousands of people on the Minnesota prairie outside Haven 6 would become hordes. His job was logistics; he knew exactly how many people the Havens could hold.

Not enough.

The seven Havens located around the country were a marvel of engineering. To call them domes was a misnomer; they were actually silos. Like LUNa City on the Moon, the domed part of a Haven was only the top floor, the penthouse of a much taller, cylindrical society extending deep underground.

They were century ships, time capsules for humanity. Once the airlocks were sealed, the entire structure was designed to be completely self-sustaining for one hundred years. Air, water, food, and all the other essentials of life had to be generated from within the structure itself. Together, the selected passengers in each Haven—the Pioneers—would form an insulated society: a new civilization for a new Earth, if that eventuality came to pass.

Graves's domain spanned levels 1 through 36: living quarters, provisions, and logistics for three thousand souls, a Haven's capacity. His mission ended at the security airlock on deck 36. Though he knew there were levels below, he had no idea how many. For all he knew, there were another thirty-six levels and another Colonel Graves provisioning them as a backup. In spite of himself, he grinned at the idea of an alter ego doing the exact same job as him in a parallel universe below his own. That guy was probably just as tired as he was.

The most intriguing part of his mission was the line in his orders that read "proceed without regard to financial constraints." In his twenty-seven years in the US Army, in postings all over the globe, he had never before been given that kind of latitude. But Graves was nothing if not a soldier who knew how to follow orders, so he did exactly as his mission specified.

Perhaps he'd taken his orders too literally and he was being called to Washington for an ass-chewing of epic proportions. Maybe it's what he deserved. While the world had fixed its crosshairs of blame on President

Teller and Anthony Taulke, they'd somehow forgotten about Colonel William Graves, the guy who had pushed the button, the officer in charge who executed the president's launch order.

Night after night, he relived that scenario in his dreams: the garbled phone call, the last-minute loss of communications. He'd done what the president ordered, Graves told himself. Twenty-seven years of unswerving military service had brought him to that moment.

He was only following orders.

But that was the problem: he never actually got the order. He'd heard the president's speech and knew the intent, but when push came to shove, he never actually heard the Commander in Chief say the words.

And he launched anyway. Now, people all over the world were dying because of his actions. He could have held the launch, reestablished communications with Washington, confirmed the orders. Given the chance, would Teller have changed his mind?

The aircar reached the transcontinental air-bahn, and the powerful craft trembled as it accelerated to top speed.

Graves tried to reset his mental state. The past was unchangeable. The only thing to do was to move forward and execute the next set of orders to the best of his ability.

He put his data glasses back on and pulled up the top secret briefing. The device automatically read his biometrics and opened the file for the report titled "Global Military Assessment." He skimmed the executive summary:

The US Intelligence Community is united in its view that military forces of the major powers—namely the People's Republic of China, the Russian Confederation, and the African National Coalition—are under intense internal pressure to take aggressive, unilateral action against the United States for its role in the disastrous bio-seeding experiment called the Lazarus Protocol. US bases outside the continental US are on full lockdown. Nonessential personnel are being evacuated.

The source of the internal strife within these potential aggressor states is unknown. There are unconfirmed reports that the New Earth Order, colloquially called the Neos, are behind this agitation. There are also rumors of a Neo communications channel undetectable to known methods of surveillance. While we stress that these claims are speculative, field commanders are advised to minimize access to highly sensitive operational information by followers of the New Earth Order.

Graves stopped reading and leaned back against the headrest.

"Jansen, how many Neos do we have on staff?"

She peered at him over the rim of her own data glasses. "On your immediate staff, sir, there's only one. Second Lieutenant Hokum. Just transferred in last week."

"Let's put Hokum on temporary duty somewhere outside the main Haven operation. And go through the rest of the military personnel, move any Neos out of the Haven."

"Yes, sir." Her eyes held a questioning look, but she said nothing. She knew he'd tell her when he was ready.

---

Their aircar landed gently outside the staff entrance to the Pentagon. Since Lazarus had launched, protestors marched regularly on the seats of power in Washington, from the White House to the Capitol to the Pentagon itself. In response, a broad security perimeter had been cleared around the military headquarters. After the briefing he had just read, Graves expected that perimeter to widen and harden with armed outposts.

While he understood the military necessity of the precautions, the situation gave Graves pause. Somewhere in a long-ago West Point history class, he recalled a quote about the right to protest in a free society.

Graves dismissed the feeling. He was outfitting a modern-day Noah's ark with the ability to save an infinitesimal segment of his country's population. Maybe he should save his self-righteousness for another time.

Their biometrics cleared before they reached the building and two MPs held open the doors for him and Jansen. They joined the throng of foot traffic in the halls of the famous military building, making their way quickly to the innermost ring and the bank of elevators that would take them to the secure underground levels. When they reached the meeting room, Jansen opened the door and Graves marched in.

The briefing room was empty save for a man lounging in an office chair.

He stood when Graves entered and extended his hand in greeting. "Colonel, good to see you again." With bared teeth, the man reminded Graves of a shark before it took the big bite. His guard went up instantly.

The man who'd first briefed them on Operation Haven some months earlier seemed determined to shake Graves's hand. He and Jansen had nicknamed the unnamed man Mr. Slick after his clothing. The man's suit, just like at that initial meeting, shifted colors subtly when he moved, from navy blue to smoky onyx to charcoal gray. Had he even changed clothes since then?

"You look disappointed to see me, Colonel."

"I don't know you well enough to be disappointed," Graves replied. Mr. Slick finally dropped his hand. "I take it from your presence here this isn't a budget meeting?"

The man's laugh was friendly but forced. "You don't miss a thing, Colonel. I thought it was time for another chat." He gestured at the open chairs.

Graves sat. His back did not touch the chair. "What is it you want exactly?"

"Things have progressed, Colonel. It's time you knew the rest of the Haven story."

"Like what's beyond deck thirty-six, you mean?"

Slick's face became thoughtful. "Maybe I should ask what you think is beyond thirty-six."

Jansen answered instead. "It's a power plant."

The man in the multicolored suit clapped twice. "Very good, Captain. But a power plant for what?" When neither officer offered a guess, he pointed at the ceiling.

Graves's stomach tightened with anger. This guy, obviously a covert ops agent, was playing some stupid game while people were dying out there. He slapped his hand on the table. "I don't have time for this cloak-and-dagger crap. Tell me your name and get to the point of why we're here."

What might have been genuine emotion flitted across Slick's features. "Your passion is a credit, Colonel Graves. It's that fire and dogged determination that'll be needed if—"

"Name. Now."

"You can call me Smith."

The small victory let just enough air out of Graves's fury for him to regain control of his emotions. The name was bullshit, but it was a name at least.

"Fine, Mr. ... Smith. How about you cut the crap and tell us what's so important we couldn't do this over secure comms?"

"We're not sure there's any such thing as 'secure comms' anymore, Colonel."

Graves took that in. Coupled with the report he'd just read, it was a chilling thought.

Smith cleared his throat. "The Haven Project began over thirty years ago. It was started under the National Science Foundation as a way to study environments in isolation, sort of like the old bio-dome experiments, but on steroids. The sites were carefully selected away from major population centers, areas where we could closely monitor access and build the domes without attracting attention. Once the initial domes were erected, they became part of the natural environment—another big government project—and people just stopped seeing them."

"But they were more than just another big government project," Graves guessed.

Smith nodded. "Much more. Over the course of decades, we excavated the land under the domes to create a self-sustaining underground silo structure."

Jansen leaned forward. "How many levels are there really?"

"Forty-two."

Graves chewed his lip. Six levels would comprise nearly two hundred feet, maybe more. That was one massive power plant.

"That's not all," Smith said with a humorous flare in his voice.

"Do tell." Graves let his sarcasm show.

"There's a new type of drive, called a GEMDrive. The full name: Grav-Electro-Magnetic Drive. The eggheads say that means you fly a ship in space while providing compensating gravity inside the vessel. Basically, it means you can accelerate without getting squashed like a bug."

Graves shot a glance at Jansen, who had discipline enough to keep her teeth together. Graves held up a hand. "Back up. You said *drive* and *ship* and *space*. Are you telling me Havens are able to fly? Like spaceships?"

Smith's expression lightened. "Exactly like spaceships, Colonel. But wait, there's more." He called up an image on his tablet and pushed the device across the table.

Graves and Jansen looked at the tablet together. It cycled through pictures of an Earthlike planet hanging in the blackness of space.

"It's an exoplanet, four light-years away, give or take, in the Proxima Centauri system. Nine years ago, we sent a probe drone, and we found a planet there that's everything we could have hoped for. Breathable air, clean water, temperate climate, and uninhabited. The gravity's a little heavier than Earth's, but we'll adapt. It's just sitting there waiting for us to colonize it."

Graves stared at the images of the planet. "What's its name?"

*A new planet, unpolluted, untouched by human hands. A global Mulligan for the human race. Do it right this time.*

"The scientists call it Proxima *b*," Smith said. His tone was soft.

"What are *we* calling it?" Jansen asked. Her eyes were glued to the images cycling across the tablet.

Smith smiled. "Haven."

# 4

## LUCA VASQUEZ • MINNEAPOLIS, MINNESOTA

Luca Vasquez stabbed at the pinkish-yellow goo in the skillet. How did Americans even call this food? She shaped the protein-enhanced egg substitute into a pile and flipped it in the frying pan.

Back home in Veracruz, breakfast was an actual meal, not a squirt of paste in a pan. A fresh tortilla, maybe an actual egg from an actual chicken, some beans, and an orange if they were in season.

An orange. How long had it been since she'd tasted a real piece of fruit? When she was growing up, her family had a citrus grove in the backyard. Every morning she'd pick one for her breakfast. But that was before the city of her birth had been wiped off the map by a freak storm...

The pink stuff in the pan was starting to char. She snapped off the tiny burner and divided the protein paste across two plates.

"Donna!" she called. "Your breakfast is getting cold."

The apartment was small enough that she didn't have to yell too loudly for her sister: a living room–kitchen–dining room adjoining a tiny bedroom that they shared. Not much, but it was safe. For now.

Luca placed the plates on the fold-down table and called again. "Donna! Now."

"¡Ya voy!"

"English, D! We have to practice!"

"*Sí*, I know, I know," Donna said from the other room. "I'm coming."

Donna had adopted the whine of an entitled teen since she'd started school in Minneapolis. The YourVoice forums Luca researched said that everyone dealt with grief and stress in their own way. With their parents gone, Luca's best path forward was to be a supportive and nurturing female role model for her sister. Easier said than done.

Donna appeared in the doorway wearing a bright blue jumper and red scarf. Getting dressed was a good start, but her long, dark hair was a mess.

"Sit down and eat. I'll brush your hair."

The girl slumped in her chair. "What's this?"

"It's called P-Eggs. The *p* is for protein, I think. It's pretty, isn't it?" Luca said, trying to sound positive. *And it's cheap.* "Looks like pink coral. Papa used to take me to the aquarium when I was your age." Their shared father had been past middle-aged when Luca was growing up. He'd remarried and fathered Donna late in life. Whatever possessed a man that old to have another child?

"I think it looks gross."

Luca pulled the brush through a resistant nest of knots. "Well, I'm sorry, little sister, but that's what we have to eat this morning. Eat or starve, your choice."

The girl grumbled again and picked up her fork.

"Single braid?" Luca asked.

Donna grunted assent through her mouthful of P-Eggs.

Luca expertly separated the strands into three plaits, then began to braid them together. When she uncovered the back of her sister's neck, her fingers lingered on the tattoo there. A round image—half a woman's face and half the image of Earth.

"Does it hurt?" Luca asked. "Ever?" Who would do that to a little girl? And why?

Donna shrugged. "All the orphans got them after the hurricane, Luca. *No es la gran cosa.*"

"English."

"It's no big deal!"

Luca hated the tattoo. If only she had made it home from school sooner, Donna never would have ended up in that orphanage. It took her months to find her sister after the hurricane. Now it was just the two of them against the world.

"Lots of kids here have them too," Donna said.

That reminder did little to calm Luca's unease. "I know. Now, finish up and get ready for school." She kissed the top of her sister's head.

Luca sat down and scooped a mouthful of the P-Eggs. They tasted worse than they looked, but at least they were cheap.

---

Luca settled onto the hard plastic bench seats of the tube transport for the three-minute ride to the University of Minnesota. Most of the traffic on the transport this early in the morning was support staff or grad students with campus jobs like hers.

She nodded politely to the haughty black woman with the bright red headdress and was rewarded with a broad smile. Luca recognized her from Foyle Hall, where the lab was located. Glancing down at her own plain brown sweater and dark pants, Luca thought maybe she'd buy a new sweater with her next paycheck. Something red or yellow to contrast with her dark hair.

Foyle Hall was a short walk from the tube station. Luca took her time, savoring the morning sunshine on her face. Dr. Markov's laboratory was in the basement, with no windows, so she always tried to soak in as much natural light and warmth as possible before descending into the EM-shielded dungeon.

Markov had explained that the electromagnetic shield was needed to ensure a pristine signal environment for his work. For Luca, it meant she was out of contact with the WorldNet. Not a big loss—all she had was a cheap pair of data glasses—but not having an instant connection to the outside world had taken some getting used to.

When she first heard about Luca's job, Donna proclaimed she would quit before giving up her WorldNet.

Oh, to be young and have such life choices.

She should level with Donna about their situation. She had a student visa and a campus job that barely paid for their shoebox apartment, food supplemented by the campus food bank, and a pair of data plans. If one of them got sick, there was always the campus free clinic, but they were balancing on the razor's edge of poverty.

Her compassionate side wanted Donna to have as carefree a childhood as Luca could give her. Why burden a twelve-year-old with grown-up concerns she couldn't do anything about?

On impulse, Luca pulsed Donna good wishes for the day as she descended the stairs of Foyle, then scanned her badge and entered the dungeon. When the door closed behind her, the signal on her glasses went dead.

She always fed the animals first: two white rats named Frick and Frack, a calico cat named Luis, and Leroy the beagle. None of those names were assigned by the lab, of course. For experimental purposes, the animals had numbers only.

When she'd first learned Dr. Markov used animals for testing, Luca almost quit, thin finances be damned. She was relieved when she found out the testing did not involve macabre experiments that might cause pain in the test subjects. To the contrary, all the animals looked and acted normal and healthy, except for the silver discs embedded in the backs of their necks.

Jules met her in the entryway. "Where have you been?" Her whisper was harsh. "Markov's got some woman here for a funding milestone meeting and he's freaking out."

"I get here at the same time every morning," Luca shot back, annoyed at the judgment in Jules's voice. "Dr. Markov knows that." Jules, with her tall, lean frame and spiky blonde hair, was just another one of Markov's unpaid graduate "helpers." Luca had seen a few like Jules cycle through the lab—and the doctor's bed, she suspected.

Jules hissed at her, her silver piercings catching the light. Jules was heavily into body art, including a Neo tattoo on the nape of her neck. Although lots of students on campus were Neos and there was a Temple of Cassandra a few blocks away on University Avenue, as far as Luca remembered, this was the first time she'd seen a Neo as Makarov's lab assistant.

Any further retort was cut off by Markov's entrance. "Luca, you're here. Good."

He was slim, with close-cropped dark hair and a wispy beard. His dark eyes sharpened when he brushed past Jules. "Please bring 763B and 986Y to the observation chamber. Immediately."

"Right away, Dr. Markov," Luca said, wondering why he wanted Luis the cat and Frick the rat in the observation tank at the same time.

The animals were glad to see her. She dashed a cup full of kibble into Leroy's dog dish and sprinkled some rat food pellets in the clear plastic carrier she used to transfer Frick to the observation tank. Then she went back for Luis.

The cat was waiting for her. He arched his back under her hand and meowed when she picked him up. Luca nestled the feline close to her chest, and he began to purr softly, licking her hand.

"If you promise not to eat Frick, I'll bring you a treat," she whispered.

Luca lowered him into a holding pen connected to a six-by-six observation corral recessed into the floor. Sensors studded the tank's inner wall for recording signal data. On the other side of the tank, Frick the rat watched nervously through the clear plastic door of his own holding pen. Once both animals were secure, she walked to the control room.

Markov was speaking in his professorial voice to a black woman not much older than Luca. Her hair was cut close, her posture upright and self-assured.

"The animals have been implanted with a nanite dose in their brain stem," Markov was explaining. "The theory I'm testing is that we can control instinctive behavior, transmit real-time sensory data, and possibly even facilitate basic two-way communication."

"The silver disc," the woman said. "How does that work, exactly?"

"It's a transceiver. The biggest problem with the signal is gain."

"You're working with subspace frequencies?"

"Absolutely. That gives us the best communication range and speed, potentially global reach—if we can solve the gain issue."

She cocked her head. "And what are you going to demonstrate with these subjects?"

"Ah, yes." Markov walked to the control panel and rested his hand on Jules's shoulder. "Aggression intervention. I'll demonstrate how we can alter the feline's natural instincts to hunt and even encourage gentle behavior toward the rat."

The woman raised her eyebrows. "I'm watching, Doctor."

Luca's heartbeat quickened. Markov triggered Frick's door, releasing the rat into the observation tank. He quickly ran to the side farthest from Luis and cowered.

The cat peered out through the plastic, eyes alert and calculating. Luca wished she had arrived just a few minutes earlier so she could have fed him.

The door to Luis's pen rose. He stalked into the open corral and dropped into a crouch.

"Doctor..." Luca began.

Luis began stalking around the tank's perimeter. The more animated Frick's whiskers became, the slower Luis moved.

"What you're seeing is natural, predatory behavior on the part of the feline and the expected fear response by the rat, its prey." Markov pointed to the sensor readout, which showed a flat line. "No intervention yet, please note."

Luis was close now, nearly close enough to pounce. Frick's growing panic came in a constant stream of high-pitched squeaks. Luca saw the muscles along the cat's sleek body ripple as he gathered his legs beneath him.

Luca's own body tensed.

"Now," Markov said calmly to Jules.

Luis leapt.

Jules engaged the transmitter.

The effect was instantaneous. Luis dropped to the floor in mid-leap, landing on all fours next to the terrified rat. Frick scrambled away to settle near the closed door to his own pen, his whiskers twitching. Luis began to preen himself.

"Amazing," the woman said. The sensor readings had spiked during the experiment, then leveled off to a new normal.

Markov smiled broadly. "Our intervention has overridden the cat's natural instinct to hunt, making him a placid, well-adjusted creature. Think of the applications to humanity."

"Mind control, you mean."

"Oh, nothing so nefarious!" the scientist said. "I was thinking of mentally ill individuals. If we can control abnormal impulses in them, we can help them lead a normal life, even assimilate into society."

The woman's eyes narrowed. "And if you discontinue the signal?"

Markov nodded at Jules, who pushed the button again. The cat's head swiveled to find Frick. His tail dropped to the floor, and he began stalking Frick again.

"Please, Doctor," Luca said.

"No need for bloodshed," the visitor added. "You've proven the tech."

"Oh, of course," Markov said, motioning to Jules. With a flick of a button, once again Luis became docile. "This technology, while more advanced than anything we've seen before, is nothing new in terms of the theory behind it. Back in the early twentieth century, doctors controlled motor functions in Parkinson's patients by installing a stimulation implant directly into their brains. That's my goal for my invention, applied to the mentally ill. Schizophrenics, even psychopaths could potentially benefit—"

"Does it work the other way?" interrupted the woman watching the animals in the pen.

"You mean forced aggression?" Markov asked. He reached around Jules to enter a new sequence, then activated the transmitter.

Frick the rat reared up on his hind legs, his red eyes glowing fiercely, and launched his small body at Luis. The cat skittered backward, yowling. Frick pressed in, ripping at the cat's fur, his tiny teeth slashing for Luis's throat.

"Stop!" Luca dashed from the room and vaulted into the observation tank, grabbing Frick by the back of the neck and lifting him off Luis. The rat's whiskers were a storm of activity. He twisted in her hand and sank his sharp teeth into Luca's thumb.

Luca stifled a scream as she wrestled the rat back into his pen, then thrust her bleeding thumb into her mouth. The visitor appeared at her side. She wrapped a clean, white handkerchief around Luca's injured thumb.

"That's a nasty bite," she said. Her voice was calm and kind. "My name's Hannah, by the way. Hannah Jansen."

"Luca," she replied, attempting to ignore the pain in front of Jansen. "Vasquez."

Markov had exited the control room, Jules close on his heels, clearly furious. "I must apologize for my assistant," he said. "She's a bit squeamish when it comes to the animals. We can conduct another—"

"Nonsense, Doctor," Jansen said. The command in her voice made Luca smile inside. "You've certainly demonstrated the efficacy of your research. If you and your assistant would put these animals away, I'll finish dressing this young lady's wound. First aid kit?"

"Control room, ma'am," Jules supplied.

Markov muttered to Jules to return the cat to its cage.

Back in the control room, Jansen removed the handkerchief and began cleaning the wound. "Well, the good news is, you don't need stitches. But this will really throb for a few days." She applied an antiseptic spray, then a quick-drying gel to seal the wound. "Leave this on for at least twenty-four hours before you check it."

"I will," Luca said with genuine gratitude. "Thank you." Through the window of the control room, she could see a frustrated Jules trying to catch Luis.

As the cat easily evaded her grasp, the readings on the panel caught Luca's attention. The transmitters were all zeroed out and the lines representing Luis and Frick were back at baseline, like they should be. But another signal was showing on the screen. A variable signal.

Jules exited the tank with the captured Luis.

The signal disappeared.

———

That night, long after Donna had gone to bed, Luca sat awake in the dark on their ratty loveseat. Sleep wouldn't come. Her thumb throbbed, despite Jansen's excellent field dressing.

All day, Luca's mind had percolated on the brief, active signal reading on the lab's control panel. Jules had been radiating a signal. How was that even possible? That was the whole point of working in an EM-shielded space. Data glasses, retinal implants, even old-fashioned smartphones were rendered useless.

There was only one possibility. The signal had come from Jules herself.

She slipped her data glasses on and eye-scanned to the WorldNet through an anonymous connection.

She hadn't visited the Pawn's Portal in weeks. It was a secure gathering spot for ex-Neos, people who claimed the New Earth Order was a recruiting method for corporate mind control on a massive scale. She told herself the people who posted there were just conspiracy theorists, crackpots with nothing better to do than to let their paranoia run away with them.

But tonight, after seeing Markov's technology in action, Luca thought maybe it wasn't such a crazy idea after all.

Luca entered the Portal. It was skinned as a hotel bar, complete with dark corners and a beery-breathed lounge singer playing a piano. Every visitor had an avatar to represent them. Luca used her favorite superhero, Wonder Woman, but dressed as her alter ego Diana Prince.

The man behind the front desk smiled. "Howdy, Dubya-Dubya."

"Shhh," Luca admonished. "It's Diana Prince, remember?"

"Ah, yes. How lovely to see you again, Miss Prince. How can I help you?"

"I need to speak with Magdalena."

# 5

## REMY CADE • AL UDEID AIR BASE, QATAR

The troop carrier rocked as they descended into the choppy lower atmosphere over the Persian Gulf.

It'd been more than six years since Remy Cade had been part of a battle unit, but it felt like only yesterday. The butterflies in his stomach, the racing thoughts recounting every detail of the mission, the obsessive way his hands checked his gear over and over again.

M24 assault rifle, Glock sidearm, carbon-smartglass knife. Check, check, check. The new Dragonskin body armor hugged his torso like a second skin, promising him invincibility. But experience taught him believing that feeling got you and those around you killed.

Most of the squad had their data glasses on, engaged in a multiplayer combat game. Only he and Sergeant Rico were passing their last few pre-battle minutes without distraction. Rico chewed a plastic toothpick.

"You ready to go, Sam?" Rico asked.

Remy clenched his teeth. "Enough with the Sam shit, okay?" He knew the Neos still harbored doubts about his loyalty. Rico was Remy's babysitter, and for some reason, he wouldn't stop calling him Sam.

"It's my new name for you, man. You're my *secret agent man*—Sam, for short." Rico flipped the toothpick end over end with his tongue, an insolent grin painting his face.

Remy turned to the window. A blooming line of sunlight crawled across the eastern Mediterranean Sea. He squinted at the horizon. There were eleven other teams out there, one from each of the Neo assault bases scattered around the world. Together, they would take on twelve US forward operating bases across the Middle East and Africa. His team was assigned CENTCOM at Al Udeid Air Base in Qatar.

Penetrate the command-and-control infrastructure and upload a virus into the central computer—that was their mission. While the generals slept in Washington, the Neos would take away their ability to wage war overseas.

The blow wasn't meant to be fatal. It was meant to send a message from Cassandra:

My people are everywhere; we can strike anywhere. You are not the most powerful force on the planet anymore.

You are not safe from me.

But there was another mission, known only to a few select team members, like Rico. The real goal of the coordinated strike was to deliver Remy into the hands of the enemy. He'd been promoted to spy. Less a vote of confidence, and more another test of loyalty. An opportunity to prove himself to Elise once and for all.

Elise Kisaan was the love of his life and he'd do anything for her, that was the harsh truth. But she had tested that faith sorely. He went along with the faked kidnapping by the Neos, even took a bullet for her. He watched her kill two men in cold blood and not shed so much as a tear of regret. Remy stood by as she manipulated the weather, putting thousands of people at risk...

All that mattered to her was Cassandra's wishes ... and Remy, of course. But if it came down to it, which one mattered more?

Months ago, he'd finally given in and tried to officially join the Neos, stupid tattoo and all, but Elise had stopped him.

"I need you clean," she'd said.

Clean? The term hadn't made sense at the time, but it did now. No tattoo, no implants, nothing to indicate to Colonel Graves that Remy had been turned by the Neos.

And now he was a spy.

Even Elise must have suspected she was pushing her influence with Remy, because she took it slow. She invited Remy to share her bed on the Temple of Cassandra space station. Her quarters had floor-to-ceiling windows that afforded them a magnificent view of Earth.

How many nights had they made love in front of that scenery before she'd sprung the question on him? Twenty, thirty? Not that it mattered; with Elise it was impossible for him to say no.

He closed his eyes and let his mind wander...

Elise straddled him, her long, dark hair stroking his face with the rhythm of their bodies. Her silhouette framed in the reflected glow of the Earth below, she dug her nails into his chest. Remy knew she could tell he was close. Her bionic thighs tightened gently against his sides and her hips rocked as she rode him.

Waves of ecstasy pulsed through him as he held her fast and close, their eyes locked together. The shared moment of heightened existence stretched until, at last, their heartbeats began to slow. When the cool air swept over their sweaty flesh, it teased out a shiver from both of them.

Elise gazed down into Remy's eyes with a satisfied, conquering expression he found too erotic for words. Then she leaned down slowly to kiss him on the lips. Remy's hands slid along her back, pulling her even closer. He never felt safer, never more complete than in the far-too-short moments following their lovemaking.

"I love you, Elise," he whispered.

She kissed his ear, her breath heavy and humid. "That's why you're here."

Carefully, she removed her body from his. He watched her pull away and out of bed. The white light from Earth made her damp skin glisten as she padded to the bar.

"Thirsty?" The curves of her body were slim and perfect, barely a ripple of scar tissue where the bionic legs fused with her hips.

Remy was conscious of the power she had over him in moments like these, but he didn't care. He only wanted more of them, forever.

She poured them each a glass of water. Handing him his, Elise walked to the huge window. The silver light bent around her. "I need to ask you to do something," she said.

Remy took a sip. "Yes."

Though she faced away from him, he could hear the smile in her voice. "I haven't told you what it is yet."

"I'll do anything for you. You know that."

Elise returned to their bed and threw one leg, warm and powerful, over his midsection. If he hadn't known she had bionic limbs, he wouldn't have been able to tell. Elise settled on her back, her head in the crook of his arm. Her hair smelled like flowers.

"You know Colonel Graves, right?"

Remy grunted. "You know he was my CO in the army. Why?"

"Would he remember you?"

"Oh, yeah. Graves was a soldier's soldier. Knew every man in his outfit. We were Graves's Diggers, and if you served under Graves, you were somebody. He even offered to be a character witness at my court-martial."

Elise rolled over and placed her chin on Remy's chest. Her eyes were dark brown and intense. "They've put Graves in charge of a project called Haven. It's a silo, a place to shield a few thousand people from an environmental catastrophe, but there's more to it. Our intel says they've developed an entirely new power source. Unlimited, clean power. Think about what we could do with that. But we can't get any of our people inside the Haven, and we really need to know—"

"You mean Cassandra needs to know."

It was always Cassandra. In those moments when Remy felt closest to Elise, Cassandra would slip between them. Always.

Elise cocked her head. "Yes, that's exactly what I mean." She pushed herself into a sitting position. For a few moments of silence, they no longer touched. Then she placed her hand under his chin and gently turned his face toward her. "We're in this together, Remy. You and me. Or are you having second thoughts about our cause?"

"I don't have any second thoughts about us," he said.

"And that's exactly why I need to know you're committed, once and for all," Elise said. "To me and to Cassandra. I'm nothing without her."

Then her demeanor melted, and she became the shy girl he'd first fallen in love with. "When you get back, there's a lot we need to talk about. I —I think it's time. I want to start a family. With you."

Remy pulled her close, banishing Cassandra from between them. "I just need you to do this one last thing for me..."

And now, he was riding a military transport with Rico. Bedroom to battlefield.

"All right, listen up!" Rico shouted, standing.

The chatter from the gamers ceased. They removed their data glasses. The tension in the cabin charged the air around them.

"Both squads will move out when we land. When Cade and I are in position, I'll cue you for the diversions. Make it good and get your asses back to the shuttle while we deliver the package. Understood?"

Grim faces nodded back.

The ship lost altitude rapidly, entering the military transit lanes. Just another routine troop transport, one of a dozen flying all over the Eastern Med and Northern Africa. They entered a holding pattern over Al Udeid Air Base. Despite his nerves, Remy knew this delay was expected. All the international US military bases were on lockdown, given the overt hostility from the Chinese and Russians—hell, the whole damned planet— following the Lazarus disaster.

In the dawn light, Remy could see the Qatari peninsula jutting like a sore thumb into the Persian Gulf. The base was a square piece of real estate, isolated from civilian cities by open desert, bermed barriers, and drones on patrol. With final clearance granted, their pilot swung to his assigned pad and landed the ship with textbook precision.

The ramp at the rear of the ship descended with a hydraulic whine. A wave of scorching atmosphere blasted the manufactured air from the bay.

"Helmets on, people," Rico called. "Good luck!"

Remy slid his helmet over his head, locking the base with his collar. A heads-up display gave him a readout of his armor status and vitals. The other twelve members of the team were tiny green icons along the base of his vision.

"Comms check, secret agent man," Rico said, unwilling to drop the snark even in a professional situation.

"Comms check sat," Remy replied. He would be the adult in the room.

Rico stepped down the ramp. He led the column toward the hangars. Once out of sight of the landing pad, the diversion squads hustled off in opposite directions. Rico and Remy continued toward the heart of the compound. Early morning foot traffic was light.

"Shouldn't we remove our helmets?" Remy asked. "Look like friendlies?"

Rico chuckled. "Check the outside temp, Sam. Most of this base is underground now."

Remy scanned his readout for the external temperature and blushed. One hundred twenty-one degrees Fahrenheit, even this early in the morning.

"That's the target," Rico said, indicating the squat brick building ahead. "We have a man on the staff entrance at the rear. He'll get us inside, then it's up to our compadres to cause some confusion."

Remy's chest tightened. There was a lot about this operation that had been left out of his briefing package.

Following Rico's brisk pace, they left the ground level, walking down a steep ramp to a pair of soldiers guarding a set of double doors. "Sergeant Ernest Rico, reporting for duty," he said to the guard.

After a curt nod, the guard activated the doors. "Elevator's at the end of the hall, Sergeant."

Rico punched the man on the arm as they entered. "Lock it down behind us."

"Her will be done."

"You got it, man." Rico waited until the door shut behind them, then said: "All squads, this is Rico. You are a go for playtime, people. Let's make it count."

Rico's pace took on a new urgency as they marched down a wide concrete hallway. A sharp right turn brought them to a reinforced elevator, flanked by another security team. One guard stepped forward with his hand up. "Stay behind the yellow line and scan in, Sergeant."

Rico nodded, placing his forearm under the scanner.

Nothing happened.

"Step back. Try again," said the soldier, annoyed.

Rico did like he was told, with the same result.

"Dammit," the guard said. He turned to his partner, saying: "Call maintenance, will you—"

Rico stepped across the line, drawing his Glock at the same time. He pistol-whipped the first guard, who went down hard. The second soldier lunged for the alarm, and Remy clocked the man in the head with the butt of his M24. The guard dropped to the ground, unconscious.

"Well, how about that, you're not just a pretty face, Sam." Rico sighed. "I hate this part."

He shot both men in the head.

Remy gasped. "What—was that necessary?"

"Cassandra said no witnesses." There was a note of regret in the sergeant's voice. "We do what has to be done for the cause."

He dragged the bodies to the security station and keyed the elevator door open. A slight tremor shook the floor. "That'll be our boys. Right on time."

———

CENTCOM command center was a bunker buried a hundred meters beneath the Qatari desert. Set up arena style, the room housed two dozen operators outfitted with high-tech data visors and hand manipulators facing a massive wallscreen. When Rico and Remy stepped off the elevator —the only entrance in or out—the room had already been placed on red alert.

Rico fired a rifle round into the ceiling.

"Everyone, may I have your attention, please!" he shouted over the blaring Klaxons.

The room stilled.

"Stand up, take off your headsets, and step away from your workstations. Now."

A young woman in an Air Force uniform reached forward and Rico fired a slug into her workstation. "The next one goes in your ear, little lady."

She ripped off her data visor and scooted back.

Behind them, a solid sheet of steel slammed down over the elevator doors.

"Who did that?" Rico's voice was casual, which made him seem even more dangerous. He appeared unconcerned about the fact that they were now sealed in the bunker.

"I did." An officer in her mid-forties raised her hand. Her dark hair was streaked with gray and her jaw was set. "I put us in lockdown. You're trapped here, you piece of—"

Rico shot her through the heart.

The room froze as one, the alarm pulsing like a grating heartbeat. The officer's mouth hung open as if she might continue, then she crumpled to the floor. A younger woman moved to catch her.

"Nope!"

Rico aimed his rifle at her. The woman stopped midstride.

"Anyone else want to play the hero? Anyone?" He waited. "All right, then." Motioning with his rifle, Rico said, "Everyone into the meeting room, back there." He followed the personnel and closed the door behind them, then slid his M24 rifle through the door handles to lock them in.

Remy's mind reeled as he followed Rico back into the main bay. Security footage from the rest of the base played on the massive wallscreens. One outside camera showed a column of smoke rising into the brassy yellow sunlight. A full platoon of armored soldiers engaged a Neo squad in a heavy firefight. Drones crisscrossed the sky overhead.

"What do we do now?" Remy asked.

"We put on a show."

"What?"

Rico gestured at the ceiling-mounted cameras. He leaned in close to Remy's ear. "We try to upload the virus, we get frustrated, I shoot you and you shoot me. Bing-bang-boom."

"I don't understand," Remy said.

"It's theater, Sam," Rico said. "Think of this as making a film for posterity."

He extracted a slim probe from his belt and inserted it into the nearest workstation. After a few moments of supposed effort, he slammed his fists down on the console and cursed for the cameras. Then, to Remy in a low voice, "Okay, Sam, you ready for your big moment?"

"Ready for what?"

Rico spun around, drew his Glock, and fired point-blank into Remy's chest armor. The shot lifted Remy off his feet, slamming him backward. He slid to the floor.

Remy's mouth worked in the dry, conditioned air of the bunker. The cement floor was cool against the back of his head. Remy pawed at the fasteners on his armor, anything to be able to catch his breath. When he pulled his hand back it was slick with blood. His blood. Frantically, he probed at the armor and felt his fingertip slip into a hole.

Rico's shot had penetrated the Dragonskin armor. How was that possible?

Rico's face floated over him. "Stay with me, buddy."

Rico turned his back to the nearest camera. Remy felt him unfasten the restrictive armor, then Rico inserted something into the wound. A spike of chill in his chest, and all at once, he could breathe again.

"That should stabilize you for now," Rico whispered. "Buy you enough time for them to open the bunker. It's not too bad. We only weakened your armor in that one spot. Cassandra did the calculations herself. She's never wrong."

"Why?"

Rico gave a low chuckle. "To sell the defector story. You just got betrayed on camera. You're as pure as the driven snow now, secret agent man." He pressed two fingers against the chest wound and a bolt of pain made Remy's eyes snap open. "Stay awake, now. I need you to do one last thing."

The world was swimming. Rico's face faded in and out.

"What?"

Remy felt Rico unholster his sidearm and guide the muzzle under Rico's chin. There was a strange trembling light in Rico's eyes.

"You need to kill me. Cassandra says no witnesses, remember?"

"No—I can't," Remy gasped. "Won't."

Lips quivering, Rico said, "Her will be done."

One of them pulled the trigger. Maybe it was him; Remy wasn't sure. All he felt was the dead weight of Rico's body on his, and blood everywhere.

Then blackness.

# 6

## ANTHONY TAULKE • EN ROUTE TO MARS

After his extended stay in the Alcatraz of the Rockies, Anthony Taulke deemed himself a changed man.

He spent the first entire afternoon of the three-day trip to Mars in the galley of Adriana Rabh's yacht, the *Staff of Isis*, sampling dozens of organic fruit juice combinations just to see how the different flavors mingled on his tongue.

After his incarceration, Anthony figured Mars was the best option to ensure his continued freedom, but even that was debatable. If the governments of Earth really wanted to seize him, they had the military capability to do so. Taulke Industries wouldn't be able to protect him.

Teller wanted Anthony free to find a solution to the "climate problem," as the president called it. Anthony had to laugh at that euphemism. There was no *climate problem*—the governments of Earth were being held hostage. Someone had stolen Viktor's cryptokey and used it to wreak weather havoc all over the planet. But who was doing it, and why?

Viktor had joined them before they departed Earth's orbit. Anthony felt a strange rush of nostalgia upon seeing his rumpled friend—another indication that his time as a jailbird had permanently changed him.

Viktor laughed at his reaction. "You were in jail for two months—"

"Seventy-four days," Anthony snapped back. "I counted."

"You counted! In Russia, you can get six months for a traffic ticket. And real jail, not a holiday in the mountains." Viktor let his native accent slip through to emphasize his point, but Anthony could tell he was glad his friend was safe.

After the Lazarus disaster, Viktor had been returned to his homeland for trial and sentencing. But Viktor Erkennen had many friends in Russia, and his incarceration had been more like home arrest—with full access to his lab.

At dinner that evening, Anthony tried to turn the meal into a working session. "I want to be ready when we get to Mars," he said as Adriana's servant poured white wine for each of them. "We need to hit the ground running."

"There is bad news and worse news," Viktor said, taking a healthy pull from his glass.

"That's a 2082 Pinot Grigio," Adriana said with a look of frustration. "Part of the last of the wines produced in the Lavaux vineyards overlooking Lake Geneva, before the region went fallow."

Nodding appreciation, Viktor slurped another mouthful.

"So, tell me, Viktor," Anthony said.

"The bad news is that the cryptokey was stolen from my Moon facility—"

"Your super-secret, impenetrable Moon facility," Adriana interjected.

Viktor grimaced.

"We already know the bad news," Anthony said. "What's the worse news?"

Not waiting for the manservant, Viktor refilled his own glass. "The nanites are working as designed."

"That's not a headline you want to see on YourVoice," Adriana observed.

"Indeed not," Viktor said. "Someone is controlling local gradients to cause these disasters. These climate insurgencies are quite localized—and deliberate."

"But who's behind it?" Anthony said. "That's what we need to figure out."

Viktor set his glass down. "My government says it's your government."

"Teller?" Anthony said. "That makes no sense. Weaponizing the weather has rallied every other country on Earth against the United States. And why would he break me out of jail to try to fix the problem if he's the one causing it?"

Viktor curled his lip, a sign that he had achieved a state of inebriation where words were fungible. "Maybe his hands are ignorant."

"What does that even mean?" Adriana asked. Her voice had an edge of impatience.

Fortunately, Anthony spoke fluent Viktor-ese. "He means the right hand doesn't know what the left hand is doing."

Adriana rolled her eyes, then took comfort in her wine.

"Maybe it's not Teller," Viktor mumbled. "Maybe someone else inside your government—"

"Russian conspiracy theories," Adriana said. "Look at the facts: who benefits from all this chaos? No one. The world economy is in shambles, including the US. No one is making money off this situation, not even the climate change industry. There's too much anarchy cascading too rapidly. Countries can't keep up with the costs of resettling refugees anymore."

She moved the Pinot Grigio out of Viktor's reach and spread her hands on the snowy-white tablecloth. Her red nails gleamed in the soft, tasteful light of the dining suite. "Well?"

The Russian eyed the wine bottle. "I'm a scientist, not a political philosopher."

"It puts every country in the world at each other's throats," Adriana continued. "Think of it like a business takeover. What's the first thing a smart businessman does before cornering the market?"

"Undercut the competition," Anthony said.

"How?"

Anthony thought for a moment. "Destabilize the market. Play one competitor off another."

Grunting, Viktor said, "Like a criminal syndicate. Get the competition to eliminate each another, then step in and take over."

"Exactly. Criminal empire or business conglomerate or international politics, the strategy is the same: divide and conquer."

The three fell silent. Adriana ticked her nails on the table. Viktor stared at his nearly empty wineglass. Anthony turned to the window, centering himself in the vastness of space.

Adriana broke the silence. "My sources tell me the attacks on the US bases were all Neos, except for one soldier, and they captured him."

"The religious cult?" Anthony said. "You think they're behind all this weather manipulation? That seems farfetched to me."

"There are two billion followers of Cassandra in the world," Adriana said. "She promises them a new Earth, but she never promised them they'd live to see it."

Anthony sat forward. "Fine, it's worth looking into. But I don't want to make the same mistake that happened with Lazarus. When we solve this nanite problem, I want us to be in control of the solution."

Adriana folded her hands. She knew a business pitch was coming. "What did you have in mind?"

"A council that can protect our interests, made up of the people in this room: business leaders with vision and resources who don't kowtow to every shift in public opinion. Adriana, you bring the financial backing and the relationships with Earth's governments at the United Nations. Viktor brings the R&D capabilities. I bring Mars and the resources of Taulke Industries. Once we deal with the Earth problem, there's Mars, the Moon, asteroid mining, even Titan as a refining colony. We can be the invisible hand that guides humanity's growth."

Adriana jerked her head and the manservant departed the suite. "You're forgetting one thing. We need to solve this Earth problem first."

"I have idea," drunk Viktor said, tapping his glass.

Anthony waited as Adriana relented and filled it The Russian drank deeply before he spoke. "I can make new nanites to kill the old nanites. Then we're back where we started." He toasted himself.

"Bold," Adriana said. "Expensive, but bold."

Viktor shrugged. "Lab research is the next step. Like before, I will need Qinlao Manufacturing to help me."

Anthony realized with a pang of guilt that he hadn't thought of Ming Qinlao since being incarcerated. "Where is Ming? Is she safe?"

Adriana toyed with her wineglass. "Unknown. Her aunt—with backing from the Chinese government—moved against her, but she escaped. Xi

Qinlao is the de facto CEO in her niece's absence." She eyed Anthony. "We'll have to deal with Xi."

Anthony stood and paced the room. They didn't really need Ming, but part of him wanted her to play a role in this grand plan he was enacting. She was the kind of leader who could help shape the new world Anthony wanted to build. "Get the design done, Viktor. I'll handle contact with Qinlao. In the meantime, Adriana and I will focus on taking back control of the current situation."

Adriana folded her arms. "How do you suppose we do that? I have some of the best networks out there and we're coming up dry."

Anthony spun his seat around and straddled it. "You said the US military sustained a Neo attack. We start there. There's a reason why the Neos are on the offense. Find the reason, find the Neos."

Adriana nodded slowly. "I'll see what I can find out."

A soft whistle sounded. "Ms. Rabh, this is the captain."

"Go ahead," Adriana replied.

"Mr. Taulke asked to be notified when we were within visual range of the Mars magnetic shield generator. You can view the generator from the observation lounge now."

Rising, Adriana said, "Shall we?"

Viktor brought his wine.

They made their way to the observation lounge, a bubble at the very top of the yacht, free of the ship's structural lines.

"It's the key to terraforming the Martian surface," Anthony said, climbing the winding staircase to the lounge. "The MSG uses a magnetic field to deflect the solar winds, protecting the atmosphere. It should be finished by now and undergoing stress-testing—"

He halted on the top step so fast Viktor bumped into him. The shield generator, which should have been bright with activity, stood dark, almost invisible in the blackness of space. Parts of the massive device had been cannibalized.

"Captain, Taulke here."

"Yes, sir?"

"How fast can you get us to Mars?"

"At top speed, we can be there in approximately eight hours, Mr. Taulke, but the ride will not be very comfortable."

Anthony shot a glance at Adriana, who nodded.

"Do it," Anthony said, his eyes still on the now-defunct MSG.

Adriana took Anthony's arm, her touch gentle. "Do you want to speak to Tony before we get there?"

"No. This is an in-person conversation. But I do have a call to make before we arrive."

---

The connection with Earth was crystal clear, making it possible for Anthony to appreciate Xi Qinlao's beauty. She was older now, yes, but her dark hair had the rich body only obscenely expensive scalp conditioning could buy. Her skin was flush and supple.

"Anthony Taulke, what a pleasant surprise. Prison is treating you well." Surgically altered to the color of jade, her eyes also carried the gem's hardness.

"And you're as beautiful as ever, Xi." He leaned forward. "Can I tell you a secret?"

She nodded, letting the flattery float by.

"I'm not in prison."

Xi lifted her chin. "That explains the tasteful décor behind you. I hadn't heard anything in the news. Aren't you afraid I'll share your secret?"

"Not once you know why I've called."

"Oh?" Xi quirked a painted eyebrow. "Tell me, how can I help a free man like yourself, Mr. Taulke?"

"Anthony, please," he insisted. "If we're going to be business partners again, we should be on a first-name basis."

"Are we going to be business partners ... again?"

"It's my hope, yes. Very soon I'll need manufacturing services, Xi. Discreet, fast, high-quality services."

The woman's thin smile stretched thinner. "In that case, you should contact—"

"Very discreet, Xi." Anthony hesitated. "A variant on a previous order."

Xi's jade eyes grew cold. "My niece's indiscretion, you mean. I'm not interested."

"Not yet, maybe. But if you'll allow a member of your board a moment—"

"Former member. My niece invited you to the board, and the board stripped you of that privilege when you went to prison." Xi gathered her wrap around her. "Anthony, you are wasting my time. I will do you the courtesy of not alerting the authorities, but don't contact me again."

"What about a trade?"

Xi Qinlao diverted the hand about to cut their connection. "You know where she is? Ming?" The woman's eyes gleamed with sudden fury.

Anthony shrugged. "I know more than you do."

It took Xi a moment to regain her composure. "I'm quite concerned about my nephew. His mother's worried sick and my niece is not fit company for a young man of his breeding."

She was lying, of course, but Anthony decided to play along. He hoped his face showed the proper concern. "If I can return him to the bosom of his family, would that change your mind about an arrangement?"

Xi's eyes went to slits. "If you can find my nephew, then you can find Ming."

"My offer is for the safe return of your nephew in exchange for manufacturing services," Anthony said.

The two stared at each other's image for a long time.

"No," she said. "My niece or nothing." Her perfect lips tightened into a painted smile. "Call me when you have her."

———————

*Staff of Isis* entered orbit around Mars seven hours and forty-seven minutes later only to be intercepted by an escort.

"Unidentified vessel, this is the corvette *Revenant* of the Mars Security Force. Your transponder signal is not broadcasting. State your registry or prepare to be boarded."

Mars Security Force?

Anthony's head ached from dehydration. They'd finished off Adriana's stock of Swiss wine, and his eyes were sandy from lack of sleep.

Corvette?

The ship setting itself in their flight path looked like a refitted freighter. An armed, refitted freighter.

Rail gun placements hung under the escort ship fore and aft, forcing Anthony to question his sobriety. There were no armed ships on Mars. The United Nations strictly regulated armed spacecraft to prevent an international arms race in space.

"This is the yacht *Staff of Isis*, under the ownership of the Rabh Conglomerate," the captain responded. "Since when does Mars have a security force?"

Anthony rubbed his eyes. "Captain, if I may?"

After a glance to Adriana, the yacht's captain nodded.

Anthony stepped center-camera in the middle of the bridge and faced a grizzled-looking man in a paramilitary uniform with the Taulke Industries logo on the left breast.

"*Staff of Isis*, we're looking up your registry now. Why are you running silent—"

"On whose authority do you challenge ships in the name of my planet?" Anthony demanded.

The corvette captain regarded him curiously. "Sir, if you're a representative of the Rabh Conglomerate—"

"I'm Anthony Taulke! And you work for me! Who the hell put you in charge of an armed spacecraft?"

The captain of the *Revenant* stared at the screen. "We're here on Mr. Taulke's orders, sir—"

"I *am* Mr. Taulke!" Anthony roared back. His own words pounded his aching brain.

"Stand by, sir."

Anthony consciously willed his jaw to relax, his fists to unclench.

"You are cleared to land, sir. Pad sixteen. Sending coordinates now."

Pad sixteen? There were only three landing pads on Mars.

Anthony stalked to the window, anxious to catch sight of the Taulke

Atmospheric Experiment Station. When the station showed over the horizon, he had to remind himself to breathe.

Domes. Two of them, under construction, each easily ten times the size of the experiment station.

Anthony's grand plan for Mars had always been terraforming. In the long term, there would be no need for domes. Mars would have its own breathable atmosphere. A fresh start for the human species. To date, the station had only needed a modest dome capable of housing a few thousand engineers and scientists while they did their work resurrecting the Red Planet as a new Earth.

But the sight unfolding below him was not that vision. An army of large crawlers were excavating soil for the pylons to anchor the domes. And there was evidence of a subterranean mining operation digging out crisscrossing maintenance tunnels to run beneath the habitat level. Tony was creating another LUNa City.

He shook his head. That was not the plan. Mars was not going to be an underground city like the Moon. Future citizens of Mars would live in the open air, free of pressure suits and radiation warnings. That was the dream. *His* dream. This ... this was a commercial operation.

The yacht banked, angling toward the landing zones. Twenty landing pads dotted the planet's surface, and all but one was occupied. Freighters, their bellies gaping open, disgorged pallet after pallet of supplies and materiel.

Tony had done all this in a little over six months? How was that even possible?

The *Isis* settled onto its assigned pad. A team of workers hustled out to attach an atmospheric tunnel to her docking port.

"Mr. Taulke, we're connected to the station. Standing by to open the airlock."

He descended the steps, his head thudding. Putting Tony in charge of Mars had been a devil's bargain to make Lazarus possible, a way to keep Taulke Industries alive.

And now, Tony had made its crowning jewel, the Mars Atmospheric Project, into something else entirely. An inferior vision. A settle-for solution of manufactured domes. Anthony nodded at the tech to open the airlock.

The young man on the other side had his father's curly hair, dark eyes, and strong jaw. If the elder Taulke had looked in a mirror a quarter century ago, he would have seen this reflection staring back at him. The main difference now could be found in their expressions.

Taulke the younger smiled, a row of perfect white teeth between perfectly sculpted lips. He opened his arms wide and stepped forward.

"Pop," he said. "Welcome home."

# 7

## MING QINLAO • LUNA CITY, THE MOON

Ming dropped gently to the ground from the jungle of overhead pipes.

"I love how you kids do that," Alvin said, putting the spanner she'd tossed him in the toolbox. "Just hoist yourself up into the pipes, no ladder or nothing."

Ming hadn't been showing off, merely taking another opportunity to keep her muscles from going moonsoft. She had to be ready to go home, whenever that was possible again.

Alvin consulted his work orders. "Well, we fixed the aerator scoop, adjusted the humidity regulator, and completed calibration on the water separator. We can pack it in for the day."

"Good. I wouldn't mind getting to Rodney's school a little early to pick him up. He's grounded. Don't want him to be idle for too long."

Alvin raised an eyebrow. "Grounded? What for?"

"Fighting at school. There was a bully in his class, and Rodney decided it was his job to do something about it."

"Trying to impress a girl." Alvin swung into the driver's seat. "That's a teenage boy for you."

The scooter lifted off. "No, I don't think so," Ming said. Then again, Ruben had casually mentioned a girl with red hair a few times. Ming had assumed her to be a study buddy, but it hadn't even occurred to her that Ruben might be interested in girls. Angel, that was her name.

"Whatever's going on with him, I hope he grows out of it soon," she murmured. Maybe Alvin, who'd never met Ruben, knew her brother better than she did.

"Give him time, Mary. He's just a boy."

Time was the one thing they had plenty of right now, as long as they stayed hidden. She half-listened to Alvin as he listed the next day's work orders. When they reached her stop, Ming hopped off the scooter and waved him a quick goodbye.

She took the steps two at a time up to the inhabited levels. It was second nature now to keep her head low and face angled away from the ever-present cameras. In the time since she'd arrived on the Moon, Ming had grown her bangs long and wore a pair of data glasses augmented with the expensive face-blurring tech celebrities employed to confuse facial rec programs. Only in the anonymity of crowds did she feel truly safe from Xi's unlimited resources trying to find them.

Ming stepped inside the brightly colored open doorway of the school. Children's drawings decorated the walls of the lower grades, and a video of two girls singing a nursery rhyme played on the kiosk near the vacant front desk.

"Hello?" she called down the hallway of eight open classroom doors. She checked the time. Classes shouldn't be out for another twenty minutes. And yet, there was no one, child or adult, in sight. A woman with a tousled spray of brown-gray frizz poked her head out of the last door along the corridor. Ruben's classroom.

"Mary," said the woman, "what a pleasant surprise."

"I'm here for Rodney." Ming looked around. The hallway and the open community area were normally crawling with children of all ages after school. "Where is everyone?"

The heavyset teacher stepped into the hallway. She wore a shapeless dress and walked with a plodding tread, even in low-gee. "Half day, remember?"

Ming did not remember. "Did Lily pick him up, by any chance?"

The teacher shook her head. "No, Rodney left with Angel. They were holding hands." She winked at Ming. "Young love, you know? I remember my first kiss—"

"Do you know where they went?" Ming interrupted.

The woman paused, considering. "I know a bunch of kids were talking about the new sim-parlor up on level ten. They say the Mark-6 holos are really good. Didn't your uncle tell you?"

Ming's heart beat faster. "Uncle?" Scenarios began to unfold in her head. All of them ended badly for Ruben.

"Yeah, he came by about fifteen minutes ago, looking for Rodney. Big Earth muscles, seemed to still be adjusting to lunar gravity. Cute, too. Another guy, too. He was shorter—"

"Thanks," Ming called over her shoulder.

She hustled through the throng of foot traffic in the main thoroughfare. Two men looking for Ruben? Not the LUNa City marshals—that bill had been cleared. Cops for hire, maybe, or Xi's agents.

Picking up her pace, Ming pushed aside the dark possibilities arising in her mind's eye. The men had a fifteen-minute head start but were likely unfamiliar with the city's layout. They'd use escalators, ask directions. All that took time.

There was a maintenance deck between housing levels ten and eleven in this part of the city. No one went there, she could move fast. Ming headed for the nearest maintenance door and used her passcode to enter. Inside, the tunnels were deserted, and a clear lane ran between rows of machinery. As Ming started running, she pulled out her data glasses and called Lily.

"Is Ruben with you?"

"Well, hello to you too, dear." Lily's voice sounded petulant.

"Lil, please! Is Ruben with you?"

"No, why? Did he ditch you? Don't worry about that marshal. I've got him wrapped around my—"

Quick anger flared at Lily's clear attempt to make her jealous.

"Listen, Lil, listen to me very carefully. In our closet is a green go-bag. Get it and wait for me there. Stay in the apartment and lock the door. Understand?"

"Yes, but—"

Ming cut the connection.

It felt like she'd run across half of LUNa City before finally spotting the marker for the sim-parlor's neighborhood. She cracked the door and peered into the corridor, then slipped into the stream of passing residents.

Level 10 on a Friday evening always had a festive feel. Philby's Fun House, the sim-parlor, sat nestled among the shops, restaurants, gambling houses, and bordellos along one of the busiest recreational corridors in LUNa City. The entrance to the sim-parlor was a sea of people, all hoping for a chance to escape the dull reality of lunar life with a half hour's distraction.

Ming kept her head down, edging through the scrum of people lining up for Philby's Mark 6 holos, closet-sized VR pods where singles or couples could dial up whatever fantasy they desired. Bodies jostled against her as she pushed her way through the crowd to the front desk.

The young man behind the counter handed her a personal access data device.

"Sign in, please. The wait's two hours and change—"

"I'm looking for my brother," she said, pushing the padd away. "He came in here with a girl, red hair, maybe an hour ago."

"Are you kidding? Look at this crowd." He looked past her, anxious to help a paying customer instead.

Ming reached out and snagged his hand, pressing paper scrip into his palm.

"I want to speak to the manager. There's an underage boy here. Think how that will play with the marshals." In fact, she had no idea how it would play with them. On the lunar frontier, morality was a fluid concept.

The clerk eyed the crumpled cash. He flipped up a divider and Ming walked through, customers grousing behind her. She followed him into a narrow hallway.

The manager sat behind an array of two dozen displays showing interior views of the holo pods. Ming had a fleeting glimpse of pumping buttocks and flailing legs scored by a soundtrack of grunting and gasping before the man minimized the display wall. She hoped that was not Ruben and Angel.

"I'm here for my little brother. He's underage. Help me find him quickly and I'll be on my way."

The manager nodded at the clerk to go and raised his palms in surrender. "Look, we guarantee privacy to our customers. I can't just let you look at anyone's holo—"

Ming punched him in the face with the heel of her palm. Once, sharp and hard. Then, with her Earth-strong muscles, she pulled him out of his chair.

"Ow! Jesus!" The man's voice had an echoing, nasal quality now. "I think you broke my nose!"

"Let's keep it to just that body part," she said. "Find my brother. He came in with a redheaded girl, both about fourteen."

He held his nose as he scrolled through the thumbnails of the live feeds.

"There!" he said, stabbing a bloody finger at the wallscreen. "Is that him?"

Ruben and Angel were sitting on a fallen tree in a woodland park, surrounded by ferns and mature oaks with Spanish moss hanging from them. A horse grazed in the background, and birds flitted in the lower tree branches. Ruben had one arm wrapped around Angel's shoulder. Her red hair flowed down her back like a river of shimmering silk. They were locked in a teenager's awkward, passionate kiss.

"Pod seven," the manager said. "That way." He pointed to the sliding door on the wall.

Ming stepped into a hallway that ran between Philby's two rows of holo pods. Quickly locating pod 7, she disregarded the red occupancy light and jerked the door open. The 3-D VR projection fooled her depth perception, and there was a moment of disorientation.

The two teens broke apart immediately, Angel gasping. Ruben rose and moved in front of her.

"We need to go," Ming said. "Now."

Ruben shook his head, his eyes wide.

Ming reached for her brother. "We need to go!"

It took Ming a split second to realize he wasn't looking at her, he was looking over her shoulder. And she missed the fear in his eyes.

Two hands clamped onto her shoulders.

"Ming Qinlao, you're coming with me." The voice was deep and menacing.

Years of training with Ito paid off in instinct. She stepped backward, set her feet, and head-butted her attacker's face with the back of her skull. Her right elbow slammed into his gut, then she jackhammered a fist into his groin.

Butt, gut, and nuts. Ito's go-to sequence for an attack from behind.

The grip on her shoulder loosened and Ming spun into a kick that swept his feet out from under him. He crashed into the side of the pod, the idyllic image around them glitching from the impact. She pistoned kicks to the side of his head until he stopped moving.

Ming stepped into the hallway, ready for the second attacker. Ruben's teacher had said there were two men.

The door on the pod across from them opened. A young woman saw the prone assailant and quickly shut the door.

Ming seized Ruben's arm. "We're leaving, now!"

Ming jerked Ruben into the hallway. Xi, Earth authorities, the UN— whoever the hell had sent these men, they knew she was here. The Moon wasn't safe anymore.

Still holding on to Ruben, she hurtled to the back of the sim-parlor.

A lifetime ago, when Ming had been an engineer on the LUNa City project, she'd approved the specs for every one of these buildings. They were cookie-cutter designs, with the power distribution center and the exits located in the same place.

She found the panel and killed the power for the entire block. Main lights went out everywhere, drawing screams from the crowd. Then sparsely placed banks of emergency lights came on, casting a harsh white glare and ghostly shadows. Ruben's face was a rigid mask of fear as he gripped Ming's hand.

The room behind them filled up as the sim-parlor patrons evacuated their pods. Ming waited for maximum confusion, then opened the maintenance level access door.

"It's okay," she said. They were hidden behind the walls of LUNa City. She could feel him shaking, cold sweat on his palm. "I have a plan."

The boy worked at speaking a moment. "Angel..."

Ming wiped strands of sticky hair from Ruben's forehead. "She'll be fine."

She hoped it wasn't a lie. Whoever was after them, if they worked for Xi, they wouldn't bat an eye at interrogating a teenaged girl. Even if Angel knew nothing of any real value, they wouldn't stop questioning her until they were sure of that.

"Her parents will look after her, don't worry." Ming urged him down the dimly lit hallway.

"Where are we going?" Ruben asked.

"Home."

Though they maintained a steady pace, getting to their habitat level took longer than expected. The maintenance corridors were built for utility, not as convenient shortcuts between levels. And there were always the security cameras to be avoided, especially now.

Finally, Ming knelt inside the access door looking out on their apartment door. "Stay here," she said. "I'll get Lily and—"

"I don't want to stay here by myself, Ming," Ruben said. He seemed ashamed to admit it.

"It'll just be for a few minutes, I promise. I'll be right back."

Ming waited until a neighbor and his wife debating dinner choices turned the corner at the far end of the corridor, then slipped from behind the access door. She walked the few short steps to Lily's front door and keyed in her passcode.

The apartment was brightly lit but silent. The hackles on Ming's neck rose.

There was a black Chinese tiger crafted out of sintered Moon rock on an end table inside the door. A welcome-home gift from Lily. Ming picked it up.

"Lil?" she whispered. It was like her voice was afraid to disturb the silence.

Ming stepped into their quarters. A grinding sound erupted from the kitchen, making her jump. The sonic dishwasher had kicked into high gear, its whine loud in an otherwise soundless apartment.

The sliding door to the small office off the living room was closed. The bedroom door was open, the light on.

Ming cleared her throat, calling louder, "Lily?"

In the bedroom, one lamp on the near side of the bed was on. The other lay broken between the bed and the wall. Ming stopped in her tracks. It looked like a windstorm had hit. The bedcovers lay tangled on the floor. The reading chair had been knocked askew. The mirror on the outside of the en suite bathroom door lay shattered in pieces on the floor.

"Lily!"

Ming ran to the bathroom, glass crunching beneath her work boots, the broken mirror pieces casting crazy reflections over the walls.

Lily lay in the tub, her left leg splayed over one edge, her right twisted beneath her body at an odd angle. She was still as stone.

A cold layer of gooseflesh prickled Ming's skin. Her mind closed in on itself.

*Lily.*

A red stain was spreading slowly across the white of Lily's blouse. Her vacant gaze pierced through Ming.

Glass crunched under her boots, and Ming felt the bite of glass in her knee as she knelt next to the tub.

"No. No, no, no..." Ming held her lover's hand. The flesh was cooling quickly. "Oh, Lily ... I'm so sorry."

A sound met her ears. A grinding noise, the sound of a sliding door in need of oil...

Ming was not alone.

Soft footfalls in the bedroom. Cautious noises.

*You're wasting time, Little Tiger,* Ito's voice told her. *Take the initiative ... before it takes you.*

She stood and spun, the glass under her feet screeching in protest. The tiger statue felt heavier than it should in the lower gee of the Moon.

A screech came from the kitchen as the dishwasher switched cycles. And she knew exactly how long the sound would last.

*One ... two ... three.*

On *four*, as the dishwasher resumed its low drone of sonic scouring, Ming stepped into the bedroom.

A thin man stood in the doorway, waiting for her. He was lean and wiry, and he held a knife with the ease of someone who knew how to use it.

The blade was dull. No, not dull. Stained with blood.

*Lily's blood.*

"She tole me you'd left LUNa City," the man said in a reedy voice. His lips stretched, revealing sharp yellow incisors. "Didn't believe her, me."

Ming clutched the sculpture in her right hand. The thin man noted it.

"Don't matter how this ends," he said. "Come on two feet or we ship your body. Get paid either way, we."

We. The man in the sim-parlor was his partner.

*Take the initiative, before it takes you.*

His eyes taunted her, told her she was trapped. But Ming had worked hard to keep her muscles from going moonsoft. He didn't know that.

Ten feet between them. She crossed the distance in two bounds.

Ming raised the tiger with her right hand as a feint, then slammed her feet into the thin man's right knee. She felt the joint pop as they tumbled together into the living room. He grunted at the pain, slashing at her. Ming avoided the blade and rolled to the opposite wall. She sprang to her feet.

He took longer to get upright and favored his knee when he did. His back was to the main door. If Ming was going to get away, she needed to go through him.

"Last chance, you," he said. "My partner gets here, it's carryout only. No delivery deal."

The dishwasher screeched for several long moments.

"You killed Lily," Ming said, closing by inches the distance separating them. "You didn't have to do that."

"Beggar, she," the thin man said, turning the knife over in his grip. "Pathetic. Pretty, too. Shame no time for nothing but the knife."

The chime on the front door rang. *The partner.*

The thin man lunged. Ming turned in profile. *Small target, big miss,* said Ito from a thousand years ago.

The thin man wasn't used to the lower demands of the Moon's lesser gravity and his momentum carried him too far forward. Ming brought the tiger statue, Lily's gift, crashing onto the back of his skull. A thick sound like a hammer on a board, and the thin man dropped.

The door chime sounded a second time.

She brought the tiger down again, and the wet, crunching sound of his skull fracturing made her lip curl. The fingers of his knife hand twitched.

He was still breathing, Ming saw. She could run—should run—and get to Ruben.

Fury settled into her stomach, the hard center of a dark sun.

The thin man stirred. He held up a hand to ward her off.

"Please," he said, levering himself up on one elbow.

"Don't beg," Ming said. "It's pathetic." She lifted the stone tiger a third time and finished him.

The beeping at the door meant someone was overriding the lock.

The door opened. Ming readied her legs to launch herself at the doorway, then saw it was Ruben standing there.

"I got tired of waiting," the teen said. His eyes descended to find the dead man on the floor.

"Get in here," Ming cried.

Ruben's gaze stayed locked on the thin man and the gore staining the carpet, but he did as he was told. The door shut behind him.

"Lock the door, Ruben." He complied mechanically. "Now, don't move!"

Ming reentered the bedroom for the go-bag she hoped was still there. She paused in the doorway of the bathroom. She wanted to stop and talk to Lily, to arrange her body so her leg wasn't so painfully bent behind her, to say how sorry she was, to cover Lily's face with a bath towel—*something*.

But there was not time for that now. They were coming for her.

# 8

## LUCA VASQUEZ • MINNEAPOLIS, MINNESOTA

Christmas is just around the corner, Luca realized, stepping off the tube. Ho-ho-holy shit.

She ignored the festive decorations hanging from the lampposts along University Avenue as she rushed to Foyle Hall. She was late for work. Again. The people on the slushy sidewalks all seemed joyful, embracing the holiday and its infectious optimism. She ignored them, too.

There was little cheer in Luca. Doctor Markov had been curt with her after the demonstration for Hannah Jansen. Luca had put his grant in jeopardy, he said, by interfering with the experiment. Once the semester was over, he'd be requesting another lab assistant. To top it all off, she'd called in sick two days in a row.

Donna, suffering some virulent forty-eight-hour flu, had needed her at home. The urgent care on campus prescribed bed rest, liquids, and a shotgun dose of antivirals for both of them. But two days away from the lab meant two days without pay. If strained finances had made the holidays look glum before, a short paycheck and losing her campus job made it ten times worse. And then there was the real problem: this was their first Christmas without their parents. They were strangers in a strange land with little hope and less money.

Her shoe slipped on a patch of ice, and Luca windmilled her arms to keep her balance.

A perfect metaphor for her existence. One patch of ice away from a broken arm and total insolvency.

She wrenched the door open and hurried down the stairs to the dungeon, thinking about all she had to get done before her ten o'clock class. Feed the animals, download the data from the previous day's work, prep the tank for the…

Luca paused in the foyer. A stocky man in a university security uniform stepped out to meet her.

"Can I help you, ma'am?" His beady eyes narrowed under a broad brow and his uniform appeared a size too small for his beefy frame. He reminded Luca of a gorilla with a badge. Broad shoulders, hairy arms that hung like thick parentheses over stumpy, powerful legs.

"Ma'am?"

"I—I work here. Who are you?"

"She's okay, Matt." Jules appeared in the doorway, her blonde spikes catching the light. She wore her usual tight tank top, but instead of the normal snarky bite to her tone, she spoke in a professional voice. "Leave your purse and data glasses here and follow me, please."

The security gorilla stepped aside, his eyes tracking her as she followed Jules inside. Luca caught a glimpse of a Neo tattoo on his nape.

"What's going on?" Luca whispered.

"Markov's project is being shut down," Jules replied. Her voice was flat. She might have been talking about the weather. "He's on sabbatical. Licking his wounds, I guess, after his funding got pulled. I'm supposed to take care of everything here."

"His funding got pulled?" Luca reached out and turned Jules around. Her pupils were enlarged—near-black pools framed in bone-white sclera. Was she high?

"What about the animals?" Luca asked.

Jules cocked her head, thinking. "Destroying them would likely elicit unwanted attention," she said in that same creepy, flat voice. "Kidding."

She didn't sound like she was kidding.

Jules said, "Protocol is that post-experimentation, all animals, failing other arrangements, are to be turned over to the College of Veterinary Medicine. Can you call them today? Before they're closed for the weekend?"

"Sure. Have the animals been fed yet today?"

"No, I've been too busy. Can you take care of it? And tonight too? I've got to be somewhere."

"Sure. But Jules—what's going on? Why's the project being shut down? We were supposed to be funded for two years."

Jules looked past her. "Markov broke protocol. He must've been talking online with other researchers or something. Some of his data leaked on the WorldNet, and that made the people who write the checks really unhappy."

Luca swallowed hard, suddenly wishing she hadn't brought up the subject. "He leaked his own data?"

"Yeah. He tried to cover his tracks online, but they know it was him."

"Who's they?"

Jules hesitated a fraction of second too long for Luca to believe her. "The university, of course."

Luca gave her a half smile, uneasy. "I'll feed the animals."

"And call Vet Med."

Luca backed away. "I'll take care of it."

As she made her way to the kennel, she passed a team of workmen disassembling Markov's observation tank. One man was on his hands and knees with a cutting tool. She noticed a Neo tattoo on the back of his neck. Just like Jules had. Just like the security guard.

Just like Donna.

Luca practically ran to the cages on the far wall. Had her exchanges with Magdalena in the Portal been discovered?

Filling the rats' food dishes, she shook her head. She was overthinking things. Jules was right: Markov got sloppy. Probably bragged to some colleague after a few drinks.

She dropped kibble into Leroy's bowl and the beagle buried his head in the food. His tail wagged as he ate. Luis didn't seem hungry, so Luca pulled him out of his cage and held him, stroking his fur. The cat purred against her rib cage while she fingered the silver disk implanted under his collar.

No, Markov was a professional and very protective of his work. There was no way he would have talked about his results before he published. He had too much riding on the outcome. She stared through the doorway, watching the workmen beyond. Jules was packing boxes. When she caught Luca's eyes lingering on her, Luca glanced away.

She stroked the cat's fur faster. This was her doing. Magdalena had betrayed her. That was the only logical explanation. Magdalena had shown up a month earlier in the Portal, asking about the wild theories the members tossed around about the Neos using implants for mind control.

And Luca had responded. She'd shared some of Markov's data. Only a few observations, nothing really.

Magdalena hadn't seemed like so many of the others in the Portal. She wasn't a raving nutjob. She was reasonable, a thoughtful person ... a friend. Luca had trusted her so much she'd shared her concerns about Jules and the weird transmissions that day during the demonstration.

"Did you call Vet Med yet?"

Luca jumped at the sound of Jules's voice in her ear. Luis meowed his displeasure at being clutched so closely and dug his claws into her stomach.

Jules was staring at her hard. "Nervous much?"

"Sorry," Luca breathed. She tried to soothe Luis. "The lab closing—it's got me freaked, I guess. It's my job. I'm not sure what I'm going to do in the spring." Luca hoped Jules might give her some idea of how long she still had a paycheck.

Jules shrugged, her expression cold. "Well, for now, I need you to take care of these animals. Before the end of the day, remember?"

Luis hissed at Jules's retreating back as she walked away, the Neo tat almost lost in the rest of her body art. She put Luis back in his cage and booted up her terminal.

Since she'd shared the data with Magdalena, she'd gone back to her analysis a hundred times, and the simplest explanation was the most plausible: the transmission wave was not from an unauthorized data device or an EM field failure.

The transmission had been on the same wavelength as Markov's animal implants, but it hadn't come from either of the animals.

The transmission had come from Jules.

After classes, Luca stopped in a coffee shop for a cup of hot chocolate. She ignored the pang of guilt she felt about spending money on the luxury. She needed something to turn her mood around before going home to Donna.

The drink was creamy and rich with a pile of snowy whipped cream on top. The close, gray sky was finally yielding snow, fat flakes clumping together in the gathering twilight. The winter gloom did nothing to quell her nervousness.

In her shirt pocket, her data glasses blinked once. Donna was probably wondering where she was. She shouldn't have stopped for the cocoa. Luca slipped on the glasses, prepared for her little sister's wrath.

The message was from Magdalena. Luca felt the warmth drain out of her face. The only time she'd ever communicated with Magdalena was in the Portal, anonymously. How had she broken two levels of encryption to access Luca's personal email?

She hesitated, afraid to open the message. The incoming address was from a verified account with Magdalena's name on it. This was not spam, this was a real person with a real message. She opened the message with a blink.

*"You are in danger. This is what they did to Markov. Your friend, Magdalena."*

Below the single line of text was a link to a Canadian newsfeed. Clicking it played footage of a smoking wreck on a snowy hillside. An announcer's voice droned in the background: "Authorities have identified the driver of this aircar killed in a crash early this morning as Doctor Anton Markov of the University..."

Luca yanked the glasses off, trying to catch her breath. Any doubts about her complicity in Markov's death vanished. She was responsible. She was the leak.

She looked around the coffee shop, expecting to see armed police men advancing on her. A couple tangled together in an overstuffed leather chair, a student who looked vaguely familiar lost in his data glasses, and an older gentleman in an overcoat reading a tablet while he sipped his coffee. His eyes flicked up to meet hers, then dropped back to what he was reading.

Luca donned her glasses again and deleted Magdalena's message, then gathered her things and exited the shop. Charged with adrenalin, her senses screamed at every detail. The ankle-deep snow muffled the city sounds around her. Her shoes were soaked from the first step on the sidewalk.

"Oh, do be careful, dear," said a woman walking her dog. "It's very slippery."

Luca stopped in her tracks. She'd forgotten to feed the animals and she'd failed to call Vet Med. Now it was closed for the weekend, leaving the animals stranded in the dungeon.

She slogged through the heavy snow back to Foyle Hall. Brushing away nagging feelings of dread, she descended the stairs to find the too-big guard in the too-small uniform still on duty.

"What are you doing back here?" His attitude had not improved over the course of the day.

"I'm here to feed the animals," she said. "Jules told me to."

He scowled at her. "Make it fast."

Her footsteps echoed in the shadowy, half-deconstructed lab. The rats chittered when she turned on the light. They weren't used to night visitors. Leroy whined inside his crate, and Luis half-stood and stretched to greet her.

"I promise I'll feed you guys as soon as we get home," she said.

*Home?* But what choice did she have? Vet Med was closed, and someone had to take care of them for the weekend.

Luca packed food for each animal in her backpack, then placed the rats and cat into their carriers. When she put on Leroy's leash, his tail wagged with excitement at the prospect of a walk. Slinging the backpack over her shoulder, she loaded up Luis's larger crate in one hand and the two rats' shared smaller one in the other. Leroy's nails clicked on the linoleum floor as he led the way through the darkened lab.

The security guard looked up when they walked into the foyer. He put out a hand to stop her. "Where do you think you're going?"

"I'm taking the animals home." Luca decided her best course of action was to act like she knew what she was doing. "Unless you want to feed them and clean their cages all weekend."

"I dunno," he said. "They're wearing proprietary tech. I don't think you're supposed to be..." He stopped speaking, his pupils dilating like Jules's had that morning. His head cocked before his gaze fastened on Luca again. "Put the animals back."

She tried to stand her ground. "It's okay. I do this all the time."

The gorilla-guard advanced. Luca took a step back, laden with the animal cages.

"I said, put them back."

She continued retreating into the dark lab. His bulk filled the doorway, blocking the light. "I was supposed to call Vet Med, but I forgot. This way, I can care for—"

"Put them back!"

His body spasmed, jerking upright, then crumpling to the cold linoleum floor. Electrode darts made a pattern in his back. A lithe black woman with a shaved head stood in the doorway, a stun gun in her fist.

"Luca, are you okay?"

Leroy growled.

Luca blinked, not believing her eyes. "Hannah?"

Jansen nodded. "We have to hurry. Here, give me the cat." Luca handed Luis's cage to her without thinking twice. It felt natural. In exchange, Jansen handed her a Wi-Fi Microdrive.

"I want you to sync this up with Markov's personal terminal and download everything you can. Then you're coming with me. I have people picking up your sister."

"You want the data? You—you have Donna?" Luca repeated, trying to grasp the meaning of her words. The man on the floor twitched. "Wait ... you killed Markov..."

"No, Diana," she said carefully, deliberately. "We tried to protect him, but we failed."

"Diana..." How did Hannah know her avatar name from the Portal? The light dawned. "You're Magdalena."

Jansen smiled.

Her earlier fears drained away, replaced by a calm security.

"It's the Neos, isn't it?" Luca said. "Everything they're saying in the Portal is true."

"I'll explain, I promise," Jansen said. She gripped Luca's shoulder. "But we have to go. And we need that data."

"I'll have to sign in as myself. They'll know."

"It won't matter. You're not coming back here."

Luca blinked, wondering what that meant. For her and her little sister. "We can take the animals with us?" she asked.

"I'm counting on it. You'll need them to help Donna."

Luca exhaled a breath she hadn't realized she'd been holding. Hannah would take care of them. Hannah would protect them.

Help Donna. Now that would be the best Christmas present of all.

# 9

## WILLIAM GRAVES • HAVEN 6, BLUE EARTH, MINNESOTA

Graves had outfitted a makeshift secure room in the oversized closet next to his office. After installing the shielding for a Faraday cage along the walls and a small generator to power the jamming field, there was just enough room for two chairs facing one another.

The space lacked ventilation, but Graves decided to prioritize security over comfort. As a result, he normally stripped down to his T-shirt before entering the "hotbox," as he liked to call it, and he kept the meetings as short as possible.

Jansen sat across from him, similarly attired, their knees almost touching. A sheen of sweat gleamed on her dark brow. His head throbbed, a side effect of the New Year's Eve party the previous evening.

"We lost Markov, sir," she said.

Graves cursed. Markov had been the furthest along of three covertly funded research efforts aimed at understanding how Cassandra controlled the Neos. Figuring out how to disrupt their communications would have been his next step.

"Well, if he hadn't been close, they wouldn't have risked offing him so publicly," Jansen said.

"That's a hell of a silver lining, Hannah," Graves said. But Jansen was right. Their ham-handed murder of Markov spoke of an emotional reaction, not a strategic one. "You really think Markov's lab assistant can finish his work?"

"No one knows his research better."

Graves detected a note of hesitation in the captain's demeanor. "What is it?"

"Well, sir, Luca Vasquez is complicated. I guess that's the best way to describe her." She waited for Graves to indicate he wanted more, then plunged ahead. "Recent immigrant on a student visa, but she has a younger sister, Donna, who's implanted. We have Donna under sedation, of course. Luca damn near got herself killed trying to smuggle the test animals out of the lab. She's got guts, I'll give her that."

"And she has a personal motivation: the sister," Graves said. "Put her in the lab with the guy from UCLA. Same deal. You figure out how to disconnect all these people from Cassandra and you get a free ride to a new world."

"The sister too?"

Graves eyed her. "Eventually, our scientists are going to need human test subjects, right? The sister too."

He wiped his brow with his forearm. After a few sessions of like this one, the tiny space had the sour ripeness of a locker room. Across from him, he could see sweat soaking through the underarms on Jansen's shirt.

"How's the housecleaning going?" Graves asked, anxious to tick off items from the agenda in his pulsing head. Since they'd come to suspect the capability of the Neos, Graves had slowly been sidelining any key personnel who were marked with Cassandra's tag. It had to be done carefully, by moving them into new jobs of equal responsibility but outside the Haven project.

"Complete. The command staff is clean. I can't guarantee the other six Haven sites, but your staff here is clean."

She left the obvious flaw in Graves's plan unspoken. If they didn't find a way to break the Neo implant connection, everything would be revealed once Graves used the Havens as they were intended. Even now, he doubted this enormous structure could fly, much less travel to a distant planet, but that part was beyond his control. Whatever they had going on past the airlock on deck 36 was not his responsibility. Yet.

Jansen cleared her throat.

"Something to add, Hannah?"

"At the risk of beating a dead horse, sir—what are we going to do with Remy Cade?"

Graves scrubbed the side of his jaw with his fingernails. He was starting to smell himself now, and not in a good way.

"You have a recommendation?"

She shrugged. "He doesn't have a tattoo, so as far as we know, he's clean. And he wants to talk to you. In fact, that's damned near all he says: 'I want to see Graves.' He was seriously injured. Almost died, in fact. Shot by his own man, so that gives him some credibility."

"Bring him in."

Jansen sat back in her chair. "Here, sir? I didn't mean—"

"See if Ms. Vasquez can develop a more thorough test, but you say he's clean, no implant, which means he's either a defector or a double agent. Let's figure out which one we're dealing with."

Graves stood, and a wave of body odor rose with him. A bass drum beat loudly inside his skull.

"Now if you'll excuse me, Captain, I have an appointment with the president and I seriously need a shower first."

---

The sight of Washington, DC, from the air still put a lump in Graves's throat. Yeah, it was old-fashioned. Nobody really professed to be a patriot anymore, but to him, these symbols of America still mattered.

The aircar swung around on its final approach. The Capitol dome and the White House glared at each other from opposite ends of Pennsylvania Avenue. Beyond the levees, the Potomac surged around the District of Columbia, a muddy brown worm gorged on eroding soil.

A decade ago, the Washington establishment had given serious consideration to moving the US capital inland, but that movement fizzled. Everyone liked the idea of moving the capital, but everyone also had their own take on where it should be moved. Not surprisingly, every member of Congress favored their own district, and in the absence of a clear and present danger to the capital—no monuments or institutions had yet tumbled over—the status quo prevailed.

Graves's young pilot apparently fancied himself a bit of a hotshot behind the wheel. He flared the landing with a touch more power than was necessary and dropped the front pad of the aircar with an authoritative *thunk* onto the White House macadam.

"Let's keep it less showy next time, Lieutenant," Graves called.

The back of the young man's neck reddened. "Yes, sir. My first trip to the White House. Got a little carried away."

Graves scowled, more for show than out of real annoyance. "Give me a minute, Lieutenant."

The young man climbed out of the cockpit, leaving Graves alone with his thoughts.

He wasn't nervous about seeing the president. He'd long ago shed his sense of wonder about the people in high places. His interactions over the past year had taught him they were just people. Usually trying to do the right thing, sometimes for the wrong reasons, and sometimes with disastrous results.

But the secrets. That was the part that bothered him most. Graves would gladly trade his colonel's silver eagles for the gold bars of a lowly second lieutenant right now to avoid the compartmentalized mess his life had become. He knocked on the window to signal the pilot to open the door.

Graves stood, squared his shoulders, and set his beret on his head at the regulation angle. He was off to lie to the President of the United States.

All in a day's work, he told himself. You do what you have to do to help the most people.

The marine guard on the door popped a sharp salute, and Graves returned it. Inside, Helena Telemachus waited for him, dressed in a dark blue suit and skinny tie.

He offered her a shallow smile. "You didn't have to dress up for me, Helena." He addressed her by her full first name, knowing how it would bother her. Petty, but Graves was past caring.

H smirked back at him. "He's waiting." She set off with a long stride that forced Graves to double-time to keep up with her.

"Do we have an agenda?" Graves said to the back of her head. One did not refuse a summons to the White House, but the White House did not always deign to offer a reason for the summons.

"Not here," she muttered back, popping two sharp raps on the door to the Oval Office before entering.

Teller rose from behind the *Resolute* desk. Teller was a history buff and he'd made a news cycle out of moving the historic desk, fashioned from the British Arctic exploration ship, from the Smithsonian back into the Oval Office.

Smiling broadly, the president advanced, hand extended. Graves took it, studying Teller's face for any sign of what might be heading his way. Despite the micro-cosmetic treatments, Graves detected a new spray of worry lines around the president's eyes. With his second swearing-in only a few weeks away, Graves could only imagine how old he would appear four years from now. Assuming he wasn't crucified by the United Nations before then. Or Russia and China declared war.

Teller's smile felt genuine and his handshake warm, but Graves knew better than to judge this man based on those factors. He was dealing with a world-class political animal, a man who could change his skin faster than a chameleon in a kaleidoscope.

"Mr. President," was all Graves said.

"Sit, sit." Teller waved at the couches Graves had seen in media stories so many times. The striped cushions were firm, forcing an upright posture. He accepted an unsolicited cup of coffee from H and set it down on the table between them.

"Tell me about Haven," Teller said without prelude. His face was open, patient.

Graves froze. Did Teller know about the true nature of the project? He picked up his coffee again to stall for time, then set it down. H was watching him with narrowed eyes.

"Logistics are ninety percent complete, sir," Graves said, recounting the most innocuous details from Jansen's last report. He spoke slowly, pretending a need to recall the information. "The last ten percent is the hardest in any project, of course. But I expect to be fully supplied and ready to seal the dome within the next thirty days."

"How many can you take inside each dome?" Teller asked.

"Three thousand apiece, sir, including staff."

The president's posture sagged. "Seven Havens. Twenty-one thousand people. Half a billion people in this country, and the best we can do is save twenty-one thousand. That's pathetic."

Graves said nothing. Teller rose and began pacing, punching his fist into an open palm as he walked.

"I don't need to tell you that we're in the shit here, Graves. The UN is going to come after me again, and you're no doubt aware of the attacks on the US bases overseas. First, the New Earthers attack our overseas bases. Now, I've got the Russians and Chinese on my ass. If they rattle their sabers any louder, we'll need earplugs."

Graves shared a look with H. Her expression was inscrutable.

"Haven in its present form is a defensive play," the president continued. "We're just burying people in the ground and hoping things get better. I refuse to sit here and let innocent Americans die. We need to take action." He drove his fist into his palm one last time, then spun on his heel to face Graves. "That's where you come in, General."

The president stared hard at Graves, waiting for a reaction. H cleared her throat.

Wait ... the President of the United States just called him a—

Teller handed him a small velvet box. Graves opened it to find two silver stars, the insignia of a brigadier general. He looked up at Teller in disbelief. "Sir, I don't know what to say."

Teller's grin was grim. "Oh, don't thank me yet. You haven't heard what your new job is."

Graves pried his eyes away from the box in his hand. "New job, sir?"

"Brigadier General William Graves, you are in charge of the newly formed CONUS RELOCOMM."

Graves stared at the commander in chief, who'd just pole-vaulted him over a number of other, grayer heads in the command structure. "Continental United States Relocation Command? We already have units providing shelter and food to inland migrants, sir."

"Surely you can see we're beyond that, Graves. Think bigger." Teller returned to his seat. "I need you to save people. When the history books talk about Howard Teller III, I want Lazarus to be an unfortunate footnote to the story of the man who saved humanity. Look at those stars and that field of black velvet they're sitting on." He waited a moment until Graves obeyed. "That's not just a symbol of your new rank, General. That's a symbol of your new job. The Moon, Mars, wherever we can set up a colony. Save people, man. Save Americans."

The room fell silent. Even H gave the moment the respect it deserved. The tick-tock of the grandfather clock in the corner seemed anxious for Graves to answer.

Teller leaned forward, hands clasped together, gaze intense. "They still teach Dunkirk at West Point?"

"Of course, sir," Graves replied.

"When the British army was pinned on the beaches of northern France, the ocean at their back and the Germans breathing down their neck, Churchill didn't give up. He knew if he lost those soldiers, there was nothing stopping Hitler from taking Britain. The entire history of Western civilization would have been different. So, what did he do?"

"He rallied," Graves said.

"Exactly. The English requisitioned anything that would float—private yachts, fishing boats, anything—and sent them across the Channel. Saved more than three hundred thousand soldiers when it seemed all was lost." He stared Graves down. "I am the Churchill of our time, and we are going to save as many Americans as we can. I need you with me on this journey, General."

H continued, "You'll have the authority to requisition any off-planet transport necessary to move refugees. And the power to enter into negotiations with LUNa City to take them. We'll be transferring two companies of combat engineers under your command to assist in setting up additional lunar colonies."

"But, sir," Graves said. "The UN is already on the verge of declaring war against us. Why would they help us with LUNa City?"

"I'll handle that part," Teller said with a politician's smile. "We're sharing our intel on the New Earth Order with our closest allies. They've seen the attacks on our bases around the world and they're as worried about the Neos as we are. We can use that fear."

But Graves wasn't done yet. "You mentioned Mars before. Anthony Taulke is in jail, Mr. President. You put him there. Why would his company help us?"

The president grinned again, wider this time, and nodded to H.

"Taulke has been on Mars for the past month," she said. "Working on a way to reverse the weather problem. We have intelligence suggesting the Neos are the ones controlling the weather. I think you'll find Anthony Taulke receptive to helping with our refugee issue—as long as you are willing to share some intel about the Neos. We both want the same thing."

Graves took a deep, slow breath.

"Are you with me, General?" Teller asked, standing up and extending his hand.

Graves snapped the box shut and shook the president's hand firmly.

"Absolutely, sir. You can depend on me."

"I'm counting on it, General."

Graves followed H out of the Oval. For the first time in a very long time, Graves felt a sense of growing confidence. He had the resources. He had the authority. He had the mission to save the maximum number of human lives.

More than that, he had unlimited ability to launch anything he wanted in the continental United States. Without even knowing the true nature of the Havens, Teller just made his job a whole lot easier.

# 10

## REMY CADE • WALTER REED MILITARY MEDICAL CENTER, WASHINGTON, DC

Remy felt the sledgehammer blow of the bullet against his Dragonskin armor, smashing him back against the wall. He gasped, his mouth gaping like a fish in the sunshine. His strength leaked away, his joints turned to water, and he slid to floor.

*Need ... air.* He told himself to stay calm, but the air was not coming back. His reptilian brain screamed in panic. *Breathe now! Breathe now!*

A seal broke inside him, and his gasping yielded a creaking trickle of air, then like a bellows expanding, he sucked in a complete lungful of atmosphere. Remy's reptilian brain reversed polarity, shrieking with joy.

But there was a new noise, a sucking gurgle that matched the tempo of his labored breath. It took great effort to swivel his head to the right and down. A neat hole in his armor, ringed with red. When Remy exhaled, the hole turned into a tiny bubbling spring of rich crimson. His brain took painful seconds to connect the dots.

*Armor-piercing bullets... I've been shot in the chest with an armor-piercing bullet.* Another burble of bright red. It filled the grooves in the armor and tracked away from the wound, drawn by gravity.

*I'm going to die.*

As if summoned, Rico's face floated into view. "You're not gonna die, buddy." He released Remy's armored vest, drew a tube from his pocket, and tore the wrapping away with his teeth. Rico positioned the tube over the hole in Remy's chest and squeezed with both hands.

A finger of ice shot through Remy's torso, even more painful than the initial wound. He tried to scream but his breath was gone again.

Rico rolled him halfway over to make sure the injected first-aid gel had gone all the way through his chest. That would stabilize and sterilize wound, stop the internal bleeding. His breath was hot and fetid, like a panting animal hovering over him. Remy started to close his eyes, but Rico slapped his cheek.

*Elise.* Her face came to him unbidden, mixing with the images around him. Starlight flared over her shoulder.

"I just need you to do this one last thing for me," Elise said.

But it was Rico's voice.

Remy blinked. Elise was gone.

"Elise," he whispered.

"I just need you to do this one last thing." Rico's voice, strained. His pupils had expanded to consume all the color in his eyes. "Are you with me?" he said.

Remy dipped his chin. It was too hard to speak.

"Good. We need to finish this. Make it look good. Can you do that?"

Rico took his hand, wrapping Remy's fingers around the butt of his Glock. He slid the weapon between them until the muzzle rested under Rico's chin.

Rico's face, his breath, his all-black eyes consumed the space in front of Remy.

"I want you to pull the trigger, Remy." Rico's cheek twitched, and he forced the words through clenched teeth. "Pull. The. Trigger."

Remy tried to shake his head, but the other man forced Remy's index finger through the trigger guard.

"Pull. The—"

The resulting explosion turned Remy's world bright red.

He woke up with a whimper, his breath catching in his throat as if he was still back in the bunker, fighting for his breath, fighting for his very life.

His fingers found the neatly sewn hole in his chest, the wound now puckered and pink, the stitches long removed. The military doctors had done a good job. He swung his feet to the cold floor and walked to the window.

Late afternoon sunlight cast long shadows on the architectural hodge-podge that was Walter Reed Medical Center. The complex was a dog's breakfast of the latest in prefabricated structures mashed into ancient brick and limestone facades, a testament to the rise and fall of military budgets.

He was in one of the newer wings, a high-security compound for dangerous criminals, important people, and whatever they considered Remy. He swiped the smartglass dark to protect against the afternoon heat.

In the bathroom, he splashed water on his face. The mirror showed how little he'd slept. The nightmare was there every time he closed his eyes, but it always left him with the same question: had he pulled the trigger? He dried his face with a towel and avoided his own gaze in the mirror.

A knock at the door interrupted his thoughts.

"Come in," he called out. It was time again for the intel weenies to check his story. They came every day, always with the same list of questions about his time with the New Earth Order. And every day, Remy answered them the same way: *I want to speak with Colonel William Graves.*

He sighed. So far, nothing had changed.

The young woman who lounged in the armchair in his hospital room did not strike Remy as military intelligence. She was slim, with dark hair and a surly smile, and wore men's trousers. When she turned her head, Remy noticed sharp ear tips poking through her short hair.

"Are those elf ears?" he asked.

The woman flipped her hair out of the way and angled her head so he could inspect them more closely. "You like? Got them done a few years ago after I saw the remake of *Lord of the Rings*."

Remy sat down on the edge of his bed. "I'm a big fan." It had been weeks since he'd had an actual conversation with another human being who wasn't a doctor or an intel professional. And LOTR was his all-time favorite. A wave of nostalgia threatened to overwhelm him. He'd seen the holo-show with Elise, one of their first dates after she'd gotten her new legs.

Maybe that was their plan. Throw him off his game by bringing in some sassy chick instead of Dumb and Dumber from the intel shop.

He stood back up and strode to the window. Half the building facing him was in shadow now. "If you're here to question me, I've got nothing to say. Not until I see Colonel Graves."

"Well, that's gonna be a problem, soldier boy."

Remy turned, surprised that she was disagreeing with him. The text-book move was to say yes, build rapport. "Why's that?"

"Because Colonel Graves is now General Graves and he doesn't waste his time with traitors." The woman got to her feet. "Me, on the other hand, I'm used to the underbelly of humanity. In fact, you could say I prefer it." She put her hands on her hips. "Well, are you ready to go?"

Another surprise. "You're just going to take me out of here? Just you?"

The woman winked at him. "Jailbreaks are my specialty."

⸻

After a half hour in the aircar, the woman finally told him her name was "H, just capital H."

"How'd you get me out?" Remy asked her. With the sun almost down, the horizon had taken on a blood-red hue.

"Not my doing," H answered. "This one is all Graves. You're his problem now."

A long silence passed, scored by the white-noise hum of the aircar's engines. "Where are we going?" Remy asked.

H shook her head. "You answer my questions, I'll consider answering yours." She drove manually, which Remy found unusual, and judging by the color scheme and personal touches to the cab, the car seemed to be her personal vehicle.

"Why do you want to see Graves?" H asked.

Remy squinted at the horizon. "He's the only one I trust. If I'm coming in from the cold, it's gonna be to him."

"You've kinda put the cart before the horse, haven't you?" H said. "You came in from the cold not knowing if he'd want to see you or not."

Remy snorted. "And yet you're taking me to him."

H flashed him her perfect teeth. "Touché."

"My turn," Remy said. "Where are we going?"

H made a tiny course correction. "Know what a Haven is?"

Remy's heart skipped a beat. He kept his eyes focused on the night sky. "The survival domes? I've heard of them." He maintained a nonchalance to his tone. Elise wanted him to find out about Haven and here he was being taken right to one of them. This was beyond good luck.

"They've been activated and Graves is in charge." He could feel H watching him in the dimness. "Lots of people who matter think the Neos are behind the weather wars. Your little stunt attacking our air bases was an attempt to make the president do something stupid and strike the host nations—that's the prevailing theory. And then you show up. Convenient, huh?"

"Stop classifying me with those nuts," Remy answered, plugging into his old disdain for the New Earther movement. "I was the one who took a bullet in the chest, remember?"

"Yeah," she said. Her voice was flat, unreadable.

The lights of Haven 6 appeared in the distance. The last of the dying sun glinted off the arc of the dome, making the object look like a bubble pushing out the landscape. He tried not to gape. "Jesus, it's big."

"That's what all the boys say."

As H busied herself with clearance permissions, he watched as the dome grew larger in the windshield. In the dusk below, there was a blank circle around the perimeter, then thousands of lights scattered in random groups. He squinted as the ship dropped lower. The lights were from people and vehicles.

"Refugees," H said. "Everybody wants into the dome. Very few get cleared."

"Cleared?"

A pair of military drones flanked her vehicle and H lifted her hands from the wheel, allowing the flight control computer to take over. Remy could tell by the sour look on her face she much preferred controlling her own destiny.

"There's room for a few thousand in each dome and each person is selected on a needs basis. Genetic history, ethnic makeup, skill sets, fertility —there's hundreds of categories. If we're preserving the best of mankind, we need to be selective."

"Do you really think it'll come to that?" Remy said. "You think this bio-seeding will wipe out humanity?"

"You've spent time with the Neos. You tell me, Remy."

The aircar passed through the upper airlock and was guided to a preassigned landing spot. Inside the dome, it was bright as day and the port was bustling with activity. The drones peeled off.

A young black woman with a shaved head and dressed in an army uniform with captain's bars waited for them. H popped the aircar doors open and stepped out. "He's all yours, Jansen. Tell the general I hope he knows what he's doing."

The young officer glared at Remy with intense brown eyes. "Follow me, Mr. Cade." She spun on her heel and strode away. Remy trailed after her to a passenger door manned by an armed MP. She stepped aside to let Remy enter first.

Inside, the room was bare save a sturdy worktable crowded with electronics, a chair with restraints, and another young woman with long, dark hair. She started when the door opened and fussed with the equipment as Remy entered.

The captain closed the door behind her and Remy heard the bolt lock.

"Strip," the captain said.

"Excuse me?" Remy said.

"Stri-i-i-ip," she said again, drawing out the word in a mocking tone.

Slowly, Remy stepped out of his boots, unbuckled his belt, and dropped his pants. Then he tugged the shirt over his head. He heard the nervous young woman draw a sharp breath when he uncovered the fresh exit wound scar on his back.

"Boxers, too," the captain said.

Remy shrugged and stepped out of his underwear.

"Take a seat," she said when he was completely naked.

Remy surveyed the chair, ignoring the furtive looks from the red-faced technician. "How do I know it's sanitary?" he asked, more to stall for time than out of any real concern. He eyed the machine on the table. What was that thing? A torture device, a mind probe? He licked his lips.

"Oh, it's clean, don't worry," the captain said with an edge of malice in her voice. "You're our very first patient."

Remy hesitated, and the captain said, "I can always arrange to do this the hard way, you know."

He nodded. If they had been planning on using some sort of brain-scrambling device, why bring him all the way out here to do it? When he sat down, the cold steel of the chair chilled his naked buttocks.

The captain strapped his arms and legs in place. The tech busied herself attaching two leads to his temples, then held a plastic mouthpiece in front of his lips. "Bite down on this."

Remy felt his pulse spike. "Why? What are you going to do?"

She looked at the captain, who shook her head slightly. "Please, bite down on this," she said again in an apologetic tone.

Remy opened his mouth and accepted the mouth guard. His mouth was so dry his tongue rasped against the plastic, making him gag. The woman's fingers ran across the back of his neck, applying some sort of gel, then a hard metal clamp touched his skin. He jumped when the clamp tightened suddenly.

"You're going to feel some slight discomfort, sir," the tech said in a timid voice.

A high-pitched whine started, then leveled out. The sound drilled into his brain in waves of color, brilliant tones that washed into his vision and made him gag. Reds, neon yellows, flaming orange. He tried to scream, but the plastic in his mouth reduced the sound to a strangled yelp.

The sensory overload ended abruptly, the clamp on his neck fell away, and he heard the tech say to the captain: "He's clean, Hannah. No implant."

"You're sure?" the captain said.

The young woman appeared out of the corner of his vision, nodding, and extended an open palm under his chin. Remy spit out the mouth guard.

The captain, her arms folded, studied Remy's face. Finally, she leaned down and whispered in his ear. "Listen to me, Cade. I don't know what your game is. If you screw over Graves, I will make it my life's work to end you." She unbuckled his restraints and let him stand up. "We're done here. You can get dressed."

As Remy pulled on his clothes, he said to the officer, "Why did I have to strip? You only looked at the back of my neck."

The captain opened the door. "I just wanted to see what kind of man I was dealing with." She offered a thin, mocking smile. "Now I know."

As he followed the captain across the flight deck to an elevator, Remy tried again. "So your name's Hannah? I'm Remy."

She ignored his outstretched hand. "You can call me Captain Jansen. I work for the general. And I don't trust you as far as I can throw you."

"Anytime you want to try that," Remy said, buckling his belt, "you just let me know."

They walked down a Spartan hallway to an elevator. Once inside, Jansen pushed the button labeled *10*. Remy noted the floors went from G to 36. He tried to do the mental math about the overall height of the structure and gave up.

Jansen was on the move again as soon as the elevator opened. She strode down the wide passageway, nodding to people they passed. Remy noted an even mix of civilian and military. She paused at a set of double doors and tapped a keypad.

"Come." The doors slid open.

Graves sat behind a desk with a glass top that served as a massive touchscreen. He swiped the contents away, and Graves stood, his eyes going first to Jansen. Whatever signal passed between them, Remy couldn't read its meaning.

He was thinner than Remy remembered, and grayer, his silver hair matching the stars on his collar. There was an uncomfortable moment as the iron gaze of his former company commander raked over the soldier-turned-traitor in front of him.

"Congratulations on the promotion, General."

Graves acknowledged Remy by pursing his lips. "Leave us alone, would you, Captain?"

Jansen hesitated. "Sir, I would prefer to remain—"

"I'd prefer you didn't," Graves said. His words sounded harsh, but Remy saw his expression was anything but. Graves and Jansen were close. Another fact to squirrel away.

"Very well, sir," Jansen said. "I'll be just outside."

The doors closed behind her, and Graves motioned to a chair. "Sit, Corporal."

Remy took the chair, and Graves resumed his own seat. The distance of the smartglass desktop stretched between them.

"I wanted to say, before anything else, how much I appreciated your testimony after Vicksburg," Remy said.

Graves scowled. "Vicksburg was a mistake, Cade, and I'm sorry for it. But that's ancient history now." He studied Remy's face. "Some hold the opinion I should shoot you. That you're a traitor aiding and abetting an enemy of the United States."

"Sir, my allegiance has never been to the New Earth Order," Remy said. Stick to the truth as much as possible. It sells the lie. "The upshot is this: I fell in love with the wrong woman."

"Elise Kisaan? The UN Secretary of Biodiversity?"

Remy nodded. "I knew her long before that. Nursed her back to health when she had her legs attached."

Graves arched his eyebrows.

"Bionic, sir."

"The daughter of the most powerful agriculture magnate in the world goes over to the Neos." Rising, Graves began to pace. "And you've been with her since Alaska?"

"Yes, sir."

Graves changed the subject. "Why did that man, Rico, shoot you?"

Remy let a breath fill the space. "I couldn't go through with it," he said. "Rico considered me a traitor to Cassandra."

"Explain that statement to me, son."

"I wouldn't help him upload the virus, sir. I knew it would put thousands of US military troops in danger. If that virus had gotten into the DoD core ... that's where I drew the line. That's why he shot me."

The general sat down on the edge of his desk, looming over Remy.

"And the girl?" Graves said. "What about her?"

What about Elise? Remy didn't have to lie about that topic. "She's gone, sir. She's one of them now."

The general nodded, saying nothing. After a long time, he extended his hand.

As Remy gripped the hand of his former commanding officer, he felt the first twinges of doubt. He'd found Graves and gotten access to a Haven site—now what?

"Mr. Cade, I believe we can help each other."

# 11

## MING QINLAO • LUNA CITY, THE MOON

It took Ming three days to figure out how to get off the Moon. She was lying on her back in a hammock strung between two columns of sewer pipes in sector 12, tunnel 6, bay 4, when the solution came to her.

Her preplanning had worked perfectly. She'd stashed food and water and other necessities all over the warren of maintenance tunnels, and she used a clean pair of data glasses to check the work schedules every shift to ensure they could stay out of the way of any maintenance crews.

What she hadn't counted on was the boredom—and the guilt. Always lurking in the back of her mind was the specter of Lily.

So she planned their escape. As much for her sanity as her survival.

Option one was staying in LUNa City and living on the down low. Not a terrible plan, but with obvious risks. The city had enough population and transient personnel activity to hide them, but someday, somehow, through some tiny mistake, one of them would be recognized and they'd be on the run again. Also, as a pair they were more recognizable than they were separately, and she wasn't about to leave Ruben to fend for himself.

She heard her brother shift in his hammock. "You still awake?" she said.

"Can't sleep," Ruben said from his matching hammock a few feet away in the pitch blackness. "I miss Lily. I wish I'd gotten to see her again."

*No you don't, Ruben. No you don't.*

"Ming?"

"Yeah." The mention of Lily conjured up images that made her want to scream into the dark, but she kept her voice low. Sweet Lily, whose only crime was loving Ming.

"I'm sorry. About everything. I—I was selfish. This all happened because of me."

"Yeah, it did," she said. He needed to hear the truth. "But you didn't ask for any of this."

"I'm a Qinlao," he said. "It's part of who I am."

Ming reached her hand into the darkness, found Ruben's hammock. He reached back and touched the tips of her fingers. He was doing a lot of growing up in a very short space of time.

Option Two was obvious: find a way off the Moon. Easier said than done. Even if she could get them to the docks and even if she could find someone to take them on an outgoing vessel, the bounty hunters would be watching for them.

Ming scratched at the grime behind her ear. If there was only a way to get out of LUNa City without being seen, maybe through one of the mining camps that dotted the lunar surface. If she could bribe enough of the right people, they had supply shuttles that ran regular routes off-planet...

*Point Bravo.* She sat bolt upright in the darkness, her fingers searching for the LED light she'd stuck to the pipe over her head. Cold illumination flooded over Ruben, huddled into a ball in his hammock. His dark eyes gleamed from beneath a ragged fringe of hair.

"Pack your stuff," Ming said. "We're moving."

She unstrung her hammock and stuffed it into her backpack. Her hands automatically checked the food and water supplies on hand. Including what Ruben had in his pack, they were good for three days. More than enough time to get to Point Bravo and arrange for a ride off this rock. Ming was even a little annoyed at herself for not thinking of it before. After all, she had been a construction engineer on LUNa City long before she was a fugitive.

When the concept for LUNa City was first established, the first engineering task was to decide where to site the new lunar metropolis. A series of vertical tunnels were dug at five points twelve kilometers apart around the Albategnius Crater. The tunnels, named Alpha through Echo in military speak, were used to study the stability of the underlying rock strata, the available minerals, and the presence of sublunar ice. The final decision placed LUNa City on Point Charlie, but not before there was a connecting tunnel dug between Bravo and Charlie to further explore the underlying rock.

And just like the ad hoc maintenance tunnels under LUNa City were only mapped as an afterthought or not at all, the existence of the Point Bravo tunnel was not on any topside engineering drawing she'd ever approved.

Ruben waited for her patiently. He'd become adept at moving quietly in the dark and making sure they minimized any trace of their existence in the tunnels. The acting out she'd been dealing with before the bounty hunters arrived was gone.

Ming touched his forearm. "I never said I was sorry about what happened with Angel."

Ruben smiled shyly. "At least I'll remember my first kiss."

Ming tried to return the sentiment, glad the light was dim. *If you live long enough to get a second kiss.*

They traveled with a dim light and sharp ears, listening for any maintenance crew that might stray across their path. Ming did not worry about the bounty hunters following her into the tunnels. They could bring a platoon of hunters down here and she could avoid them. No, she was convinced the hunters would use face-rec bots on the vid-feeds and focus their efforts on choke points, like the docks.

The whirr of a scooter and a pair of voices arguing made Ming stop and press Ruben into an alcove. Her hand found the handgun in her backpack. The sounds drifted away.

The entrance to Point Bravo was an unmarked steel door at the end of a long winding tunnel. She shined the light on the gauge to see if there was atmosphere on the other side. Slightly below one atmosphere. Ming swore to herself. She could equalize pressure between the two compartments slowly, but that would take hours, maybe a full day. Too risky.

She needed to force the door open and minimize the time it took to get through. The sudden equalization in pressure would cause a slight atmospheric dip on the LUNa City tunnel-side. Not much, a slight popping of the ears at most, but enough to alert an astute maintenance crew to come looking for the cause.

But Ming was committed to Point Bravo now. This was their best chance of getting off the Moon—or being trapped.

"Help me," she said to Ruben. She detached a heavy metal bar from a bracket and inserted an end into a wall socket to form a lever. She ratcheted the bar down, each cycle adding a tiny amount of force to a spring that could manually open the tunnel door.

She worked until sweat drenched her body, then stepped aside to let Ruben have a turn. As the boy pumped, she checked the spring gauge. A quarter charged. "Keep going," she said. At half charged, she signaled him to stop. They only needed to get the door open enough for them to slip through. His heavy breathing echoed in the confines of the tunnel.

Ming positioned him close to the door. "When I trigger the spring, it will force the hatch open for a few seconds, until the spring loses charge and the door closes. It's going to be noisy, so be prepared."

Ruben nodded. Ming took a deep breath and triggered the spring. A noise like rapid-fire gunshots sounded, and the hatch cracked open. A rush of wind was sucked out of the tunnel around them into the blackness beyond. Ming's ears popped from the pressure change.

The hatch was open about six inches when she forced the backpack through. The spring noise seemed to peak, and Ming thought for a heart-stopping second that she had miscalculated the amount of force needed to open the hatch.

When the gap had widened to twelve inches, she slapped Ruben on the back. "Go!" The boy worked his shoulder into the still-widening slot, then disappeared.

Just as Ming slipped her arm into the gap, the spring noise stopped. She felt the hatch start to press on her thigh. Panic set in as the thought of being crushed took over. Ming froze, then started to back out. From the other side, Ruben seized her arm and heaved her through the narrowing gap.

The hatch closed with a resounding boom.

Ming sprawled across the rough stone floor, pitch darkness all around. She held her breath to still the sobs that threatened to burst out of her. For the first time since all this had started, Ming had felt afraid, really afraid. Afraid of dying, afraid of getting maimed, afraid for Ruben ... just more scared than she'd ever been in her life.

"Are you hurt?" Ruben said tentatively.

Ming shook her head, then laughed as she realized he couldn't see her. "No." It came out part sob, part laugh. Then: "Thank you. For pulling me through, I mean."

"I didn't want to be alone, Ming. I'm scared."

The air in the dark tunnel was damp and stale, but she breathed it in like a tonic. She found her light and switched it on. "Me too."

---

Point Bravo was a twenty-by-twenty room at the top of a long climb from the tunnel. Besides the airlock to the lunar surface, there was a single porthole, a rack with three emergency pressure suits, and a pile of junk left over from the geologists who had done the soil evaluation years ago.

Ming slumped against the wall and slid to the floor, her thighs burning from the climb. She was officially moonsoft now. Ruben clambered out of the hole in the center of the floor and crawled to sit next to her. His face was smudged with dirt and he needed a haircut. He panted at her. "This is it?"

"Welcome to Point Bravo." She hauled herself to her feet to look out the porthole. It was good to see the stars again after days in the lunar underground. The surface was ablaze in daylight, the sun's rays bending around the rocky cliffs of the crater. Ming watched a transport lift off from LUNa City.

Ruben joined her at the window. "What now?"

Ming dug into her backpack for her glasses and eye-scanned to a secure uplink. "Now, I make some travel reservations."

Zeke Bronksi's day job was supervisor of the Helium-3 extraction crews on the Moon. In that capacity, he controlled all mining operations flights on and off the Moon. If you worked on an extraction crew outside of LUNa City, you went through Zeke. His part-time job was of more interest to Ming: Zeke Bronski was the King of the Darkside, the Moon's thriving black market.

Theirs was a casual relationship, one borne of necessity when Ming was the lead construction engineer on LUNa City. She'd learned to take a pragmatic view of the black-market economy. The UN's policy of price controls on incoming materials made for bureaucratic inefficiencies that worked against the larger goal of completing LUNa City. There were times when Zeke needed some adjustments to the bills of lading for incoming shipments of construction materials and times when Ming needed certain materials expedited to meet her schedule. In all her time on the Moon, Ming never took a bribe or cut corners on quality, but she frequently bent the bureaucratic rules in the name of efficiency.

Zeke owed her, Ming told herself. They had enough of a relationship to warrant a favor, but how large of a favor might that be?

Only one way to find out. She used an anonymizer program and triggered a call to his day job.

Zeke's jowly face had a perpetual five-o'clock shadow and his shaggy dark hair was more salt than pepper since she'd last seen him. He was looking away when he answered her call. "Bronski."

"Zeke, it's me."

The man's eyes snapped to the screen and he opened his mouth.

"Don't say my name." It was a near surety the bounty hunters had the ability to scan voice comms for keywords. Ming prayed the anonymizer fooled their voice-rec bots.

He closed his mouth. "Holy shit."

"Don't hang up, Zeke. I'm in trouble."

"Holy shit," he said again, his face a war of emotions. What might have passed for goodness won out. "You okay?"

"I'm okay, but I need a ride."

He shook his head, his jowls wobbling. "You're crazy. There's no way you can get to the docks. These guys are dropping serious coin to find you. You wouldn't last five seconds—"

"I can pay. And you owe me."

Zeke's eyes narrowed with interest, then he shook his head. "Too risky. Sorry, I'd really like to help you, but—"

"What's the bounty on us?"

His eyes ticked left, a sure sign he was lying. "Six fifty. Cash."

Ming had no alternative, and Bronski undoubtedly knew that. "I'll double it," she said. "As long as you get us off this rock in the next twenty-four hours."

She saw greed flicker in his eyes. "You got that kind of scratch?"

"A hundred now, the rest when—"

"Two fifty now," Bronski interrupted. "In ByteCoin."

Ming did her best not to wince. That amount would all but clean her out.

"Two hundred in coin, take it or leave it," she said in a voice that brooked no compromise.

Bronksi hesitated and she played her trump card. "I know where your skeletons are buried, Zeke. One call to the marshals and we're sharing a cell."

"Deal," he said after a pause.

"I'm at Bravo. We need a pickup here."

Zeke's lips twisted in thought. "Point Bravo? Smart girl." His eyes defocused as he scanned the list of ships on his retinal display. He grunted.

"What?" Ming said. Every second she stayed connected to the network, even with an anonymizer, put them at serious risk.

"Your best option is not really an option."

"Tell me."

"The *Lucky Baldwin* is leaving in the next shift for an ice-mining job on Mars. This is not the nice side of Mars, girl, with all the domes. This is a low-rent shithole operation. The manifest on this crew looks like a bunch of degenerates."

"Book it."

"You don't want this—"

"I don't have a choice. Make the deal, Zeke. Two new crew members, no questions. We'll be outside at 2300. A simple touch-and-go landing and no one's the wiser."

"All right, I'll get it done. Been nice knowing you."

"I owe you, Zeke."

"Only if you make it."

Ming helped Ruben into his pressure suit. He'd never been on the surface and this was as good a time as any to let him enjoy the experience. The suits were older models but still serviceable, and they were charged with two hours of air, enough in theory to walk back to LUNa City if there was an emergency.

The suits were sized for a full-grown man, so they hung on both their frames like clown outfits. Ruben giggled when he saw Ming in her suit. It was the first time she'd heard him laugh in days.

"You don't look much better, kid," she said, laughing along with him.

By Earth reckoning, this side of the Moon was twenty-six days into its twenty-nine-day cycle of daylight, and the long shadows of the coming night stretched like black shark's teeth. Earth shone in three-quarter view, a blue and white jewel suspended in the twinkling velvet of space.

"It's beautiful," Ruben said. His voice was tinny through the comms of the old pressure suit.

"Yeah, it is." A wave of loneliness passed through Ming. "That's home." She slid her arm around the loose folds of Ruben's suit, pulling him to her.

A transport lifted off from LUNa City, veering in their direction, staying close to the lunar terrain.

The ship drew close enough for her to read *Lucky Baldwin* on the side of the scarred hull. It was an older model, with angular lines never intended for atmospheric entry, known in the trade as a MOAB, or Mining Operation in a Box. In theory, a team of miners could land a MOAB anywhere in the solar system and start mineral extraction.

The transport touched down, and a side airlock cycled open.

"This is us," Ming said. "Stay close."

---

The *Lucky Baldwin* was a dirty ship full of dirty people who leered at the new arrivals with dirty thoughts evident on their faces.

Ming and Ruben stayed to themselves, holed up in their quarters for the first couple of days of their journey to Mars. Tobias Johns, the *Baldwin*'s captain, let his last-minute passengers—now known as Hui Luong and her nephew Ricky—have their space. He'd been paid well enough by Zeke to take them aboard, but in her one and only interaction with him, he'd made it clear he wanted nothing to do with them or their troubles.

By the third day of the voyage, just when Ming had lulled herself into believing they'd gotten away safely, a loud banging on the door woke her from a dead sleep. She opened her eyes to find Ruben standing in the middle of their small room.

"Should I open it?" he asked.

Ming roused herself from the single rack they'd taken turns sharing. "Hang on," she said. Her every move felt sluggish in the presence of a continuous one-gee burn toward Mars and her knees popped when she stood. She moved Ruben behind her, then opened the hatch.

"Johns wants you on the bridge," said a skinny woman. She stood aside, waiting for them.

Ming slung her backpack over her shoulder. The weight of the handgun inside was reassuring. On the bridge, she found Johns waiting for her with a withering scowl.

"We have company," he said, motioning out the window.

It took Ming a few seconds to figure out what he was talking about, then she saw it. Another ship, matte-black and unmarked, with paramilitary lines.

"They're armed," Johns continued, "and they made sure we saw them fire their rail guns in target practice."

Ming swallowed. "What do they want?" She dropped the backpack casually to the floor, leaving the top halfway open.

Johns touched a button, passing the incoming comms to the loud-speaker. "*Lucky Baldwin*, this is *Revenant*. We are seeking two illegal passengers, a young woman and a boy. Stand by to be boarded."

Ming tried to get to the handgun, but it was too late. Two muscular arms encircled her from behind, pinning her arms to her body. The pistol dropped to the deck. She reacted quickly, Ito's *butt-gut-nuts* mantra singing in her head. But her attacker dodged the head-butt, making the follow-on strikes impossible.

Ruben cried out, caught in the grip of another crew member.

"Let him go!" Ming shouted. She stomped on her captor's foot. His grip loosened, and she squirmed free.

"That's enough," Johns said quietly. She looked up to find her own handgun pointed at her. "Comms, signal the *Revenant*. We'll turn over the cargo."

"We had a deal," Ming hissed. She sized up the odds against her: a handgun and three crew. Not good. "I can pay, Johns. Hide us and I'll pay you more."

"You're already going to pay." Johns tossed the backpack to the thin woman who'd brought Ming to the bridge. "Call it a surcharge."

"Give me that!" Ming said, lunging at her.

Johns cracked the pistol barrel across her cheek. Her vision exploded in a riot of color, then faded to black. The last thing she heard was Ruben's frightened voice screaming her name.

---

The smell of coffee woke her. Real coffee.

Ming attempted to open her eyes, but only one eyelid responded. The right side of her face felt fat, swollen. She groaned.

"Ming? Can you hear me?" Ruben's voice.

Her monovision took in the scene. Half reclined, all she could see was a well-lit cabin outfitted with two double beds. So much space. Definitely not the *Baldwin*.

"Where are we?" Her question scratched like dry wood in her throat. Ruben worked the controls on the chair to help her sit up, then handed her a glass of water. She gulped it down without tasting a drop.

"You have a concussion. He said you need to rest."

"He who?"

Ruben tapped on the wallscreen. After a few pings of the ringer, the face of Anthony Taulke appeared larger than life. His expression brightened at seeing her and he smiled widely, the world-famous billion-Byte smile.

"Ming," he said. "I'm so glad I found you."

## 12

ANTHONY TAULKE • TAULKE ATMOSPHERIC
EXPERIMENT STATION, MARS

Even as his lips automatically formed a smile of greeting, Anthony tried not
to stare at the screen. In his mind's eyes, Ming Qinlao was a beautiful,
vibrant young woman, not this beaten wreck. Her dark hair, once styled
and flowing like black silk, was a ragged, matted mess. Her skin was
mottled with bruises like a piece of overripe fruit and sallow in the places
in between. The right side of her face was swollen beyond recognition.

Her eyes—eye, rather—seemed to have trouble focusing on him.
"Anthony?" That was definitely Ming's voice. "Where are we?" she asked.

"You're safe. You're on a Taulke vessel on your way to Mars."

She moved toward the camera. "I was already on my way to Mars.
Johns, the captain of the *Baldwin*—he thought you were pirates. Bounty
hunters."

"That's what we wanted him to think. It's safer that way. If your aunt
manages to track him down, she'll find another dead end."

Ming gave a slight nod. The boy moved in beside her, trying to pull a
blanket over her.

"I see you're in good hands, Ming."

The boy smiled into the camera. "Yes, Mr. Taulke."

"Anthony, please. Remember?"

"Okay, Anthony."

Ming stirred again. "How did you find us?"

"You would've been hard to miss. YourVoice has been blowing up for days about the deaths of Lily Wallace and some lowlife named Branch Moeller. They don't have a lot of murders on the Moon." He paused, realizing the flippant way he'd just spoken about Ming's former lover. "I was sorry to hear about your friend."

Anthony continued, "It's Viktor you should really thank. He hacked into LUNa City's shipping records. We made a calculated guess that you wouldn't return to Earth and we began stopping any ship headed from the Moon to some other destination. We kept the Taulke name out of it, of course."

"Thank you, Anthony." Ming's good eye teared up and she gripped Ruben's hand. "From both of us."

Anthony flushed, but inside him something heavy and slick slithered around. He had the sudden impulse to tell her the truth about the deal with Xi.

"It's nothing, Ming," he said, anxious to end the conversation. "We were partners. That still means something in my book. Get some rest. I've told Captain Lander to use an easy burn back home. I'll see you in a few days."

Anthony swiped the connection closed, hating the prickles of guilt crawling under his skin. She had hidden herself and a boy for months on the run, living by her wits, supporting herself. Could he have done that at her age? Could his own son, Tony, do that even now?

And he was going to betray her.

His virtual alerted him to Viktor's arrival, a welcome distraction to that line of thought.

Anthony spun in his chair. Time to get on with his next agenda item of the day: saving the world.

Viktor entered at his normal shambling pace, more bear than man in his movements. He liked to affect an air of detached intellectualism, but today his gaze sought Anthony's as soon as he walked through the door. "You found Ming? She's safe?" he said.

Anthony was touched. Ming had even earned a place in the heart of a Russian oligarch. The young woman was truly special. "Yes, thanks to your trolling bots. She and her brother will be on Mars in another day or so."

"Good, good. She'll be able to convert the manufacturing facilities here to make the new nanites?"

"With Tony's help, yes," Anthony said with more confidence than he felt. Tony's expansion plan for Taulke Industries on Mars had every available second of manufacturing capacity booked for the next year and beyond, but that would just have to change. This was still his company and the Earth project was vitally important.

"The test bed is ready?" Anthony asked. "I'm anxious to move to the next phase."

Viktor's flyaway gray hair bounced in agreement. "Very good numbers on the sims. Dispersing with satellites this time makes achieving global coverage much easier. I think we are nearly there, my friend. Come, come —I show you!"

As they walked to the testing center, Anthony took notice again of how much Tony had developed the facility. It was a far cry from the simple testing station Anthony had entertained potential investors in last year. If Tony had his way, Anthony was convinced, he'd brand the whole planet, maybe even rename it Taulke. He found himself not hating that thought outright.

"Talk to Tony yet?" Viktor asked.

"I can handle Tony."

He bumped into Viktor, who had stopped in the doorway to his lab. Anthony looked over his friend's head into the room with annoyance, then surprise.

What should have been a scene bustling with engineers and scientists involved in the last frantic minutes before a major experiment was instead a lab almost devoid of personnel. In the center of the room, one man spun around on a stool and stood to greet them.

Tony Taulke moved with the languid, easy grace of unshakable self-confidence. He smiled in a way that bared teeth but lacked warmth.

"Hi, Pop," Tony said. "We need to talk."

"Tony," Anthony said. "What the hell have you done to my testing center?"

Tony glared at his father. "You used one of my ships to board an innocent mining vessel in transit. What were you thinking? You could have caused an international incident."

"*Your* ships?" Anthony snapped. "Those are Taulke ships, Son. Company ships. We kept their identity hidden. It was worth the risk, in my opinion."

"Your opinion doesn't matter here, Pop. You need resources, you ask permission. From me." Tony's lean frame had gone rigid as he faced his father.

Anthony's frustration of the last few weeks began to boil. He felt the heat of embarrassment and rage creeping up his neck. "Fine. Since you brought it up, Viktor and I need—"

"No." Tony bit off the word with a snap of his teeth.

"But you haven't even heard what I was going to say."

"Priorities have changed, Pop." Tony swept his fingers in a dismissive motion toward the lab around them. "This little sideshow you're running here. Trying to save the world again. It's over. That place we came from is finished. Mars is the new center of the universe for mankind. We're building a new world from scratch and we only let in those we want to let in."

"This is still my company, boy!" His fury took the wheel from his intellect. Anthony knew he needed to calm down.

Tony's face went still. "You know what the board calls me behind my back, Pop?"

Anthony knew, but feigned outrage. "What the hell does that—"

"Junior," Tony said. He might have just announced he was about to vomit. "Some even call me Tony Two-Point-Oh, like I'm the second coming of *you*."

"What the board calls you—"

"I *saved* this company!" Tony advanced on his father. Despite his own rage, Anthony stepped backward. "While you were sitting on your ass in prison, I brought the stock back from a wave of panicked sell-offs. I restructured our debt. I convinced shareholders that colonizing Mars was the way of the future. I did that, Pop. Me, by myself. If not for me, there wouldn't be a Taulke Industries today."

Anthony's anger short-circuited, and he sat down in one of the empty chairs. What Tony was saying held the virtue of being true. His son *had* saved the company, had even grown it. Tony's wasn't his vision for Mars, but it was a vision many others had bought into—literally. And that had saved Taulke Industries.

"I don't want to be Tony Two-Point-Oh, Pop." He straddled one of the chairs opposite his father, his voice softer now. "I'm my own man. I'm going to build a new world from scratch." He touched Anthony's hand.

Anthony stared at his son's hand overlaying his own. Tony had his own ambition, his own desire for greatness. His own future to shape from the clay of opportunity. Maybe Tony was more like his old man than Anthony had given him credit for.

"I admire your motivation, Son, but I'm still chairman and I get a say in this grand vision of yours."

Tony sat back. "We're beyond the boardroom now, Pop. This is a new age, and it calls for a new kind of governance. I say we do away with the board and we form a new one. We'll call it a council, a roundtable of business leaders to shape this new opportunity for our benefit. We choose our peers. There's you and Viktor, and Adriana. Maybe even Ming if she gets her company back. We write our own destiny."

Anthony sat back in his chair. He'd had the same thought, and now Tony was endorsing the idea. "I like where your head's at, Son."

Tony's easy smile returned. "I thought you might."

"Now, I do think that this council owes it to Earth to—"

"The answer's still no, Pop," Tony interrupted. "If you want to run this little science experiment on your own time, that's fine, but you're going to have to fund it and equip it on your own. Mars resources are focused on building the Mars of the future."

Tony leaned forward and patted his father's knee. "Pop, you know I love you, but you have to get your head out of the clouds. When you came to Mars, you wanted to terraform the planet. You nearly bankrupted the company on a pipe dream. For a fraction of the cost, I am building a set of domes that will house a million people. A *million*. We don't need to save the world, Pop, we only need to save the ones worth saving."

"And who makes that determination?" Anthony said in a cold voice. "Who determines the ones worth saving?"

"That's why we have a council. To make sure everyone's interests are protected."

"I see," Anthony said. It all made sense in theory, but real leadership required more than cold logic. What about humanity?

"So Viktor and I can keep working as long as we minimize the use of company resources?" he said.

Tony stood, his signal that the meeting was over. "The staff you have now is the staff you have. Period, end of story. Don't ask for more—and no manufacturing capacity."

"On Mars."

Tony stretched his lips without humor. "On Mars. You find some off-planet partners, Pop, knock yourself out."

---

The latest recreational hobby for the younger set on the Taulke station was biking on the Martian surface.

"Single or tandem, sir?" said the kid at the airlock.

There had been a time in the history of Taulke Industries when Anthony had known every employee and vice versa. Despite Anthony's custom pressure suit, the kid obviously didn't know who he was talking to. Anthony decided he liked it that way. He needed to get away from people for a few hours. Clear his head. A change of scenery and some exercise seemed like just the right combination.

"Single," he said through the external speakers on his suit.

"Stall seven."

The airlock cycled and he stepped into the bright, brassy barrenness that was Mars. He stooped to pick up a handful of loose soil, letting the rust-colored sand run through his fingers. So much potential oxygen for the taking. If only he could break those chemical bonds, he could turn this place into an oasis of green and gold.

He rubbed his hands together, then strode to the stall marked seven.

The "fat bike," as they called them, looked like a cartoon tricycle. Three enormous balloon-like tires, each as tall as a man, with a gimballed saddle-and-pedal arrangement perched on top. The rider had the option to pedal or ride along using the electric motor buried somewhere in the center of the contraption. The heavy engine had the additional purpose of keeping a low center of gravity for the entire machine, which allowed it to ride over rocks and up and down steep mountains.

He snorted at the absurdity of the moment. His son allowed his people to make tricycles but refused his own father permission to manufacture a device that might save an entire planet.

This was just another speed bump on the way to greatness, he told himself as he mounted the bike. He pulled out of the space and headed across the open plain toward the half-finished dome. The bike synced with his retinal implant and recommended a track to follow around the dome for optimum viewing. He eye-scanned his acceptance.

Anthony pumped his legs, letting the sound of his breath fill his awareness. The dome was farther away than it looked; it kept growing as he pedaled until it towered over him, the sides nearly vertical.

It was truly a masterpiece, an endeavor worthy of the Taulke brand. The terraforming dream had more sex appeal, but this was solid—and it was here now. Maybe Tony was right after all.

Tony had struck a chord with Anthony in articulating the idea of the council—he was already capitalizing the entity in his own mind. Maybe it was time for Anthony to regroup, follow his son's lead for a while.

After another dozen pumps of the pedals, he discarded that idea. He could have his cake and eat it too. Divide and conquer. While Tony established the Taulke brand on Mars, he, the father, would conquer the Old World. If he could save Earth from the scourge of this climate menace, he would bring even more prestige and power to the council.

Father and son, the Taulke powerhouse, creating the first system-wide form of governance that was both profitable and humane. Together, they could be first among equals on the council.

But he needed resources separate and apart from his son's bailiwick. That meant Earth resources. That meant Qinlao resources.

If Ming were back at the helm of Qinlao Manufacturing, this would be easy. But she wasn't, and the political capital he would have to expend to get back in power was not within his grasp—not yet at least.

Anthony pedaled another two kilometers before he gave up, letting the electric motor take over. He engaged the autopilot back to the station and relaxed, alternating his gaze between the glassy sheen of the new dome and the outline of the ochre mountains against the black sky.

By the time the bicycle had reached its destination, Anthony had come up with a plan.

⸻

Xi Qinlao's image on his screen brought to mind the cat who had devoured the canary. Her elegant fingers tucked a strand of stray dark hair into her elaborate hairstyle.

"Anthony." A thin smile, no teeth. "I didn't expect to hear from you so soon."

"Xi."

She waited for him to speak, her glittering green eyes trying to find an edge in his demeanor. Anthony stayed silent.

"I assume you're calling to give me good news, then," she said finally.

"I have your nephew."

Her eyes widened for a split second. "And Ming? You have her?"

Anthony shrugged.

"Don't be coy with me, Anthony! Do you have her or not?"

"Temper, Xi, temper. I have her."

"Good, then we can—"

"But she stays here for now."

The woman's nostrils flared. "We had a deal, Anthony."

He sat back in his chair. "No, you had the opportunity to make a deal when you had me at a disadvantage, but you refused. Now, I hold the advantage and there are new terms."

Xi's green-lacquered nails tapped her glass desktop. Anthony suppressed a little surge of glee.

"What do you propose?" she said.

"The safe return of your nephew for the manufacture of an initial batch of my nanites. If I'm satisfied with the quality of your work, we can discuss more work—and further payment."

Xi steepled her fingers together. "I propose—"

"This is not a negotiation, Xi," Anthony interrupted harshly. "This will go one of two ways: either you accept young Ruben and the possibility of getting Ming in the future, or I will announce on YourVoice that Ming Qinlao, the current CEO of Qinlao Manufacturing, is alive and well and under my protection. How would that play with your board, Xi?"

The soft skin of her neck fluttered as she swallowed. Xi nodded curtly. "You can send the specifications back with my nephew."

"Thank you. I'll be in touch with the arrangements."

Xi's smile had all the warmth of an arctic sunrise.

"Thank you for your business, Mr. Taulke."

Anthony killed the connection, but his fingers worried at the glass edge of his desk. It was done. He didn't expect Ming to understand, but he would not accept failure as his legacy. Sacrifices must be made.

He strode to the windows. Tony had assigned him a new office overlooking the ruddy canyons of Valles Marineris. From orbit, the collection of rocky regions appeared as a jagged scar across the planet surface. From this vantage point, during the soft Martian twilight, it almost felt like he was looking across the vista of a rocky seabed.

His retinal display pinged. A message from Earth. General William Graves. Anthony eye-scanned acceptance.

"General Graves, I've been expecting your call," Anthony said.

Graves looked worn, his face lined like tanned leather. Saving the world was taking its toll. Anthony could relate.

"Mr. Taulke," Graves said. He sounded uncomfortable, like he'd made the call against his better judgment.

"Anthony, please." He took in the silver stars on his collar. "And congratulations on the promotion, General. Well deserved."

"No rest for the wicked is what my grandmother would have said," Graves replied with a faint smile.

"H told me about your new role in the president's plan to relocate people off-world. I'd like to offer my assistance."

Graves seemed relieved to be getting down to business. "Right. How many can Mars take?"

*Fifty thousand, max,* Tony's voice said in his head.

"One hundred thousand," Anthony said. The positive press alone would sell Tony.

Graves's eyebrows shot up. If he had considered holding a poker face during negotiations, he'd failed.

"Not enough?" Anthony suggested.

"No, sir," Graves said. "I mean—it's more than we hoped for."

"Tony's doing incredible things on the planet," Anthony said, hoping his smile looked sincere. "Rapid construction, modular housing, prefabricated, 3-D printing of—well, I won't bore you with the details."

"I wish he'd been the contractor on my last house."

Anthony chuckled. "How are you set for transport? I can send ships if you need them."

"Anything you can spare," Graves said. "No one thought we'd be moving this many people this quickly."

"Understood. I can send escorts, too."

Graves appeared both concerned and curious. "Escorts? Military escorts?"

Raising a placating hand, Anthony said, "Security vessels only, General. Converted freighters and mining ships mostly."

"That's very generous of you, Anthony, I'm glad we're on the same side here."

"Indeed." Anthony cleared his throat. "And speaking of sides, I could use some help on my end..."

"Yes?" Graves crossed his arms and waited.

"The New Earth Order, General," Anthony said, plunging ahead. "I need to know what you know. *Everything* you know."

# 13

## LUCA VASQUEZ • HAVEN 6, BLUE EARTH, MINNESOTA

Luca scooped up Frack the rat and placed his frail carcass in a small box. She detached the electrical leads, looped them around her hand, and placed the neat coil on the workbench.

"Maybe the pulse was too strong," Jeremy Cabbot said. To him, the animals were just tools in an experimental process, no different from Bunsen burners or computers.

Luca grunted a noncommittal response, not trusting herself to speak just yet.

*It's just a stupid rat.*

Her eyes roved over the lab, looking for something to do. She moved to the sink, rearranging the test tubes and the packages of unopened hypodermics on the counter. Anything to keep her hands busy, her mind occupied with other things.

Jeremy followed her. "We could use the other rat and modify the—"

"No," Luca snapped. She controlled her breathing before turning to face her lab assistant. "No," she continued in a gentler tone. "They're too important, too valuable, to waste on guessing. We need a better hypothesis."

Jeremy let out a huff that made her want to strangle him. Then, after a moment: "Want me to put it in storage?"

"Sure," she said, realizing Jeremy probably thought he was doing something kind for her.

Technically, they were equals, but General Graves considered Luca the lead researcher in charge of finishing Markov's work. Jeremy had resented her position in the lab from day one.

"I'm going for a walk," she called after him. She opened her office door and whistled for Leroy. "Just so we're clear, you do *not* have permission to conduct animal tests while I'm out."

Jeremy's expression contorted, confirming her worst fears.

She considered taking the cat and the other rat with her. "I mean it," she said in as menacing a tone as she could manage. She stared at him until he nodded.

Luca led Leroy from the lab, his nails clicking on the metal floor. Haven 6 was more industrial in design than military, with molded, heavy-duty plastic walls and plain, block-lettered signs. Leroy held his head high, like he knew he was the only dog allowed on the medical deck.

The pair passed the security station that marked the entrance to the secure wing where Luca worked. The guard nodded as his eyes dropped to his scanner. Luca was not allowed to take any notes out of the lab and Hannah said it was very important she not speak about her research to anyone, which was a little ironic considering that's how she met Hannah in the first place.

Officially, they were investigating medical implant devices. Unofficially, they were trying to figure out a way to disconnect a Neo's brain from the subspace network run by the religious mystic Cassandra.

At the nurse's station, Elly, the nurse on duty, peered over the high counter at Leroy. He knew his audience and wagged his tail.

"How is she today?" Luca asked.

Elly's expression fell. "Same as yesterday."

Walking into her sister's room, Luca wondered if all the nurses thought she was an idiot. There was nothing wrong with Donna. But, at Graves's order, she was being held in a medically induced coma until Luca could figure out a way to turn off the Neo implant in her head. At her current rate of progress, that would be a very long time.

"*No te preocupes por mi, hermana mayor,*" Luca imagined Donna saying, followed by a snort of teenage bravado.

*I'll always worry about you. And English, D!*

She sat on the edge of the bed and stroked Donna's forehead. The girl's pale skin was warm and responsive. At times like these, the weight of Luca's choices crushed her. Donna was a child, not a doll to be kept in storage until…

She stopped herself. If not for Jansen and Graves, they might both be dead already. She needed to set aside emotional, irrational, short-term thinking and focus on the future. She'd made a deal: Donna could stay, but her implant had to be made "inert"—Captain Jansen's term. When Luca figured out a way to turn off the nanites infecting her sister's brain, then Donna was her first patient.

Luca gritted her teeth. Donna was just another lab rat to these people, no better than Leroy, who was now scratching at her knee.

"Am I interrupting?" Jansen stood in the doorway, her rank insignia glinting on her collar, sleeves rolled up on her workday jumpsuit. "I heard about the rat, Luca. I'm sorry. I know you two were close."

"His name was Frack." Luca laughed in spite of herself. "I know I'm being all emo, but I'm worried, Hannah. I'm running out of ideas." She blinked back tears. "If I can't figure this out…"

Jansen shut the door behind her and sat next to Luca on the bed. Leroy rested his chin on the top of the captain's boot.

"Don't think like that, Luca. You'll figure it out. Markov had the pieces of the puzzle. You just have to put them together."

"I don't think this puzzle has edges!" Luca said. "He talked about a trigger signal that could turn the nanites off, but he never found it. It could be anywhere in the EM spectrum—blue-light waves or ultra-high-frequency gamma pulses. We're just guessing."

Hannah stood and held out her hand. "C'mon."

Luca looked back at Donna. "Where are we going?"

"Just come with me. You need a break." She looked at Leroy. "You too."

Hannah walked at a quick pace as if she knew the exercise would be good for Luca. "Where are we going?" Luca asked again. The other woman flashed her a fleeting smile over her shoulder but no reply. Leroy trotted along happily, glad for the adventure.

In the elevator, Hannah said, "Garden level."

They began to descend.

"There's a garden level?"

"Wait'll you see it."

When the doors opened, the scent of freshly turned soil and green things flooded the lift. Luca inhaled deeply and followed Hannah. Simulated sunshine bathed her face with warmth. Leroy's nose hovered over the deck, his nostrils quivering with delight.

"This level is twice the normal height of most, and we plant everything in these stacked rows for efficiency." Jansen pointed to row after row of plants reaching upward. "Above this deck is a fish tank. We pump its nutrient-rich water into the hydroponic levels to grow vegetables."

Luca sniffed again. "But I smell dirt."

Hannah grinned. "So you do. Follow me." She led them through so many different types of vegetables that Luca lost count. As they neared the last row, the scent of dirt grew stronger and another familiar smell tickled Luca's senses.

"I smell oranges," she said.

"Yes, you do." Jansen stepped through a doorway into a grove of fruit trees.

The tart, sweet smell transported Luca back to her home in Mexico. "Where I grew up in Veracruz, we had an orange tree in our backyard. In season, my father would send me outside—Donna was just a baby then—to pick an orange for breakfast." She stopped, the words catching in her throat. "I haven't had an orange since I left home."

"Go pick one," Jansen said.

Luca approached the tree and stood on her tiptoes to reach the fattest orange she could find. Hannah offered her an open pocketknife to cut the stem. The orange dropped into Luca's hand, heavy with juice. She held it to her nose and breathed in the memories.

"Thank you, Hannah," Luca said.

Even the normally stoic Captain Jansen looked a little misty-eyed. "You gonna share that orange?" she asked, her voice husky.

They walked and ate as Leroy ran in circles, his nose to the ground. "If this place had squirrels and rabbits, he'd be in heaven," Luca laughed.

"Sorry, Leroy," Hannah called, "no bunny rabbits for you." She smiled at Luca. "Wanna see something cool? We keep bees as pollinators for the groves."

"Real bees?"

Jansen nodded. "Much more efficient than pollinator drones. NSF has kept bee colonies in controlled living conditions for decades. Plus, we get honey." She drew in a sharp breath. "Look, they're swarming!"

A heavy droning sound filled the air, and Luca followed Hannah's pointing finger to a thick tree branch that seemed to be moving. Luca squinted. The limb was covered with thousands of bees. "Are they dangerous?"

Jansen walked forward cautiously. "No, their stingers have been genetically deleted. I've never seen it, but I've been told touching a swarm is an amazing feeling." She reached out, and hundreds of bees swirled around her arm. Hannah's mouth opened in surprise. "Try it, Luca."

Luca's fingers shook as she extended her arm toward the bees as Hannah had done. When she touched the mass of insects, a few braves bees crawled down her fingers. Soon, her hand was consumed by a mass of yellow and black. She imagined thousands of tiny feet and antennae probing at her skin. "It tickles."

Jansen grinned. "My grandfather kept bees back home, before they went extinct. He told me how bees communicate. They exude pheromones, and they dance and send each other tiny electrical signals about danger and where the best nectar can be found."

The air around them grew thick with flying bees, their wings beating a soothing harmonic. Leroy sat off by himself, watching them warily. A group swarmed toward him, then veered away when they got close. The air around the dog remained clear of bees, as if he was sitting in a bubble.

Luca watched this happen a few more times. Then, still covered with bees, she approached the dog.

At first singly, then by the handful, the bees peeled away from her arm. The closer she got to Leroy, the faster they fled. By the time she knelt beside the beagle, her arm was bare.

"Hannah, look at this."

Jansen walked over and watched her own bee collection dissipate.

"What the hell?"

Luca's hands shook. She put on her data glasses and placed a call to Jeremy in the lab.

"Where have you been?" he demanded.

She ignored him. "Find everything you can on how bees communicate. I'll be there in fifteen minutes."

Four days later, Luca's workspace more resembled an apiary than a laboratory. Like so many complex problems, the answer was blindingly simple in hindsight.

True to their ethos, the New Earth Order had taken a lesson from nature. Building on how *Apis mellifera*—western honey bees—communicate, Luca discovered the Neo tattoo was actually a bio-based transceiver tuned to 190 hertz, the average frequency of a bee beating its wings. The pattern was clear in Markov's data when she knew what to look for. Leroy's implant had caused a constructive interference signal which drove the bees away when they flew near him.

Luca's theory assumed the Neos had adapted the chordotonal organ from the insect's antenna to create modern bio-circuits laid down in the organic ink of the tattoo itself. Injected through surgically precise tattoo needles, nanites—a brilliant hybrid of living organisms and programmed bots—embedded themselves in the brain stem to form a biochemical symbiosis with the host. Powered by the body's naturally generated EM field, the nanites replaced certain DNA sequences with pre-programmed genetic coding that, once activated, made the host pliable to suggestion.

"You mean Cassandra figured out how to hack humans?" Graves asked.

"More or less," Luca explained. "The Neo signal can piggyback on any commercial transmission anywhere in the solar system."

Jansen flashed Graves a horrified look. "Holy shit."

"The nanites are integrated within the victim's brain stem." Luca flinched at her use of the word *victim*. That made Donna a victim. "They could be forced to do anything, and they might not even know it."

"Like walk into a hurricane or dust storm, where their lives were in danger?" General Graves asked.

"Exactly. You could tell someone to shoot themselves and they'd have to do it. They'd be unable to resist. Because the nanites are powered at the cellular level, when cellular activity in the host ceases, the nanites disappear. That's why no one has been able to identify them before."

"Except Markov," Jansen said.

"He created a rough prototype of the nanite tech," Luca explained. "It functioned, crudely, in the same way. But the Neo implant is much more sophisticated. It's like a work of bio-engineering art."

"But you've figured out a way to turn them off?" Graves pressed.

"The bees gave me the first clue," Luca continued. "Leroy's implant repelled them, so I figured I could use that same frequency to overload the antenna and attack the nanites."

Graves arched his chin, thinking. "The tattoo, you mean."

"Exactly," Luca said. "The brand relays signals between Cassandra and the host, like the mechanical versions Markov placed on the animals' necks. Whenever Cassandra decides to activate an acolyte, she 'wakes' them by transmitting to the tattoo. If we hit them with a large enough signal on the right frequency, we cause a feedback loop and overload the system."

"And you've tested this?" Graves said.

Luca nodded. "On Frick—the rat. The procedure stunned him, but he lived." She hesitated. "But there's a genetic component in this. A rat is different from a dog, and a dog is different from a person. The sequence and the dosage might not be the same. If I'm wrong..."

"And if you're wrong?" Graves prompted.

Luca swallowed, unwilling to acknowledge what Graves was asking.

The general let out a sigh. "You performed the procedure successfully on a rat, so the next step is to try it on a different species, right? You have a dog?"

Luca nodded but stayed silent. Graves turned his attention to Hannah.

"Captain, we're running out of time. We're in a war here. The Neos are armed and dangerous and it's just a matter of time before they decide to attack. Take the next step. Get it done." Graves turned on his heel and left them alone in the lab.

"Luca," Hannah began.

"I know, I know." She opened her office door and let Leroy into the lab.

The beagle happily ran in circles around them until Hannah picked him up and put him on the table. "Stay," she said. Leroy watched her with glowing eyes, only the tip of his tail wagging. "Good boy," Hannah said with a catch in her throat.

Luca dialed in the right genetic sequence, her stomach roiling. She checked her numbers, then checked them again.

This was what real scientists did. They made hypotheses, then validated their results in the real world. Except in this case, the real world was an innocent dog named Leroy who loved tennis balls and happened to have a brain full of potentially evil nanites.

She positioned the transmitter to point directly at the dog's head. Leroy stretched out his neck to sniff at this strange thing pointed at him.

"Stay," Hannah said. Leroy drew his head back, a guilty look in his eyes for having disappointed her.

"I'm ready," Luca whispered.

"I'll do it if you want." Hannah took her hand.

Luca shook her head, tears already forming. "No, it's my responsibility." She clenched Hannah's hand.

*I'm sorry. I'm so sorry, Leroy.*

She triggered the pulse.

With a yelp, Leroy collapsed.

Luca closed her eyes and gripped the cold steel table to steady herself. She could hear Hannah's labored breathing.

*What have I done?* Luca clenched her eyes shut, her whole body shaking. *What have I done?*

"It's okay, Luca." A warm tongue licked her hand. "He's okay. He was just stunned for a second."

Luca used the scanner to test for active nanites. There was no response.

"It worked." Luca scanned him again, just to be sure. "It worked!"

Hannah hugged her. "Congratulations, Luca. I knew you could do it."

"Yeah." Luca bent down, letting the dog lick her face. She tried not to think of the next demand from General Graves.

To test the treatment on her sister.

# 14

## REMY CADE • HAVEN 6, BLUE EARTH, MINNESOTA

"Hello, Mr. Cade? Are you with us?" Jansen's tone dripped with enough condescension that Remy thought he saw other people in the room shift uncomfortably in their seats.

"Sorry. I was distracted."

"Now that you're here again," Jansen said, "what's the status of the South Carolina refugee evacuation?"

Remy tossed a graphic onto the wallscreen. He'd been given a hard target of safely moving nearly half a million residents from the South Carolina lowland country into neighboring states, mostly Georgia, to prevent uncontrolled migration.

The chart showed he was less than halfway to his goal.

"What seems to be the problem, Mr. Cade?"

He sometimes worried Jansen was onto his espionage mission for the Neos. She certainly didn't trust him, that much was clear. The irony was, he was taking seriously this relocation assignment by Graves. The South Carolinians just wanted a home again, somewhere to feel safe. He got that.

"Ma'am, I'm not getting a lot of cooperation at the local level—"

"I didn't ask for excuses, Mr. Cade. You are at this leadership level to deliver results, not whine about local politics. Now, what about the LUNa City quota?"

Remy swallowed. That situation was even worse. He'd been tasked with finding billets for 2,000 refugees on the Moon base and he'd found exactly fifty.

"We are behind quota, ma'am."

"'We'? The other relocation officers seem to be meeting their targets, Mr. Cade. All of them except for you."

Remy felt himself redden under Captain Jansen's glare.

Jansen looked around the table. "That'll be all for today, everyone. Mr. Cade?"

Remy stopped on his way to the door.

"Please stay for a moment."

He reluctantly took his seat again as the room emptied out, pretending to study a spreadsheet.

"Mr. Cade?"

Remy looked up, and to his surprise, Jansen was actually smiling at him. "I have an opportunity for you."

"Ma'am?" Remy was on his guard.

"I'm running a humanitarian mission up to the border in the morning. I need another body on security."

A ray of hope opened up in Remy's mood. "Security? Off-site? I'm in!"

Her smile widened. "I thought you might say that. Meet on the flight deck at 0800 for the pre-mission brief." She paused. "We'll need to make sure you're up to date on your shots."

"I'm up to—"

Jansen cut him off. "Remy, it's not optional." She stood and strode out of the room before he could say anything else.

Remy sat back in his chair. That was odd. She'd called him Remy. Jansen had never called him Remy before. Maybe this was a sign that they were reaching some kind of equilibrium in their relationship after all.

And he was going off-site! After weeks cooped up inside Haven 6, he was no closer to knowing about the mysterious power plant the Neos cared so much about. His security badge gave him access to most of the Haven with the exception of one R&D deck and anything beyond level 36. As far as he could tell, there was nothing of interest to the Neos here. Just a few thousand people willing to throw their lives away to live in a hole in the ground for the next hundred years.

The ark of humanity, they called it. Well, they could keep it, as far as he was concerned. All he cared about now was finding something—anything —about this project that could justify a trip back to Elise.

<br>

The flight deck of Haven 6 was crowded with three heavy air transports. Two were packed with supplies, and the ground crews were in the process of closing the loading ramps. A crowd of mostly civilians clustered near the open ramp of the third transport. Captain Jansen, dressed in civilian clothes but looking every inch the military officer, stood at the top of the ramp. She began to speak just as Remy joined the crowd.

"This mission will be traveling approximately three hundred miles north to the Canadian border crossing at Emerson, Manitoba," she broadcast to the data glasses in the crowd. Remy slid his glasses on and saw an aerial flyby of a large crowd of people hunkered in the snow. A temporary border wall of cyclone fencing delineated the Canada–US border, a political barrier slicing through the flat, snow-covered, wide-open prairie. "In the past week, the crowd has grown to more than fifteen thousand people, forcing the US government to close the border crossing."

"What do they want?" someone called.

Jansen shrugged. "Our biggest fear is that this group is headed here, to the Haven. We have enough crowd control issues already without adding to the misery, so we're going to play offense. We're taking supplies and a portable medical unit to the border to see if we can encourage these people to stay where they are." She highlighted three spots on the Canadian side of the border. "We'll set up two supply depots and a medical unit. This is strictly a humanitarian operation. We have light security with us, but they'll be making themselves scarce. This is a milk run, people. We make a drop-off, do some good, and get back in time for dinner."

Remy sought out Jansen after the briefing. "Remy, glad you could make it. See Sergeant Whittaker for your gear and you can check in with

Vasquez"—she nodded to a dark-haired woman with the medical team—"for your shots."

"I tried to say before, Captain, that I'm up to date on my vaccinations—"

"See Vasquez, Mr. Cade, or head back to your desk." Jansen walked away.

He resisted the urge to snap back at her. She was doing him a favor by letting him out of the Haven for the day. The woman she had called Vasquez was facing away from him, so Remy tapped her on the shoulder. He was surprised to see it was the young woman who had scanned him the day he arrived at Haven 6.

"Well, hello again," he said.

"Hi." She met his eyes for a second, then looked away.

"I feel like I'm at a disadvantage here," Remy continued. "You've seen me naked and I don't even know your first name." He stuck out his hand. "Remy."

"It's Luca." She took his hand. "Hannah told me to give you a shot."

"I'm up to date, I just spent some serious time in a hospital—"

"This is new," she interrupted. "A new ... disease. Gene-hopping vaccine. Very new." She fumbled in her bag and drew out a heavy hypo-gun.

"Whoa, you use that on people?" He meant it in fun, but it was not like any hypo he'd seen in the hospital.

Luca smiled at him nervously. "Yeah, it's a big dose. I'm afraid it'll sting a bit. This is best if it goes in the back part of your shoulder. It dissolves slowly over time."

"Okay." Remy stripped to his T-shirt and rolled up his sleeve. But instead of attacking the fleshy part of his shoulder, she slipped the gun under the collar of his shirt. He heard a *psst* as the hypo delivered its payload and a sharp sting lanced under his shoulder blade. He spun around, clutching his back. The source of the pain was out of reach of his fingertips. "What the hell?"

Luca reddened. "Like I said, this one's different. It needs to dissolve over time. The shoulder blade protects the capsule, er ... dose. I'm sorry."

Remy rotated his shoulder. The pain was already lessening, and he still needed to see the security officer for his gear. "It's okay, but the next time you plan on shooting me with that elephant gun, maybe buy me a coffee first."

"You're funny, Remy."

He winked at her. "That's what you say to all the boys, I bet." She was cute, and it had been so long since he'd had a real conversation with anyone here.

Her blush deepened. "Not so much."

Remy found Sergeant Whittaker and secured a light armored vest and a Glock with rubber bullets. "There's only six of us, Cade, so we'll be spread real thin. No live ammo. Last thing the captain wants is a dead body. You got it?" Whittaker had a nervous facial tic that did not bode well for a security guard, in Remy's opinion. "We'll put two men each on the supply depots and the med tent. One at the entrance, one rover."

Remy nodded. "I got it. I'll be on the med tent." Luca Vasquez was on the medical detail.

Whittaker shrugged. "Suit yourself. Just don't shoot anybody."

Remy grunted an answer and headed for the transport. He spotted an open seat next to Luca and quickly took it. She peered at Remy over the rim of her data glasses. "You again?"

"I'm like a bad penny," he replied. "Ever been to Canada?"

"No." Her cheeks grew rosy again, and she avoided his eyes. "I—I'm looking for a day out of this place, that's all. Hannah said I could go if I behaved myself."

"Funny, she said the same thing to me, Luca. Maybe we have more in common than I thought. What's your day job in the Haven?"

"Me? I ... um ... work in medical."

Remy had been to medical at least once a day for the past month for his refugee resettlement job and he'd never seen her there. "Really? Which department?"

Luca took her glasses off. She obviously wanted to talk, but every answer felt strained. "Research," she said. "Deck thirteen."

Thirteen. The restricted deck. Remy lowered his voice and leaned closer to her. "Is it true?"

"What?" She was whispering too.

"You have an alien on deck thirteen?"

Luca smiled, a real smile. "I hadn't heard that one."

"It's true. General Graves himself told me."

"You know the general?"

Remy felt his laugh grow hollow. "Oh, the general and I go way back. Old army buddies, you know."

"You're serious." Luca was looking at him intently.

"Serious as a heart attack." He leaned in again. "I know about the Neo tattoos, too."

"You do?" Luca's eyes went wide. "That's top secret."

Remy shrugged as if he didn't care, but his internal alarm triggered. "I know you figured it out," he said.

Luca looked around, then leaned closer to Remy. "It wasn't just me ... Hannah gave me the idea for how to deactivate the implant."

"Congratulations," Remy said, his heart pounding in his ears. "That's a big win for you—for us, I mean."

Luca's face clouded. "I can stop them," she said in a forceful tone, like she was spitting the words. "I know it. They won't be able to control—"

The ramp at the back of the transport started to close, interrupting their conversation. The seat next to Remy was filled by a younger member of the security team who was determined to engage Remy in conversation.

His mind raced as the younger man droned on. He had said "Neo tattoo" and she had gone immediately to "deactivate the implant."

*Elise.* A tiny flicker of hope started deep in his belly as Elise's actions suddenly started to make more sense. Elise wasn't making her own decisions. She'd been implanted. She was being controlled.

And Rico ... he'd killed himself. Was that because of the implant as well?

*Her will be done.* Rico's last words. Not a blessing, a command.

And Luca had figured it out.

Remy nodded at the security man as he talked, all the while keeping his attention on the young woman sitting beside him.

The transports circled the area twice before settling down in the wet, ankle-deep snow.

Remy got a good look at the crowds they'd be helping. His first impression was that Jansen had bad intel. Fifteen thousand was a low-ball estimate. It might have been double that number.

The Canadians had set up a sort of shanty town with crooked rows of recreational vehicles, tents and other vehicles forming a rough grid. In the center of the action stood a tall, 3-D–printed building sporting a lighted symbol of Cassandra.

Luca paused on the ramp when she saw the Neo sign, her lip curled in disgust.

"You okay?" Remy asked.

"I didn't know they'd be here." Her tone reflected her sour expression. This wasn't just a professional issue for her, this was personal.

"I know what they're like," Remy said. "I lost my girlfriend to them."

Luca smiled savagely. "I took my sister back from them." She looked out across the ragged town, columns of people already walking toward them. "They take advantage of people like these, people who have nothing. They brand them, and they use them like animals." She looked at Remy. "And I'm going to stop them."

Remy followed her to the medical unit, which was already unfolding into a multiroom assembly line for treating almost anything. The med team were seasoned professionals and the field hospital was operational within a half hour. His opposite number on the medical security team turned out to be the chatty guy who'd sat next to him on the flight up. Remy volunteered to be the roamer and spent the new few hours wandering the outskirts of the medical tent, trying to piece together what he'd learned from Luca Vasquez.

A long line of people waited patiently in the slush for their turn to see the doctor. A few nodded to him as he trudged around the med tent and the surrounding vehicles. It took him a few passes along the line to notice what should have been obvious from the first: everyone in line was branded by Cassandra.

That struck him as odd. In the general population of the US, the number of active Neos might be one or two in ten. He would have expected Canada to be similar. He walked the line again, just to make sure. Every single person was branded—and most of the tattoos looked new.

Concerned now, he entered the tent looking for Luca. At the sight of his body armor and weapon, the nurse running the floor pointed to the door. "No weapons in here. This is a hospital."

"I'm looking for Luca Vasquez," Remy said.

The nurse snorted. "You and me both. She took off thirty minutes ago on a break and I haven't seen her since—"

"Thanks." Remy stepped back outside. The gray overcast clouds seemed to press lower now. He scanned the crowd again, but she was nowhere to be seen. His gaze lighted on the Temple of Cassandra in the center of the makeshift town.

He shook his head, at war with his own feelings. She wouldn't...

Then he recalled the way she had spoken about the Neos on the transport and he knew where Luca Vasquez had gone.

It never really occurred to Remy to call it in. After all, he didn't really know where she'd gone, he just had a hunch. Besides, he didn't want to get her in trouble, and they'd made a connection of sorts on the flight up.

But mostly he wanted to know everything about how to kill the Neo implant. If he knew that, then maybe he could extract Elise from the cult before it was too late.

He started at a quick walk, but his pace increased with the tempo of his thoughts until the Temple loomed large before him. The building was meant to inspire awe amidst the squalor of the town. Nearly three stories tall and made of faux stone, broad steps swept up to a set of ten-foot-high double doors that stood open. The architecture was a clever blend of a traditional Christian church, a mosque, and sweeping futuristic lines. Something to make everyone feel comfortable. The backlit image of Cassandra emblazoned the side of the building, her half-exposed faces seeming to smile down on him.

Around the side of the building, Remy caught sight of the back end of an ancient yellow school bus, an anachronism next to the modernity of the Temple. As he watched, a group of young children burst out of the doors, trailed by a pair of teenagers encouraging them to slow down.

They all wore fresh Neo tattoos. Was it even legal to brand a child that young?

Remy mounted the steps into the Temple. It was warm inside, with a hint of incense in the air and soft music in the background. A twenty-something woman wearing slacks and a blazer with the Neo crest stopped him with a stunning smile. "Her peace be upon you," she said.

"I'm looking for a young lady, an American, long dark hair, Hispanic—"

The woman was nodding. "It is always good to welcome a new acolyte into Cassandra's flock. She is being baptized as we speak."

"Baptized? You mean..." He touched the back of his neck.

The smile grew wider. "Oh, yes, she was with the busload of orphans that came in and she insisted on being baptized with them. Immediately." She indicated a side door off the vestibule. "You just missed them. They went with Brother Alan."

Remy started for the door, but she laid a hand on his arm. "You can't bring weapons into the Temple, sir—"

He shook off her hand and pushed the door open into a narrow hallway. The sound of music was louder, and he broke into a jog. "Luca?" he called. "You back here?"

The hall ended in a broad well-lit room with pictures of smiling Neos from all over the world covering the walls and the golden image of Cassandra's seal gleaming on the wall. In front of the image was a heavy kneeler with two handholds and a pad for the supplicant to rest their forehead and bare the back of their neck.

Tied to the kneeler with his own belt was a middle-aged man, unconscious and bleeding from a gash on his temple. Brother Alan, no doubt. On the floor next to him lay what looked like a golden clothes iron, which Remy recognized as a flash tattoo device. A cord from the tattooer ran back to a closet. Inside the closet, Luca was savaging a rack of electronics with a chair.

"Luca?"

She whirled around, her eyes wild. For a second she didn't recognize him. Then, "Remy? What are you doing here?"

He pointed at the destroyed machinery. "You're asking me that?"

Her face tightened in rage. "They're branding fucking children!

Orphans. They told the kids they'd be part of Cassandra's Army, part of the New Earth Order..." Her voice trailed off and she started to sob. "Kids..."

Remy caught her in his arms. "Hey, I think you've made your point. Let's get out of here."

## 15

MING QINLAO • TAULKE ATMOSPHERIC
EXPERIMENT STATION, MARS

Ming paused outside Anthony's office and checked her reflection in the dark glass. The swelling around her eye had gone down, leaving a rainbow bruise. There wasn't enough makeup on the entire Mars Station to cover up that mess, so she didn't bother trying.

She touched the wall chime. Her palms were sweating. Anthony had been nothing but gracious to her and Ruben since their arrival, and yet she found herself unable to let her guard down.

The door opened. Anthony sat behind a wide, glass desk with a virtual display surface showing a solar system projection. His face brightened at the sight of her.

"Ming! Come in." Swiping the displays closed, Anthony stood up and stretched his lower back. He waved her to a couch and chairs surrounding a small coffee table with the Taulke Industries logo embossed in the center. She perched on the edge of one of the stiff chair cushions as Anthony offered coffee.

"Please. Cream and sugar."

Anthony's expression turned sly. "A touch of Jameson?"

"God, yes." It was after 5 p.m. somewhere.

He handed her the drink and Ming looked away when his gaze lingered on her face.

"Does it hurt?"

Ming shook her head. "Not much anymore. It's just very, um, colorful now."

Anthony's smile was understanding as he took a seat across from her. "To what do I owe this visit?"

"I came to thank you, Anthony. I—we—were in desperate straits, worse than I could have imagined." Since she'd gotten to Mars, Ming had done some basic research on ice mining and the results were horrifying. Besides the mortality rates, the crews were one step above conscripts. No wonder Zeke had warned her away. "Without you..."

"Nonsense. I owed you. Because of Lazarus, I put you in that situation."

"Someone took control of the project," Ming said. "It wasn't your fault."

Anthony's face changed. "The Neos. I know that for sure now. They're trying to destabilize world governments, pit the US against the rest of the world. We'll fix this, Ming. You and me."

Silence lengthened, and Ming toyed with her coffee. "I'd like to repay you, Anthony, for your hospitality. Maybe I could work on the domes here. I used to be a pretty good engineer before I became a mediocre CEO."

Anthony's laugh sounded as much relieved as mirthful. "If I had my way, I'd put you to work, but my son is very protective of his Mars project. He might see you as competition. We're a bit on the outs, if I'm being honest." Anthony hesitated. "Still, there is one thing..."

Ming leaned forward. "Please. You've done so much for Ruben and me."

"It's too much to ask. I shouldn't even mention."

She reached across the table and put her hand on his knee. "Please."

Anthony drained his cup before leveling his gaze at her. "I think we have a lead on how to find Cassandra. I need someone I can trust to track her down for me."

She found herself warming to the idea immediately. Something to do with her time, something constructive. And if the Neos really were behind the failure of Lazarus, then they'd also helped propel Xi to the top of Qinlao Manufacturing.

"I can do that," Ming said. "I'm sure we could do a network search from here—"

"It's not the tech that's the issue," he said. "We've tried all that, Ming. This requires someone on site. Someone I can trust."

"Surely there are transactions you can trace," Ming said. "Some digital bread crumbs to follow—"

"There's *nothing*." Anthony stood up and paced the room. "The last place we know the Neos were is Viktor's Darkside facility. There's a clue there, somewhere in that facility, I just know it. But I need someone I can trust to find it for me."

"I'd like to help, Anthony, but I couldn't take Ruben back there. Not now. Not after..."

"You could leave Ruben here." His voice was kind, understanding.

"I can't leave Ruben, Anthony. I'm sorry, but I just can't."

A flicker of some emotion crossed the man's face and then was gone again.

"Of course," he said in a clipped tone. "I understand."

"He's my responsibility. If anything were to happen to him..."

"I understand, Ming. I just really need someone I can trust for this mission." He brought his gaze up to hers. "Trust is a commodity in short supply these days."

Ming's cup clinked in the saucer. She owed him. Without Anthony's intervention, she and Ruben might very well be dead, or wishing they were dead. But she couldn't leave Ruben here alone, unprotected. Not after Lily.

"I'm sorry," she said again. The bruise on her face ached, ached with shame. "I just can't."

———

"Well, the good news, Dr. Qinlao," the med tech said as she scanned the side of Ming's face, "is that your injury looks worse than it is."

"That's what I keep telling people."

"No sign of concussion. I'd say another few days and you'll be good as new."

"So does that mean I can get my retinal implant restored?" She'd felt naked without it for months, ever since Ito had deactivated it to keep her from being tracked.

"I can do it for you now, if you want."

Ming held up the new secure implant Viktor Erkennen had provided at Anthony's request. Any identity-bots searching the WorldNet would never know she was back online.

Ming lay back in her chair as the doctor numbed her right eye and positioned the implant mechanism over her face. Robotic fingers drew her eyelids back and the cool air of the medical office made her eyeball itch. Only the anesthetic kept her from blinking.

"Now, look directly at the red circle … you'll feel a slight pressure."

Ming swallowed, trying to think about anything besides the enormous needle over her eye. Its silver tip went from sharp to blurry in her vision. She felt a pressure as the needle plunged in, inserted its payload, and withdrew again. The tiny metal fingers released her eyelids, and Ming closed her eye in relief.

"Another minute while I run diagnostics on the new implant. The new device will interface with the memory chip from your previous device while you sleep. In the morning, you'll have all your old files back."

---

An insistent ping startled her awake.

A flashing red light pulsed in her retinal display, indicating an unopened message. Ming groaned. She was still getting used to having a constant companion back in her head.

"*Later.*"

It took her a few seconds to realize the new implant was showing her an unopened file from her mother, given to her just before she fled her home in Shanghai. Ito had deactivated her implant before she had a chance to view the file. It seemed like such a long time ago now. Her mother must have assigned the file a time-sensitive push command.

No thumbnail, no metadata, just raw information. She eye-scanned it open and paused it immediately.

Her father filled the screen, his gray hair still holding the shape of a hard hat, a sheen of sweat on his face. He was looking past the camera, talking to someone. His eyes were alert, and the frozen vid had caught him in mid-gesture. A wall of greenery behind him, piles of red dirt in the fore-ground, and a crane partially assembled looming overhead.

Her breath caught, became almost a solid thing in her lungs. The frozen image was the essence of her father. The smile, the gesture, the place ... where was this?

<j-qinlao.sec> was embossed on the bottom left of the image, along with latitude and longitude coordinates. Qinlao security ran continuous surveillance on company officers except in their personal quarters or when privacy was requested. In her short time as CEO, Ming had learned to live with the constant intrusion. But why would her mother give her a raw secu-rity file?

Her mind still foggy from the recent implant operation, Ming struggled to recall the intricacies of the Qinlao security procedures from what seemed like a lifetime ago. The raw footage was uploaded every minute to a satellite relay for collation with concurrent sources and storage.

She checked the length of the vid. Fifty-nine seconds. A check of the coordinates put the scene in the Indonesian jungle. The site of her father's death.

*"Play,"* she pulsed to her implant.

Laughing to someone off camera, Jie Qinlao raked his fingers through his sweat-soaked hair. The view shifted to a work crew in rough clothes and scarred hard hats.

*"Kerja bagus,"* her father said, smiling. Her implant translated the Indonesian for *Good job*. It was so like him to offer a few words of praise in his workers' native tongue. Her jaw muscles seemed to have lost all control, and her lips trembled. She clenched her teeth together in response, willing herself to hold it together.

A distant boom shook the camera. Men shouted in Indonesian. Sharp cries, fearful. Ming heard her father's voice trying to keep the workers calm.

The camera angle shifted again, looking skyward. A cloud of black smoke rose, and Ming made out three fast-moving aircars. Oblong shadows dropped from them, followed by a whoosh of flame on the ground, then a second, then a third.

"Mr. Qinlao!" Another man's voice.

But it was too late. She caught a glimpse of the aircraft, a flitting V shape, then the screen went blank.

It took Ming a moment to realize she'd stopped breathing. If someone called in that moment, if her door chimed, if anything outside herself intruded at all, she felt she might shatter into a million pieces.

She threw the vid to a full-wallscreen.

It took a monumental force of will to restart the vid. Her father smiling and laughing, the pan of the camera to his workers and his expression of gratitude, then the explosions and the smoke and the screaming...

"Mr. Qinlao!"

Ming had never seen a firebomb, but the sudden explosion, the devastation that spread so quickly, looked like what she imagined incendiaries could do.

*An accident ... a virus swept through the work camp ... they had to firebomb the site to make sure the virus was contained.* That's what her Auntie Xi had told her, but the vid told a different story.

Her father had been murdered.

She stood up and walked to the carafe on the small table. Slowly, as if it were the most important action in the world, she poured a glass of water and gulped the liquid down.

She played it again. When the aircars first appeared, Ming slowed the video down to view the images frame by frame. She enlarged and enhanced several, but the aircars were mere streaks of reflection in the sky. She let it play at normal speed.

"Mr. Qinlao!" came the voice of the security guard, terrified, beseeching her father to heed his call. Her father was facing away, head angled up. The vid angle followed. A single aircar flew by.

Ming focused on the screen, zooming in on the single attacker. It dropped its payload, then banked. Advancing frame by frame, she watched the weapon fall, and the aircraft turn.

*"Pause,"* she pulsed. *"Five-second rewind."*

Over Jie's shoulder, smoke was sucked downward.

*"Advance."*

Slowly, the smoke rose. The aircar appeared.

*"Pause. Zoom in."* The aircar grew on the screen. Her implant employed

an algorithm, picking recognizable points from the aircar's design to fill in the rest of the image. Ming watched the incendiary bomb release from the aircar's undercarriage.

As the aircar banked, the blurry, helmeted head of its pilot flashed against the glass.

The bomb dropped another meter. The cockpit angled a few more degrees toward the camera. The pilot's helmet had a logo.

The algorithm went to work on the logo. Ming recognized it long before the program finished its work.

The Qinlao Manufacturing logo.

Ming closed the program and let the silence of the empty room ring in her ears. She ordered her thoughts carefully, methodically, like she was solving an engineering problem.

She could assume the file was genuine and her mother had given it to Ming knowing her daughter would act on the contents. There were only two people in the Qinlao organization with enough power to pull off an assassination using company resources and still be able to cover it up.

Auntie Xi and Sying.

One woman she hated. One woman she loved.

Ming forced her analytical mind to the fore. Her personal feelings for Sying did not matter now, not until she knew the truth about what had happened. Sying was a powerful woman, a queen by her own admission. She played the long game and she played for keeps. But would she murder her husband? It was hard for Ming to fathom such an action.

That left Xi. Ming's worst fears of her aunt's duplicity, of the old woman's bottomless capacity for betrayal, now seemed confirmed. She'd been so covetous of Jie's achievement in building Qinlao Manufacturing that she'd killed him for it.

And her mother had carried her secret burden of knowing for ... how long? Shame draped over Ming's shoulders for how she'd treated Wenqian upon her return to Earth.

The shame reformed in her gut as anger. Her father, murdered. Lily, murdered. She and Ruben living on the run. All to satisfy the greed of an old woman who loved status and wealth more than blood.

The engineer displaced the grieving daughter. Ming's every step now was critical. She needed information. Real, verifiable data to arrive at a plan, a plan to reclaim what was rightfully hers.

First step: she needed to get off Mars. Every communication she made here, every iota of bandwidth she consumed was monitored and dissected by Taulke security personnel. That information could be used against her —somehow, someway, someday.

She placed a call to Anthony. He was still at his desk and his face lit up when he saw her. She automatically tamped down the need to confide in him. Until she solved this puzzle, she had no friends, only variables in her life.

"I've reconsidered," she said. "I'll do the job you asked."

Anthony's smile widened. "That's wonderful, Ming!" His face clouded. "You look like you've seen a ghost. Are you okay?"

"I'm fine," she said. "I'm assuming Ruben can stay in your care while I'm gone."

Anthony nodded. "Of course. What changed your mind?"

"I've gained a greater appreciation for the big picture. I'd like to leave as soon as possible."

"I'll let Viktor know."

When the call ended, Ming stood alone in her room again. Carefully, she closed her retinal implant and its damning file. The square of light in her right eye blinked away.

Then Ming Qinlao sat down in the nearest chair and wept like a child.

## 16

### REMY CADE • HAVEN 6, BLUE EARTH, MINNESOTA

Remy rose with the rest of the staff when General Graves entered the conference room. Jansen walked behind him, her expression tight with concern.

"Seats, everyone, please." He let his gaze work the room, giving the occasional nod and smile. Finally, he spoke. "The day we've been working toward is here. I've just spoken with Washington. We're sealing all seven Haven domes in forty-eight hours. We'll be taking on final crew members by noon tomorrow. Final logistics checks are due to Captain Jansen by then."

*Forty-eight hours?* The bile of panic rose in Remy's throat.

"Once the dome is sealed, that's it." Graves paused to let that sink in. "No one goes in or out. Comms other than those authorized by command are cut off. As far as the outside world is concerned, we no longer exist. We'll rotate the staff out in thirds for a half-day leave period over the next thirty-six hours so you can say goodbye to your loved ones who aren't part of the Haven team."

Graves's gaze made another circuit around the room. His eyes met Remy's, then slid away to the next person.

Despite developing a close relationship with Luca Vasquez, Remy was no closer to completing his mission than he'd been weeks ago.

"I know this is hard, people," Graves continued. "But you knew what you were signing up for when you volunteered for this mission. We'll start the Haven countdown at midnight tomorrow. If you're inside the dome, you're here for the duration. No exceptions."

---

No exceptions.

The words rang in Remy's ears as he made his way to the mess hall for his date with Luca. After nearly a month inside Haven 6, he knew little more about what lay beyond deck 36 than when he'd arrived.

The mess hall was full of adrenaline and speculation. People swirled around him, full of quick cordialities and guarded conversations about the pending deadline. Emotions were high as dome residents wrestled with the idea that soon Haven 6 would be their entire world.

And he'd be stuck here with them if he didn't act quickly. Alone, separated from Elise, the only person he cared about in this whole shitty world. But to go back empty-handed ... Cassandra would not like that, and neither would her number-one apostle.

Remy drew a cup of coffee and took a seat. Getting to know Luca over the last few weeks had proven a mixed bag of joy and self-loathing with a side order of guilt. She was a remarkable young woman, and since Canada they'd become more than friends. He was using her, and he knew it. Every time she confided some intimacy with him, he felt the crushing weight of guilt.

But Elise was always there, in the back of his head, urging him to do whatever necessary to get closer to her. He knew exactly what was meant by *whatever necessary*.

And now the clock was ticking.

He people-watched as he waited. The Haven selection process hadn't been kind to families or marriages. The Pioneers, as they liked to call themselves, had been chosen for one of two reasons: their expertise in building a self-sustaining society or their relative fertility potential. The first group skewed older, the second younger. There were many single—or newly single—people looking for companionship, and Remy formed a mental image of Haven as a subterranean singles cruise as the Earth tore itself apart outside the silo.

Luca was halfway across the mess hall before he noticed her shining smile. Her expression diminished when she saw his face. "What's wrong?"

Remy created a smile to prove he was happy to see her. "Oh, another reaming from Jansen. You know—Tuesday."

Luca was the kind of person who always gave her full attention to whoever she was talking to. "Everyone's on edge these days, but it'll be over soon."

Remy felt the time pressure creeping in on him again. He took her hand and Luca squeezed his fingers.

"I always feel better when I talk to you," he said. "Are you ready for this?"

"I feel the same way about you, Remy," she said. "Once the Havens..." Luca stopped speaking. Her eyes flitted up to him, then looked away. She drew her hand away.

"Once the Havens ... what?"

"General Graves's announcement," she said. "I just meant that."

Remy's skin prickled. She'd been about to say something. Something secret, by the way her eyes refused to meet his now. Something valuable, maybe? Time was running out. He needed to take something back to Elise.

"But you still haven't said what *that* means." Remy tried to make his demand for information humorous. "Looks like we're going to be together for the next hundred years or so, Luca. Might as well get it off your chest now."

"I can't. I know who you are, Remy Cade, and I trust you." Then, after a beat: "My heart knows."

A wariness hit him then, like when he'd been in the field and felt the enemy around but couldn't see them. She was hiding something. Something others—Jansen? Graves?—had told her not to tell him.

"Luca, what—"

"*Buenos dias, hermana.*"

A younger, slightly plumper version of Luca plopped down in one of the two empty seats at the table. Her sudden appearance forced Remy to shift gears.

"You must be Donna," he said, the words coming automatically.

"*Sí.* And you must be Remy Cade."

"*Sí,*" he replied, holding out his hand.

"Don't make fun of my language," Donna replied. She shook his hand anyway and leaned over to Luca. "*¡Él es lindo!*"

Remy saw the color rise in Luca's cheeks.

"Want me to say the English, big sis?"

"*Silencio,*" Luca hissed, blushing harder.

Remy settled into the routine of conversation, allowing the social ritual to displace his earlier excitement. He smiled at Donna, studied her. When she glanced at the buffet line, he was startled to see the skin healing on the back of her neck. The remnants of a Neo tattoo.

"How long were you a follower of Cassandra?"

Luca reached out and took Donna's hand. "She was *never* a follower of Cassandra. She just had that stupid tattoo."

Pulling back against her sister's touch, Donna nodded. "Yeah. I just thought it was pretty. Woman is *la madre* of the world, right?"

Remy gave her a thoughtful grin. "Right."

Donna leaned across the table toward Remy. "Are you excited? Almost time to blast off!"

"Donna!" Luca exclaimed.

Luca's face had a look of panic, then resignation. Remy put his hand over hers.

"Is that the big secret?" Remy asked. "What you couldn't tell me?"

"I'm sorry," Luca whispered. "It's going to be announced when the dome is sealed, but yes, the Haven is not a silo, it's a spaceship." She lowered her voice even more. "There's a planet identified. It's light-years away, but with the new drive we can make it in a few years. We can start over. Are you listening to me?"

Remy scanned the room, then thought about the size of the flight deck on the top level of the dome and the sheer volume of this entire structure. The Haven was the size of a city. How could something that big launch into space? Not a power plant after all, but some new type of space drive. And capable of near light speeds.

Luca squeezed his fingers with a force borne of desperation. "Remy, are we okay?"

"Yeah, yeah, it's fine, I just..." Remy forced his mind to engage. He forced himself to calm down. "It's amazing, actually. I just need time to process. A spaceship..." His smile was genuine, though not for the reason Luca thought. "We'll be together."

Luca would think he was talking about her, but Remy didn't care. He had what he'd come for and Elise would love him for it.

Squeezing Luca's hand one last time, he pulled away and rose from the table.

"I need to talk to Jansen. I need a few hours' leave to settle some affairs."

"Dinner tonight?" Luca asked, her words chasing after him. "We have a lot to talk about, I think."

"Sure," Remy answered. "Sure."

---

He shut the aircar door, sealing out the noisy Chicago aerodrome. The door light changed to green, indicating an airtight seal. Remy did not sync his data glasses with the car. In fact, he'd left his data glasses under the seat of the last aircab he'd been in. If someone was tracking him via his glasses, they were in for a ride all over the Midwest.

He'd paid extra for the voice-activated self-driver, and the aircar queried his destination. "Low Earth orbit," he replied. It was a popular destination for people who wanted to see their planet from above and had well-traveled traffic patterns. Nothing to attract suspicion.

Remy's body pressed against the gel cushions as the aircar left the dock and entered the queue for departure. Privacy, like everything else, had a price. He'd paid for the destination anonymizer, and the salesman had assured him that his secrets were safe from the government.

Still, he'd stick with well-used traffic patterns for now.

The car accelerated into the flow of other aircars, its station-keeping feature holding him the regulation two car lengths behind the vehicle in front. At each interchange, they ascended another level until they were free of Chicago traffic.

Hoping to catch one last glimpse of Haven 6, he squinted toward the northwest. Part of him regretted the inevitable heartache he knew Luca would suffer. He felt smaller than small, leaving her without even the courtesy of a lie to hold onto.

Remy closed his eyes and imagined the Haven ship rising from the ground and into outer space, carrying mankind's future with it. He couldn't wait to deliver the news to Elise.

A drive capable of lifting an entire city into orbit and traveling at speeds no one had even dreamed of achieving. No wonder Cassandra wanted that technology. The New Earth Order would be an unstoppable force in the solar system.

And he would have Elise back finally. The real Elise that he knew and loved, the one before Cassandra. She was kind, compassionate. She cared about her world, she cared about people. It was Cassandra who'd opened her skull and drowned her brain in New Earther Kool-Aid. In the fantasy of his return, after he'd explained to her about the Havens, she fell into his arms and told him how much she loved him.

The land grew fuzzy with distance, and the sky above him darkened. He could feel the subtle change in his ears as the aircar adapted to the lower pressure. Traffic at this level formed into a long, shining chain of aircars and other, space-capable vehicles ringing the planet. His car joined the chain, the station-keeping program slotting him in between what looked like a comms drone in front and a late-model Cadillac behind.

High above him, the ring of permanent orbiters massed in the darkness of space. Thousands of space stations, satellites, and ship-building docks of every size, shape, and vintage formed a ragged blanket overhead. In the distance, he could make out the space elevator poking above the layer of orbitals. This was no-man's-land out here, an unregulated frontier of technology. And beyond all that, the shining silver stars glimmered like ghost lights.

Reflected light winked back at Remy from fast-moving, smaller craft while the larger freighters moved with a lazy, easy leviathan grace above

Earth. Elise was somewhere in that dark sea of man-made metal. The aircar angled upward out of the flow of traffic.

And there it was ... at first a tiny, glowing dot, then a larger, revolving synthetic world: the Temple of Cassandra station. Remy's heart leapt.

He was home.

# 17

## MING QINLAO • TAULKE ATMOSPHERIC EXPERIMENT STATION, MARS

Ming's rage had burned away, leaving in its place an icy sense of calm rationality. She distilled her thoughts into discrete packets of information, each one aimed at seeing justice done for her father's murder.

Analysis, calculation, action. That was all that mattered now.

Entering Viktor's personal lab felt like walking into an operating room organized by a hoarder. A row of articulated 3-D printers lined the wall, one of them whining as it drew its subject into being. The walls had all been converted to screens and Viktor was pacing in front of one when she entered, scrubbing his gray fringe with his free hand. With the other hand, he twisted the image on the screen, which looked like a variant on the bio-nanite design he'd used to seed the Earth's climate—with disastrous results.

"So good to see you healthy, Ming," Viktor said. The Russian scientist opened his arms wide. His grin was infectious, especially wreathed in his halo of gray hair.

"Hello, Viktor." It was hard to muster more than a tight smile. An enormous clock ticked away in her head like a time bomb. Every second she spent not pursuing those responsible for her father's death was another second wasted.

"Are you sure you're okay? You seem on edge." Viktor took her by the elbow, guiding her to the back of the lab.

*Tick-tock*, went the clock.

"Just anxious to do my part, Viktor. I'd like to get started."

He stopped at a table and swept his hand in a flourish. "I'm outfitting you with cutting-edge tech, Ming. The best my lab can offer."

She saw only a flat black box the size of a deck of cards next to a boxy pistol and holster.

Viktor opened the box to reveal what looked like a black eyepatch.

"I call this MoSCOW, short for Mobile SuperComputer, Operator Wearable. It's a self-contained supercomputer that uses your existing implant to create a direct brain interface."

Ming plucked the device from the box. It was heavier than it looked and had a piece that folded out to connect to the wearer's temple and wrap around their ear. The interior of the eyepatch was inlaid with silver circuits that caught the light. She started to fit the cup over her eye when Viktor stopped her.

"You don't want to do that until you need to activate it. MoSCOW, uh, has some side effects that must be minimized. It's experimental, but extremely powerful."

"Side effects?" Ming replaced the device in the carrier.

Viktor shut the box. "A device with this much capability requires a significant source of power. It has a tiny nuclear battery, but once activated, it cannot be turned off."

"Nuclear?" Ming asked. "Where's the shielding?"

"That would be the side effect. One of them, anyway. The shielding needed to make this safe for a human would weigh approximately twenty-two kilos." He patted the box. "MoSCOW allows you to become an extension of the computer. A hybrid. You will find there's not much you can't do with MoSCOW's help. Decryption, facial recognition, augmented self-defense—even I don't know all the possible enhancements yet."

Ming brought him back to the problem. "How much radiation are we talking about, Viktor?"

The older man fussed with the closed box. "For every hour you wear the device, you will receive approximately one year's worth of radiation.

Don't worry," he said, wagging his hands. "When you get back, we'll put you on a radiation remission therapy right away to minimize any long-term damage." He hesitated.

"There's more?" Ming said.

Viktor looked away. "Human skin is a poor conductor, so there are probes in MoSCOW to establish the best conductivity route for optimum performance."

"Probes? How far do they go into my skin?"

"It varies by user ... some of them could be uncomfortable."

His body language told Ming the word *uncomfortable* was more of a euphemism than a clinical term. "I suppose a local anesthetic would degrade performance," she said, making no attempt to mask her sarcasm.

"Exactly," Viktor said. "MoSCOW will be accessing your brain directly, maybe even remapping parts of it for efficiency. You need to make sure you minimize your integration time."

*Integration*—an interesting word choice.

"Please, Ming, you must listen to me on this. MoSCOW is—"

"Experimental. Yeah, I get it." Ming picked up the odd-looking pistol. It was much heavier than it looked and had no gun sights. "What's this?"

"Advanced stun weapon. It creates a pulse of energy that incapacitates the target."

She hefted it. It was blocky, Russian in design. "So it's a fancy Taser?"

"No!" said Viktor, sounding offended. He grabbed the weapon from her. "Tasers use energy to lock up muscles. This is designed to immobilize the nervous system. Much more refined." His tone was that of a prideful father.

"I'm still bringing a Glock with me, Viktor. That it?"

"Not quite." Viktor led her to a mannequin dressed in a black jumpsuit. The lines of the suit still had rough seams. Another experiment. "This bodysuit integrates with MoSCOW, providing a web of sensors that capture stimuli in your immediate environment. You'll have advanced situational awareness and even precognitive self-defense abilities."

"Precognitive self-defense?"

"MoSCOW can read the body language of your opponent and prompt your muscles to defend before the attacker strikes. It comes with integrated body armor. It's not pretty, but that's because—"

"It's experimental."

"*Da.* The sensors can even tell you when someone's lying using biofeedback."

She studied the suit material, which had a way of altering color as the angle changed. "Camouflage?"

Viktor shrugged. "Planned upgrade. It has some light-bending features, but at the moment it's no more sophisticated than those expensive chameleon suits some people wear."

"So you're turning me into a fusion-powered, supercomputer soldier," Ming said. "With a side order of dementia."

The smile on Viktor's face came easier this time. "Come back in one piece, Ming."

---

Anthony and Ruben waited dockside next to a matte black spacecraft without markings. The ship had the aerodynamic lines of an atmosphere-capable vessel, and the snub nose of a single rail gun hung under the bow.

The sensor suit hugged Ming's figure and added spring to her step, making her feel ready for anything. The armor, which she feared would be bulky, moved well with her body. She kept her Glock on her right hip, Viktor's fancy energy weapon on her left, and, per her last-minute request of Viktor, a carbon smartglass knife on the outside of her calf. The MoSCOW device fit securely in a pocket just below her beltline.

"I thought you were just going to find out information, Ming," Ruben said, his eyes fastened on the weapons. "This looks dangerous."

"It's just a precaution, Ruben." Anthony put his arm around the boy. "We want to keep your big sister safe, right?"

Ruben nodded, but he didn't seem convinced.

Ming pulled her brother aside. She barely needed to lean down to look Ruben in the eyes anymore. Had he really grown that much since they'd fled Earth together?

"This is only for a few days," she said softly. "I'll be gone five days, a week at most."

"Mama said we weren't supposed to be separated."

*Mama.* Sying. Ruben's mother, Ming's stepmother. The thought of her made Ming's breath catch. Her lover—and possibly a killer. Even now, the idea was too much to process at one time.

*Your mother said a lot of things, Ruben. And she'll need to say a lot more before this is all over.*

"I know." Ming touched her forehead to Ruben's. "Trust me?"

"I'll be fine," he said, though she could hear the tremor in his tone. Then, in a whisper only Ming could hear, he said, "I just don't want to lose you too. Like Lily."

Ming hugged him hard. "I'll come back to you, Ruben. I promise."

The boy nodded into her shoulder.

When she stood, Ming found another man had joined Anthony. It took her a moment to recognize the captain of the *Revenant*, the ship that had brought her to Mars.

"Captain Lander?"

"Dr. Qinlao," he said, nodding. "Nice to see you again. And it's just Lander now. I got demoted to chauffeuring you in the *Roadrunner* here." He patted the side of the ship.

Anthony sighed. "Long story. But since he's available, I'm sending him to watch your back."

Lander looked down at her from his full height of six-foot-plus. His faded blue eyes took in her outfit. "Nice ninja suit."

"One of Viktor's inventions," Anthony said.

Ming felt her cheeks burn with embarrassment at acting the part of a soldier, but the feeling was quickly washed away by her newfound mission. She had a job to do. Screw him and his male chauvinist bullshit.

"I'd rather do this alone, Anthony," she said. "Viktor's got me loaded to the gills with upgrades and gadgets."

"He's going with you," Anthony said, his tone uncharacteristically firm. "Lander's a first-class pilot. And I want you to come back safe and sound. We both do, right, Ruben?"

"Right," the boy said.

Ming considered making a fuss, but the tick-tock of her real mission was always in the back of her mind. She would never find out who murdered her father sitting here on Mars. She needed unlimited access to a real network, one unmonitored by her host.

Anthony Taulke was a cautious man, a man who protected his investments. If he wanted to send this Lander character with her, there was probably a good reason. "Well, if you insist."

She gave Ruben a final hug, then followed Lander aboard the shuttle. Conditions were cramped and utilitarian, just four crash couches and a small cargo area at the rear. Ming felt the adaptive foam of the chair cushion mold to her body.

Lander strapped himself in and popped a mock salute to Anthony before lifting off. The older man stood well back from the takeoff radius, his arm around Ruben's shoulders.

Ming waved at Ruben. The boy did not wave back.

"Where to, ma'am?" Lander said.

"Darkside," she said. "As fast as you can get us there."

"Be careful what you wish for." The shuttle's engines fired up, pressing Ming deeper into the womb-like embrace of the copilot's cushioned seat.

They rose high above Mars Station, the three domes looking like white coins against the red landscape.

"Do you trust Taulke?" she said.

Lander looked at her with narrowed eyes, as if he didn't understand the question. "I work for the Taulke family. I take orders and I get paid. There's no trust involved." His screen flashed, indicating a flight path was confirmed. "Buckle up."

---

## William Graves • Haven 6, Blue Earth, Minnesota

"We've got him, sir." Captain Jansen's voice was clipped with tension. Without even turning around, Graves could imagine the tight smile of triumph on her face, the fist pump of victory. She'd never trusted Remy Cade and this betrayal was sweet satisfaction to her.

He shared none of her elation. Instead, Graves felt a mixture of anger and sadness at Remy's betrayal. Another casualty in this never-ending war.

"Sir?"

"I heard you, Captain." He was so goddamned tired. Physically. Emotionally. Spiritually. "Well done," he added.

The tracking device in Cade's shoulder had been Jansen's idea, as had using Luca Vasquez as a way to drop tidbits of information to Remy.

But the betrayal had been all Cade's.

He watched the tiny blip on the hologram display break from the suborbital traffic pattern and join the ring of satellites and space stations in Earth orbit. Cade had followed a circuitous path before docking at one of the stations. It would take Graves a week of paperwork and court orders to find out who owned the station, much less secure the legal permission to board it. That was not going to be necessary. He had other plans for the Neos.

"Keep an eye on him. Let's make sure this isn't a bait and switch," he said. "This is not the B squad we're dealing with here."

"Understood, sir." Jansen hesitated again, weighing her words.

"Question, Captain?"

"How'd you know, sir? How'd you know Cade would run?"

Graves turned to her, studied Jansen's face. There was an ashen undertone to her dark skin and the skin under her eyes sagged. She was every bit as exhausted as he was. But their mission together was almost done. The realization registered as a slight drop in his stomach.

"When good men do bad things, they don't do them well," Grave said. "Lying, for example. Remy's a good man, but he fell in love with the wrong person. I suspected he wasn't truthful when he said he'd given up on her, despite his attentions to Ms. Vasquez. Now we know for sure."

Jansen enlarged the hologram again. "Sir, he's disembarked. That's got to be the Neo base of operations."

Graves nodded. "Analyze the comms traffic from that space station. Look for embedded, encrypted information packets. And let's see if any transmissions match up with Ms. Vasquez's Neo frequency."

"Yes, sir."

"And her eraser devices? Are they ready?" Graves had managed to screen most of the Neos from the Haven crew, but the ones who managed to slip through would need to be dealt with. Luca Vasquez had been working overtime to produce enough of the handheld devices that deactivated the Neo implants.

"Yes, sir, the last batch just left for Haven 2 this morning. We've got the Neo crew isolated in each location. As soon as you give the order, we'll start the inoculation."

"And the Disruptor?" Graves asked with a smile. He'd asked Vasquez to produce a transmitter that could broadcast a signal to disrupt Neo communications. It would produce no more than a mild buzzing sound to normal people, but to a Neo it might be enough to knock a person unconscious for a few minutes.

*Might* being the operative word. The Disruptor had not been tested.

"Yes, sir. It's pretty bulky, about the size of a small suitcase, but it's the best she can do with the time left."

"Very well, Captain. Please pass along my compliments to Ms. Vasquez as well for a job well done. She's certainly earned that spot on Haven 6 for her and her sister."

"Will do, sir. It'll be a welcome piece of good news. She's pretty torn up about Remy dumping her like that."

Graves sighed. Luca had played her part well, feeding Remy just enough information to entice him to run back to the Neos. Right up to the bitter end, she had maintained that Remy would stay with her on Haven.

She was wrong.

He returned his gaze to the holo-display, zooming in on the space station Cade had boarded. "Are we ready for this, then?"

"I'm ready when you are, sir." Her eyes glowed with a second wind of excitement. She was enjoying this, he realized. The cloak-and-dagger subterfuge that left him queasy, the unanswered questions beyond deck 36 —Jansen found all of that exciting.

They left his office together, heading for the main lift. When the doors opened on deck 36, the marine guard came to attention and snapped a smart salute.

"They're expecting you, sir." He keyed in a code, and the heavy steel door rolled aside.

# 18

## MING QINLAO • LUNAR ORBIT

It was a long two days with Lander. He wasn't given to small talk and Ming had much bigger issues to think about. Two sleep cycles had mercifully spared her the need to interact much, and that was just fine with her.

"Lunar orbit," Lander announced. He hadn't slept as far as she could tell, but he seemed fresh. He handled the shuttle like a natural, eschewing autopilot most of the time in favor of staying busy. "What's the plan, Ming?"

She passed coordinates for the Erkennen facility to the nav system. Viktor's tech had managed to scrub any mention of the facility from public records and he employed digital camouflage to obscure any chance visual sighting.

The chill inside Ming thawed a little when LUNa City appeared on the edge of the horizon, filling her with a longing for Lily and simpler times.

Lander left the commercial traffic lanes as soon as they crossed the sun line into darkness. He was cautious. The *Roadrunner*'s stealth design should keep them off sensors, but they weren't invisible to the naked eye.

"I don't see anything," Lander said when the nav system told them they had arrived.

"It's there," Ming answered. She accessed the comms and released a coded sequence on a tightbeam aimed at the coordinates. A single light pulsed on the shadowy lunar surface like a beacon.

Lander grunted. "That Russian is one clever bastard."

She whirled her finger to indicate Lander should circle the perimeter. It appeared to be a low-slung dome the color of lunar regolith with a single docking entrance, but she knew the structure extended four stories deep. One way in, one way out, just at Viktor had described.

"The place is in full lockdown," she said, "and the encryption on the front door is the best money can buy. You try to blast your way in and the place will self-destruct." She eyed Lander. "A safety feature to prevent any Erkennen secrets from getting out."

"Wonderful. I'm guessing you can get us in?"

Ming fingered the MoSCOW device in her pocket. "We'll know in a minute."

"And you're looking for what?"

"Clues. Information that will tell me who we're dealing with."

Lander eased the *Roadrunner* into the single docking port. The ship shuddered as it formed an airtight connection with the station. Once the seals showed green, he powered down the engines.

"You're up, Ming."

She eased MoSCOW out of her pocket and opened the box. The eyepiece gleamed in the low light of the cabin. She unfolded it and flipped it over, exposing the inner surface. Inside the eyecup and the strap that ran along her temple and behind her ear, rows of tiny needles glistened. Viktor's warning about the radiation seemed petty next to the array of probes ready to burrow into her skin.

Lander's gaze cut from MoSCOW to Ming. "That looks like a torture device. You're going to wear that thing?"

In answer, Ming raised MoSCOW to her eye and pressed it in place. Viktor had told her the device would turn on automat—

Like a nail into her eyeball, hot, blinding pain injected her skull as MoSCOW latched onto her face. Ming's vision went blank. Of its own accord, the temple piece formed to her skin, wrapping around her ear. A probe wormed into her ear canal, shooting an arrow of blistering agony through her eardrum.

Ming's vision returned in spasms of vivid neon color. Greens that were too green, blues too blue, reds that were a thousand shades of blood. A high-pitched keening was everywhere in the ship's cabin, making her want to shout at the source to shut the fuck up, it was hurting her ears. Then Ming realized it was her own screaming.

Her limbs twitched uncontrollably as MoSCOW mated with her suit.

Something on her face—Lander's fingers—tried to pull MoSCOW's sensor display away from her eye. She pushed him off, surprised at how easy that was.

"Leave it," she gasped.

The vivid colors lost their glow, coalesced, and sharpened again into the outlines of objects she recognized. The excruciating pain pressing into her skull dulled to a thousand points of ache. Ming blinked. Her vision had depth again. Meaning.

And more. Identifying tags popped up as her eyes passed over the pilot's console. Ops, comms, navigation, helm, and the ad hoc control for the recently installed rail gun. She knew everything about the ship's enhanced engine specs, the normal range of every readout, even how to drive the shuttle manually. All in a single glance. She just *knew*.

"Are you okay, Ming?" Lander asked.

MoSCOW fed her layers of data about him. His voice carried a faint, generations-old accent of Eastern Europe, Hungarian extraction from the region near Debrecen, modified by immigration to the eastern United States and by his time living on Mars. More than that, his voiceprint showed he was under emotional stress. She studied his face in a sweep of data. Clenched jaw, bunched brow, dilated pupils, tension in his trapezius muscles. MoSCOW's conclusion: Lander was extremely agitated, nervous. That reaction was normal considering she'd just been screaming in pain, but the MoSCOW system was telling her his physiological response had another meaning.

Lander was concealing something from her.

"I'm fine," Ming said. She rose carefully from the copilot's seat, forcing herself to filter the unending stream of data into manageable chunks. Ming focused on her body first. The suit had anticipatory functionality, meaning it would predict her movements based on the data available.

*Don't fight it. Work with it.* She opened the shuttle airlock, then made her way to the inner seal. The panel blinked red, indicating a lockdown status.

"You're sure you can do this?" Lander said from behind her. His voice had new tension now. Lander was afraid.

"Are we even sure there's atmosphere over there? Maybe we should suit up—"

"Station atmosphere is seventy-eight percent nitrogen, twenty-one percent oxygen, with trace elements of argon and carbon dioxide. And ... hydrogen sulfide and methane."

Ming was startled by the sound of her own voice. MoSCOW had offered up the analysis without prompting. And she'd recited it without thinking.

She placed the haptic sensors in her palm against the panel and interfaced with the lab's security program. Ming had to close her eyes at the flood of data as the supercomputer tried to crack the encryption on the other side. Her breath rasped in her throat. In the distance, she heard the airlock open and MoSCOW severed the connection.

"Jesus," Lander said, covering his nose in the crook of his arm.

Inside were half a dozen dead personnel, scientists and security. Dark brown stains swathed the floor and walls. MoSCOW analyzed the injuries as knife wounds from three different blades.

MoSCOW fed Ming the organic compounds contained in rotting flesh. When Erkennen's lab had gone into emergency lockdown, the environmental controls had automatically minimized to preserve atmosphere for any survivors until rescue arrived.

Just past the airlock was the security cubicle. Ming pulled a sagging body off the panel and placed her hand on the center console. She paired with the system, and a new stream of data hammered her brain. The attackers, whoever they were, had tried to fry the electronics, but MoSCOW wasn't taking no for answer. She directed her sensors into the guts of the shattered memory banks, gathering bits of information to her, assembling them like they were part of the largest 3-D jigsaw puzzle in the universe.

Seconds passed, minutes, maybe longer. Ming lost all track of time. The suit held her body in place, but her flesh cried out for relief. The bits of information formed about her like a cloud of buzzing angry bees, then slowly coalesced in her vision. A moving image emerged: she recognized the station airlock, connected to another ship. A transport.

"*UN Shuttle Model B-12,*" MoSCOW reported. "*Annan class.*"

And on the facing of the ship's airlock, a number: UN X769.

The party from the shuttle was led by a woman: tall, thin, with straight dark hair and brown skin. She wore the white civilian uniform of the United Nations. MoSCOW identified her as Elise Kisaan, United Nations Undersecretary for Biodiversity, reported missing months ago.

Kisaan's shuttle had been the last ship to dock here before the cryptokey had been stolen. Somehow this missing woman was tied to the theft of Viktor's cryptokey and the control of Earth's weather.

MoSCOW allowed the suit to lower her frame into a nearby chair next to the stinking corpse. Her body screamed for sustenance.

"Food," she whispered. "Now."

Lander pulled a gel packet from his belt and she grabbed it from him, ripping it open, devouring it. Taste was irrelevant, a non-thing. The pounding in her head slowed down.

"Did you find what you were looking for?" Lander asked.

Ming nodded.

He handed her a tablet. "Show me."

She transferred the image to the tablet with a touch of her glove, explaining who the woman in the photo was. MoSCOW interrupted her thoughts.

Lander had used his left hand to give her the tablet, his nondominant hand. The tension in his thumb spoke of an unnatural readiness, as did the stance of his feet.

She looked up as he said, "Thanks."

MoSCOW noted his elevated pulse, analyzed his micro-expressions. *Deception.* A red rectangle in her vision tracked Lander's right hand moving toward his weapon.

Ming's foot lashed out, sweeping the tall man off his feet. The light lunar gravity made him tumble wildly, his sidearm spinning away.

She pounced, her weight forcing them both to the blood-streaked floor. MoSCOW categorized the emotions flashing across his face: Surprise. Shock. Fear.

Her suit formed a knife edge from her extended fingers, and Ming pressed the makeshift blade against the base of his throat. The man's right shoulder tensed.

*"Counterattack imminent,"* MoSCOW warned.

"Don't," Ming hissed. "I will kill you."

"Who are you?" Lander focused on the eyepatch. "What is that thing?"

"You lied to me. Why?"

Silence. Ming pressed down with her fingers until she could feel the ridges of his esophagus. The tension in his right arm did not diminish; his fingers twitched toward the knife on his belt.

*"Counterattack imminent."*

"Last chance." Ming felt her blade edge break the soft skin of Lander's throat.

His eyes relented, and she eased the pressure. Lander began to speak, but Ming stopped him. "I can tell if you're lying." She leaped off his body in one swift movement. "You lie, you die. No more chances." He sat up, rubbing the fresh cut on his neck.

"He told me to kill you."

"Who?"

"Taulke," he grunted, coughing.

*"Truth,"* MoSCOW reported.

"Anthony wants me dead?"

*"Confusion."*

"Not Anthony," Lander said. "Tony."

Tony Taulke wanted her dead? That made even less sense. She'd done nothing to him.

"Why?"

"I don't know," Lander said.

*"Truth."*

"I don't understand. Anthony sent you to protect me."

Lander shook his head, the muscles in his face contracting in ways that told her he was conflicted, but not lying. "Not to protect you," he said finally. "To get you out of the way. He made a deal for the boy. I don't know with who."

Ming didn't need MoSCOW for this calculation. Auntie Xi. Anthony Taulke had cut a deal with Xi, using Ruben as a bargaining chip. And he'd manipulated Ming out of the way so he could close the deal.

"It's why we intercepted the *Baldwin* in the first place," Lander continued. "To pull you both in-house."

MoSCOW analyzed his vocal inflections. *"Truth."*

"Tony and the old man are on the outs, each trying to one-up the other. Anthony sent the *Revenant* to intercept you and Tony was pissed at me for not warning him. Now one Taulke wants me to babysit you, the other wants you to have an accident. Tony signs my paycheck, so I take my marching orders from him." It was the most she'd heard Lander say at one time. Even without MoSCOW she could tell he was relieved to unburden himself.

"I didn't want to do it," Lander said. "Executing people—women, especially—is not my style." MoSCOW said he was being truthful.

"But you would have."

Lander shrugged. "Yeah, I would have."

*"Truth."*

Her enhanced mind cycled through her options. Intercept Ruben. Go to Mars, confront Anthony. Deal with Tony.

She rejected them all. She needed a new plan, a way to change the field of play. It was time for Ming to make a move worthy of a queen.

"I can help you," Lander said.

*"Truth."*

"You don't know what I'm going to do yet."

"I know if you're going up against the Taulkes, you're going to need help."

"How can I trust you?" Ming said. "You're nothing but a hired gun. You'll shoot me in the back first chance you get."

She watched the range of emotions cross his face. He knew she had no reason to trust him and she would also know if he was lying.

He finally spoke in an even voice. "Just because I work for the Taulkes doesn't mean I'm not telling the truth. Here's my offer: I'll help you do whatever it is you've got planned, then we go our separate ways. I'll make my peace with the Taulkes on my own terms."

*"Truth."*

"You're bleeding." Lander pointed at her face.

Ming wiped her nose with her gloved hand. It came away wet.

MoSCOW recommended disengagement to minimize the radiation exposure. She ignored the warning.

Lander might be right. The universe had just gotten a lot more complex, and she would need help for this new plan. Without MoSCOW, she never would have entertained the idea of trusting him, but his biometrics confirmed Lander's offer was genuine.

"Fine, you're hired," she said and started for the *Roadrunner*. "Double-cross me and I'll rip out your spine."

––––––––––

Ming let Lander drive. Using MoSCOW, she could have flown the shuttle and done everything else she wanted to do at the same time, but it was better for Lander if she kept his mind and hands occupied.

When they were back in lunar orbit, Ming connected to the LUNa City traffic network and searched for the flight data on UN Shuttle X769. A UN ship passing through LUNa City traffic flow would not have aroused any suspicions, but it would have been tracked as a matter of routine.

She found it, but no incoming flight plan had been filed. That wasn't unusual. As a UN vessel, it would have passed security automatically. She found the logs for the outbound flight, searched for the long-range track using its transponder signature.

The UN craft had entered high Earth orbit, the traffic pattern that flowed above the space stations and assorted satellites ringing the planet like so much junk. The final ping in the record showed the shuttle descending into the orbital ring. The transponder was designed to stop when the shuttle docked.

Using standard UN flight protocols, MoSCOW laid out the projections. Five space stations—all registered to corporations—were possible docking sites. She queried the registries for each of them simultaneously, finding they were all registered to impenetrable shell companies. Ming cursed. She would need access to an Earthside database for that search and she could not risk that level of exposure.

All of the stations had repositioned since the UN ship contact and were spread about the orbital ring. Ming targeted the nearest one and shot the coordinates to Lander.

"That's where we're going," she said. "I need to make a call before you start the burn." She checked the timer built into MoSCOW. Two hours and seven minutes.

*Tick-tock.*

She permanently disengaged the radiation warning. She'd do the hospital time, but if she really was going to hunt down Elise Kisaan, she needed the abilities MoSCOW offered her—whatever the consequences.

"You don't look so good, Ming," Lander said. MoSCOW registered genuine concern in his voice. Odd, since he'd tried to kill her less than an hour ago.

"I'll be fine." She dialed her father-in-law JC Han's personal connection. The Korean man's blocky face filled her retinal screen. He looked surprised to see her.

"Ming, you're safe."

*"Truth."* She was getting more comfortable with MoSCOW's intrusions now. She could call on the added capabilities at will.

"I need information, JC. About my father. I need to know how he died."

The older man's face creased into a frown. "He died in a virus outbreak in Indonesia, Ming. You know that."

"Did you review his security logs?"

"No, the security upload link was down that entire day. Maintenance, I think. Unfortunate, but not unusual."

"There was an inquiry."

"Of course, Ito visited the site and reported back to the board. The camp had been firebombed for safety. There was nothing left, he said."

*"Truth."*

Ito was the one who had found the last fifty-nine seconds of security vid. Ito had given it to Ming's mother. But that got her no closer to knowing who was behind the attack, Sying or her aunt.

"My father was murdered," Ming said.

JC's face registered shock.

*"Truth."*

"What do you know about Ruben?" Ming asked.

"Nothing," JC said. His eyes flicked away from hers. *Lie.*

"I need you to give a message to my aunt."

"Anything."

"Tell her I'm coming for her." She ended the call.

It felt like MoSCOW was consuming her body from the inside out. Ming stuffed another prepackaged bar in her mouth.

"Ready?" Lander asked.

Ming closed her eyes. She called up the image of the Kisaan woman in her retinal display. She was the key to this whole mess. Find her, take back Viktor's cryptokey, and then she'd have the leverage to deal with Anthony Taulke on her terms.

*Tick-tock.*

"Max burn, Lander. I don't have much time left."

# 19

## WILLIAM GRAVES • HAVEN 6, DECK 36

Graves nodded his approval. The bridge of Haven 6 looked like an army command post: a captain's chair in the center, flanked by the executive officer at tactical and the helm. Comms, weapons, and engineering were behind him. All manned by competent-looking young men and women in dark blue jumpsuits.

An impressive wallscreen showed the exterior of the Haven. US Army personnel formed a wide perimeter facing the people scattered over the countryside around the dome. The people who weren't coming with them.

He turned his attention to the navy captain, who rose from the command chair. Captain Tristan Rickard had quick, intelligent eyes that made Graves feel as if he'd just been scanned and catalogued. Rickard was the man from beyond deck 36, the man who was going to take Haven 6 to the stars.

"Captain," Graves said, automatically adopting the kind of no-nonsense tone a man like this would appreciate. "What's your status?"

"We're standing by for countdown, sir." Rickard's flat, open speech placed him from the northeastern United States. "Once you give the order to seal the dome and turn over control to the engine room, we'll start the launch sequence." Rickard's smile was perfunctory, a nervous bending of the lips. "The launch, it'll be rough. Gonna feel like an earthquake in here, but that'll smooth out once we break out of the silo."

Graves shared a look with Jansen. She'd be dealing with three thousand people of various stripes, experiences, and neuroses during the launch.

The silence drew out, the bridge crew watching them. Rickard cleared his throat.

"We're ready for the change of command whenever you are, General." Rickard indicated the tablet held by the XO, who'd appeared at his side. He scanned in his biometric data, then handed it to Graves. The general repeated the procedure and passed the tablet back.

Rickard came to attention and saluted. "I relieve you, sir."

Graves returned the honor, aware that Jansen was watching. He held the salute, feeling the tip of his finger quiver against his temple. "I stand relieved, sir."

Rickard dropped his hand and extended it to Jansen. "Welcome aboard, Captain. I'm appointing you to my staff as personnel officer."

Jansen shook his hand mechanically, a bewildered look on her face. "General, can I speak to you, sir?" she said to Graves.

Rickard gestured to the door marked *Ready Room* off the right side of the bridge then spun on his heel. "Comms, make a ship-wide announcement that we're sealing the dome in one hour. Let's get the other Haven COs onscreen..."

The sounds of the bridge faded as Graves followed Jansen into the ready room and the door closed behind them. Her gait was precise, measured.

Her about-face was so fast Graves almost ran into her.

"Sir, what the hell is going on? You're being relieved of duty?"

From the hunted look and the worry in her voice, Graves was glad he hadn't told her the truth before now.

"I'm not going," he said, doing his best to keep his voice neutral. "The Havens are defenseless ships. No shields, no weapons, no protection of any kind. Thanks to Remy, we're going to take the fight right to the Neos."

"Remy?" Jansen looked at him with horror. "That's what all that was about? General, you're needed here, not leading some kamikaze attack on a space station full of religious nuts."

Graves gripped her by the shoulders. "Hannah, I have complete faith in you. You are exactly the kind of person we need on this mission, not some old, broken-down soldier like me. I have a role to play, but not as part of the Havens."

Jansen started to speak, but welling eyes made her stop. The system-wide comm system saved both of them any awkwardness. The countdown to sealing the domes had begun.

Jansen shrugged his hands off her shoulders and wrapped her arms around him. She squeezed him for a minute, then let go and stepped back.

"I'll come back for you, sir. Promise."

Graves impressed the iron line of her jaw and her handsome face into his memory. He would miss Hannah Jansen more than he ever expected. "How about you just make me proud, Hannah?"

She smiled and let her eyes find his.

"Always."

Graves watched the Haven 6 dome shrink as the shuttle left the Minnesota prairie behind. The dome had sealed closed behind him, leaving an unbroken curtain of milky-blue material.

He missed Jansen already, but instead of sadness or anger at the situation, he felt only a gnawing emptiness. The dome shrank to a pinpoint and then was obscured by wisps of cloud.

"How long to the command ship?" he called to the pilot. The sky around him darkened and the Earth's horizon began to curve. Crowds of low-orbit satellites came into view.

"Twenty minutes, sir."

"Very well. Wake me when we get there, Lieutenant," Graves said, closing his eyes.

He dreamed of the family lighthouse in Maine. The winds of the Atlantic howled as twelve-year-old William Graves bounded up a circular staircase, hot on the heels of his older sister, Jane.

When they reached the lantern deck with its massive Fresnel lens, Jane burst through the trapdoor and rushed to the railing. The brisk sea wind seemed to bar young Will, whose hands clutched at the metal lip of the trapdoor. Jane stood on the bottom bar of the railing, rested her thighs against the top rail, and leaned into space.

"Janie, don't!" Will said.

She ignored him, her long, brown hair whipping behind her. Jane closed her eyes, raised her face to the sun, and spread her arms like a bird.

Graves's heart clenched at the sight of his terrified younger self hanging back in the trapdoor. He was afraid of heights. He wanted to be brave like his big sister, but he didn't have it inside his little body.

"Come on, Will!" Jane called. "It's like flying!"

Will's lip quivered, and he ducked his head lower. Jane hopped off the railing and raced back to the trapdoor. She knelt in front of him. He might have expected scorn or even pity from Jane, but that was not her way. She held out her hand.

"Take my hand, Will," she said. "I won't let you fall. Today is the day."

Graves felt the boy war with his fears, then he reached out. Her grip was warm and strong and so very calm that some of it leaked back into him. He climbed the last two steps of the ladder and got to his feet.

Jane interlaced her fingers with his and gave her brother's hand a squeeze. Graves wished he could freeze that moment.

"You're very brave, Will."

The boy smiled up at her, confidence swelling his chest. Today would be the day.

"C'mon," she said, pulling him forward to the edge.

He gripped the railing with one hand, knuckles white, eyes wide with terror.

"Don't look down," Jane said, kneeling next to him. She pointed. "Look out at the horizon, Will. See how big the ocean is? How beautiful?"

He saw the far, blue horizon with its magical ability to draw from a young boy's imagination limitless tales of sailing ships and pirates, sea chanties and treasure chests, damsels in distress.

"Good, Will," Jane said. "Now, look down."

The lighthouse stood atop a rocky cliff and his gaze traveled down the white stone, down the brown jutting cliffs to the black rocks and foaming surf. Spray billowed as the water hit the rocks like wet fireworks bursting in the air.

His stomach clenched, and for second Will thought he might be sick.

Jane's arm slipped around his shoulders, drawing him close. "Look back at the horizon," she whispered in his ear.

He raised his eyes to the flat blue line. His nausea subsided, but his death grip on the railing stayed.

"Are you ready?" Jane asked, a lilt of humor in her voice. Jane guided the hand she held to the railing until the boy grasped the cold, salty-wet metal.

She climbed onto the bottom railing. She rested her weight against the top railing and leaned over the edge, spreading her arms wide.

"You can do it, Will. Fly with me."

In real life, William Graves had never flown with his late sister. She was the daredevil, he was afraid.

But not today.

Still gripping the top railing with both hands, Will placed one foot on the bottom railing, then the other. He felt faint when he hoisted himself a mere eighteen inches higher, but he held on. Graves felt the wind buffeting him.

"Let go," she shouted, her face bright with joy. Stray strands of her long hair whipped behind her like a pennant. "Fly with me!" She closed her eyes and screamed into the wind.

The top railing bit into Will's waist. His palms were slippery with sweat, and his knees threatened to fail him any second now.

Will peeled one hand, then the other from the railing and spread his trembling arms wide. He looked toward the blue horizon and turned his face higher, howling his accomplishment to the sky.

"General!"

Graves jerked awake.

"We're on final approach, sir," the pilot called. "You said to wake you."

Graves grunted a reply, brushing a hand across his cheek. It was numb and cool. The dream had felt so real...

But more than that, the dream left him with a sense of hope. If ever he needed that kind of confidence, it was now.

*Today is the day, Will.*

Graves leaned forward and stared out the forward window. "Is that it?"

"That's the *Dauntless*, sir."

The ship was a newer Y-class sloop, so named for the sweep of her wings. She was built for speed, not fighting, but the upgraded comms and sensor package she carried was worth its weight in platinum for what Graves had in mind.

She carried only a pair of low-mass rail guns fore and aft, the max allowed by the UN Treaty on Space Warfare. In order to prevent an off-planet arms race, the only vessels that could be armed were atmospheric-capable ships, and then only with projectile weapons. The use of energy weapons or missiles was strictly prohibited.

Graves held no illusions that a murderous cult like the Neos would bother observing international law.

Commander Daudi Ibekwe, captain of the *Dauntless*, was a man of medium height, made shorter by a perpetual stoop and blooming potbelly. Not an inspiring figure in uniform, but he came with the highest recommendations for tactical brilliance. His handshake was dry and disciplined.

"Welcome aboard, General Graves. I have the fleet commanders standing by in the ready room."

Graves searched the man's face for any sign of irony but found none. The "fleet" was half a dozen MOABs with their guts ripped out. Three unarmed dropships intended to ferry supplies between a MOAB and a mining station were parked in each of the converted mining vessels. Each dropship would carry a team of three combat engineers and a squad of six marines, the max they could fit in the space.

Hardly an invasion force, but it was all he could cobble together under the auspices of his relocation efforts. Graves just wanted to buy the Haven fleet enough time to get into orbit and make their escape. It would have to do.

The ready room, like the rest of the *Dauntless*, was a no-frills affair. He took his seat at the head of the plain plastic table facing the six MOAB commanders.

Graves scanned their faces. They were all army combat engineer professionals in their twenties or early thirties, but to his worried gaze they looked even younger. Before they'd been assigned to him, they'd flown around the world on humanitarian missions, trying to make the world safe from climate change. They built schools and dams and bridges, anything to improve the lot of their fellow man against a rebelling planet.

Now they were going into battle with the tools of their trade. Not to build but to destroy.

Ibekwe took his seat to Grave's right. "Ready when you are, sir."

Graves took a full beat before he spoke. "Ladies and gentlemen, in the next two hours we will commence a massive airlift of refugees from the planet's surface. The most prominent ships in the airlift will be the Haven sites."

A ripple of confusion ran through the room. Graves let it run its course. "The Havens are not bunkers, as you've been led to believe; they're ships. Ships that are capable of interstellar travel."

"I'm sorry, sir. Did you say interstellar?" The speaker was a young woman with her dark hair drawn back into a stub of a ponytail. Her nametag said Quincy. "You mean to the Moon?"

"No." Graves let the denial rest for a moment. "The Havens are humanity's backup plan and the technology they carry is far too valuable to fall into the wrong hands. Our mission is to make sure they make it safely away from Earth." He nodded to Ibekwe, who called up a holo of the Neo space station.

"Your crews have been carefully screened to ensure there are no members of the New Earth Order among them," Graves began.

"The Neos? You mean the religious cult?" someone asked.

"They're much more than that," Graves said. "The tattoo they carry is not some innocuous symbol of faith. It's an implant, capable of transmitting and receiving information, capable of mind control. This organization is armed and very dangerous. Cassandra will do anything to stop the Havens. It's our job to stop her."

He called up a hologram in the center of the table. "We have information that this is their command center. If we can disable this station, we can give the Havens time to get into orbit and get away safely."

All eyes were on the hologram, a long cylinder pocked with docking ports and airlocks. There was a figure of *Dauntless* for scale. The station towered over the tiny Y-class sloop.

"You want us to attack a space station?" The tone of voice of the questioner was awestruck. "With mining equipment?"

"It's what we've got," Graves said.

"Are there defensive weapons?" someone else said.

Ibekwe answered. "We've done a visual pass on the station." He highlighted a ring of wart-like protrusions around the circumference of the structure. "We believe these are concealed rail guns, and this bulge directly above the reactor"—he highlighted a domed structure like a crown on the very top of the station—"could be an energy weapon."

The room stared at the dome. "How big is that thing?" asked Quincy.

"Thirty meters," Ibekwe replied through gritted teeth. "If our analysis is right, it could take out anything in its line of sight."

Graves took over. "The Havens will start their launch sequence as soon as North America passes out of range of the Neo station. That will give them a thirty-six-minute window to get into orbit before they are visible to the enemy again. Any time they need after that thirty-six minutes has to come from us."

"How long do they need, sir?" It was Quincy again.

"Minimum sixty minutes, assuming no technical issues," Graves said.

The young faces that looked back at him were stoic but resolved.

"There's one more thing," Graves said. "The Neos are behind the weather disasters. You all probably know people who have lost loved ones. This is your chance to make that right."

Around the table, the weight of their mission registered on the young faces.

He cleared his throat. "Unfortunately, people, this is not a volunteer mission. I selected each of you for your particular skill set, experience, and ability to get the job done. I need you for this mission, period. I need to know I can count on each of you."

No one moved. He waited for a full minute, taking his time to meet the gaze of each individual, assess their mettle. They were scared, but then again so was he. It was a strange feeling, sort of like standing on top of a lighthouse, screaming into the wind.

"All right, then," Graves said grimly. "Commander Ibekwe, the floor is yours."

———

The hologram hadn't done it justice. The Neo station was huge, half again the size of its nearest neighbor in the orbital ring. Graves gripped the armrest of the command chair on the bridge of the *Dauntless*. His palms were sweaty.

"Assets are in position, sir," Ibekwe said from his perch behind the weapons console. He switched the main screen to a tactical view, showing the Neo station in red and six green MOABs moving in orbital traffic. Marked with various corporate logos, they were spread out, each following a false flight plan, seemingly headed toward one or another of the stations in orbit. In theory, by the time the MOABs were near enough to begin the boarding action, there wouldn't be much the New Earthers could do to prevent it.

The battle plan was simple. Three MOABs would attack the reactor end of the station to disable the energy weapon. The other three would concentrate on the communications array to prevent the enemy from summoning reinforcements. Graves wished for some real fighting assets, the kind that existed planetside. Missiles, and maybe a nuke or two for good measure.

"Open a channel with Haven Six," he said.

"Channel open, sir."

The compact frame of Captain Rickard came into view.

"What's your status, Captain?" Graves said.

"All Havens ready for launch, General."

Graves nodded. "Very well. What is it you swabbies say? Fair winds and following seas?"

A smile ghosted Rickard's lips. "Thank you, sir. For everything."

"Start your launch sequence, Captain. You can thank me by getting those people out of here safely. *Dauntless*, out."

The tactical screen reappeared.

"Commander Ibekwe," Graves announced in a steady voice. "Position the MOABs for the attack."

"Aye, sir." The coded orders streamed out to the MOABs in the form of an innocuous message about job opportunities on Mars. Subtly, the disconnected flight paths of the MOABs began to converge lazily on the Neo station.

"They think they have a goddess on their side," Ibekwe said.

"Well, we have the armed forces of the United States on ours," Graves said. *God help us.*

## 20

### LUCA VASQUEZ • HAVEN 6

By the time the Haven dome was sealed, Luca was so busy she had no time to think about Remy Cade. Hannah had arranged for the Neo members of the Haven 6 Pioneers to be among the last to enter the dome.

It was a simple matter to shunt them into a side room off the flight deck and deactivate the nanites in their implants. These were all people who had been poked and prodded in all manner of ways as part of their acceptance into the Pioneer program, so they thought nothing of another test. After the first group, she had dialed the correct dosage in so that the effect on the patient was no more than a tingling in the nape of their neck. Two men objected to the treatment and she used the broadband signal—Graves's so-called Disruptor—to knock them unconscious.

"We've processed the last of the Neos," she reported proudly to Hannah Jansen. "We're clean."

"Well done, Luca. I'll let the captain know." She peered at Luca's image. "How're you doing?"

Hannah meant how she was feeling about Remy, of course, but Luca feigned indifference. "It was never going to work out with us, you know? Me a single woman, him a single man, trapped together for a hundred years. Really, Hannah, what was I thinking?" Her tone sharpened into bitterness at the end, and she saw Hannah react to it. She also saw her friend glance away from the screen. Jansen was busy; Luca was being selfish.

"Don't worry about me, Hannah. I'm fine. I just thought it would work out different for us—for me." She felt heat creeping up her neck and pressure building behind her eyes. "I need to go," Luca said, ending the call.

She busied herself with packing away the medical supplies and loading them on a cart to take back to the medical deck. A three-tone chime sounded over the all-ship intercom.

*"All Haven personnel, report to your pod assignments."*

In preparation for sealing the dome, the Pioneers had been organized into pseudo-family units called pods, a cross-section of age, gender, and skills that was supposed to stand in for the lack of nuclear families aboard the Havens. Whereas Luca and Donna had no other family left, many of the Pioneers had volunteered to leave theirs, difficult as it was, in the hope of starting a better future life.

All the Pioneers knew what they were getting themselves into. Once the domes were sealed, they stayed sealed for the next century, completely cut off from the outside world. All the living and dying and loving and loss happened under the dome. All they had was each other.

Luca made her way swiftly through the hallways to her pod's assigned meeting place in the level 10 mess deck. The emotional electricity in the air was palpable. Excitement, fear, resolve, and a true realization of what they had given up to be here at this moment in history.

The next few minutes were critical. The true nature of the Havens would be revealed to everyone. How would they react?

Over the past two weeks, select members of the Pioneers had been briefed about the upcoming space flight. Like her, they had already given their feedback about which crew members might react badly to the news. A few—very few—Pioneers had been ushered out of the Haven before the dome was sealed. The rest were here for the duration.

Donna waited for her at their assigned table. Luca scanned the other faces in her pod. Damien, a mid-twenties redheaded engineer; Althea, a psychologist from Berkeley; Quinn, a quiet female biologist from Canada who spent most of her time gazing at Damien; and Mundo, a black army sergeant who was talking with Luca's younger sister.

Luca inserted herself between Mundo and Donna.

"What the hell, sis?" Donna said under her breath.

Luca smiled at Mundo in a way that said *back off*.

The three-time chime sounded again, and Luca saw a new feed come into her data glasses. They had all been issued new glasses equipped with a command override for the Haven senior staff. When she opened the feed, the image of a trim military officer in a dark blue jumpsuit filled her screen.

"Good afternoon, Pioneers. My name is Captain Tristan Rickard of the United States vessel Haven Six." He paused and Luca scanned the members of her pod. Althea and Mundo had already been briefed, but Quinn and Damien had perplexed looks about why they had a captain and why he was calling their new home a vessel.

"The Haven project is more than just a passive program to wait out the next century underground. It is a proactive plan for the preservation of our species. Scientists have identified a planet in the Alpha Centauri system that is suitable for human life. The true mission of the Haven program is to colonize that planet. You have all been selected for your skills, your intelligence, and above all your grit to attack this new challenge. You are true Pioneers in every sense of the word."

He paused again. An animation sequence showed a flyby of a planet and then a cylindrical spaceship, presumably a Haven, in orbit. Luca caught Quinn's eye and smiled. The young woman's face shone with excitement. "This is so cool," she mouthed to Luca, who nodded back and reflected her smile. Mundo and a frowning Damien were involved in a deep sidebar conversation, with Althea eavesdropping. So far, so good.

The animation sequence showed a flock of small spacecraft disassembling the Haven ship into segments and taking them down the planet surface.

"Inside each Haven vessel, we have the people, the tools, and the resources to establish a viable colony on our new home. Each ship is equipped with a next-generation propulsion system called a GEMDrive, which is capable of taking us faster and farther than any spaceship in the history of our planet. We have a long trip ahead of us, Pioneers, but with your support and your courage, we will ensure that the human race lives on."

Luca was surprised to hear a wave of applause ripple through the lounge over the hubbub of excited voices.

"We'll be lifting off in the next thirty minutes," Captain Rickard continued. "The transit from the planet surface into orbit will be rough, so please, all nonessential personnel are asked to return to your cabins, strap into your bunks, and wait for further instructions."

Luca quickly reported the results of her pod observations back to the monitor and took Donna's hand. The atmosphere in the lounge was euphoric, with high-fives and hugs and plenty of tears. She passed a few shocked faces, a few angry ones, but the mood overall was positive.

She did not release Donna's hand until they were back in their shared cabin. The girl made a great show of flexing her hand as if Luca's grip had been too tight, but she was smiling too.

"Mundo's cute," Donna said, needling her.

"You're too young," Luca replied.

Donna spread her hands, palms up. "Hey, sis, I'm the next generation. I got my whole life ahead of me."

Luca felt a sudden stab of panic. She had made this choice for her sister without regard for what she wanted. What kind of person did that?

Donna wrapped her arms around Luca. A solid hug, a real hug, not some lame teenage half attempt at affection. Donna kissed her. "Thank you, sis. You gave me a second chance. This is the right thing for us. There's nothing for us here on Earth, right? Let's try a new planet for a change."

The tears came unbidden like water cresting a dam. Luca hung on to her sister and sobbed into her shoulder. The stress of the last months with Donna in the hospital, the work in the lab on animal—then human—subjects.

And Remy. She had thought maybe, just maybe, he was the one for her. He understood the real danger of the Neos, understood it in his gut like she did—and he wasn't afraid to fight back either. She agreed to feed him information because she knew he wouldn't let her down. She *knew*.

But he did. And that broke her already fragile heart.

"Hey." Donna pried their bodies apart and pressed her forehead against Luca's, her hands on either side of Luca's face. The girl was nearly the same height as her big sister now. "It's okay, Luca. It's okay. We have each other."

Donna took her sister's hand and placed it on the back of her neck. Luca could feel her sister's slender nape under her thick hair. She could imagine the now-dead Neo tattoo under her fingers.

"You saved me, big sis," Donna said fiercely. "Hannah told me what happened. Without you ... I don't know where I'd be, but because you didn't give up ... we're gonna be okay."

The three-tone chime sounded. "Countdown commencing in five minutes."

Luca splashed cold water on her face, then held the towel against her eyes for a few seconds. Her whole body shook as if she was coming down from an adrenaline rush. She did not resist as Donna guided her to her couch and strapped her in.

Donna got into her own chair just as the countdown started.

Ten ... nine...

Luca was still having trouble catching her breath. Donna reached over and laced her fingers with Luca's.

Five ... four...

Luca rested her head back into the cushion, exhausted. From somewhere far beneath her couch she felt a tremble, like a distant rumble of thunder. The sound grew closer and she felt it in her bones.

"Let's go home," Donna said.

---

## Remy Cade • Cassandra Station

Brother Donald met Remy at the airlock. The monk's thick face was bland, and he'd traded in his orange robes for a black uniform with the symbol of Cassandra embroidered over his heart.

"You're back," was all he said.

"I need to see Elise," Remy said. "Right away."

The warrior-monk's arm went up like a barrier. "She asked me to debrief you."

Remy didn't try to hide his disappointment. In the trip back to the Temple station, he'd let his imagination run amok. Elise meeting him at the airlock, eyes full of love, throwing herself into his arms. More Harlequin romance than reality, he knew, but he had really expected her to at least meet him.

Remy shook his head. "I speak to Elise only."

The monk's face radiated calm, but his arm didn't budge. "Follow me." Donald turned and led the way.

The thousands of refugees clustered around Haven 6 came to Remy's mind as they walked. He saw the station with new eyes. He'd witnessed firsthand the havoc Cassandra had wrought planetside. Real people, real consequences. Before, at Elise's side on the station, he'd been able to distance himself from the human costs, secure in her rock-solid belief that there was a higher purpose to what Elise was doing. He loved and trusted her and, by extension, what she was doing.

But now, the entire planet felt like another Vicksburg massacre writ large. Not a higher purpose in sight. Human beings may have brought this on themselves, but nobody deserved what was happening down there.

Enough, he told himself. He had to trust Elise. She'd sent him to find out about the Havens and he would deliver news that would make her head spin.

After that, he and Elise could start over again. It would be like it was in the early days of their relationship, back in India, when they'd had so many long, meandering conversations about nothing at all and everything that mattered. Most of all, they'd be together again, for good. That's what really mattered.

"She'll meet you here," Donald said once they'd entered the observation lounge. "Might be a few minutes." His broad back disappeared through the door and Remy thought he heard the lock engage as the door closed. He crossed to the door and scanned his badge. The door remained locked.

A flutter of unease swept through him. Remy thought about pounding on the door and making a scene, but what would that accomplish? His security access had probably been deactivated while he was off-station. An admin mistake he'd get corrected as soon as he met with Elise.

*It's fine. It'll all be fine. She just has to listen.*

Through the clutter of orbital traffic, Earth hung in front of him, suspended among the stars. How many times had he stood in this exact spot with Elise by his side? He could almost feel her hand in his.

Egypt passed into view, and he spied the Nile River's winding brown stain. He tried to discern in the clouds the difference between normal weather patterns and whatever the Neos were doing but failed. It all looked the same to him. He began to pace as he waited.

The planet below passed into darkness. He could see the devastation now. Whole swathes of the globe were blots of solid black where small cities used to be. If people were still there, they'd been reduced to using more primitive forms of light with their infrastructure gone. The remaining cities seemed more intensely lit, as if the population had been concentrated into certain areas. Oddly, the remaining population centers appeared to be concentrated in latitudinal bands, resulting in stripes of brightness in the dark.

The sun appeared on the horizon and still Remy waited. Another dusk-to-dawn cycle was complete before the door opened again.

At last, Elise strode in, her lean frame clad in the same black uniform Donald had worn. Remy met her halfway across the room—his motions frantic and anxious, hers more reserved, resulting in a clumsy tangling of limbs that more resembled a wrestling match than the joyful embrace he'd imagined in his head.

"I missed you," he said into her ear.

"I missed you too," she whispered back. Their foreheads touched.

Elise's lips were what he remembered from the earliest days of their romance, and hope flared in Remy.

*We will have that again.*

She gave his hand a squeeze, then led him with loose fingers to the bank of windows. "You found out about the Havens?" she asked.

Now that she was here and listening, part of Remy wanted to delay telling her the secret he'd learned. He wanted to draw out the anticipation of her reaction.

"Well?" she asked.

"The Havens are being sealed now," he said.

A look of frustration flickered across Elise's face. "We can see that much, Remy," she chided him. She toyed with the cryptobracelet on her wrist, and Remy's thoughts flashed to the raid on the Moon facility, where he'd seen her kill two men in cold blood.

"They're ships, Elise. Not survival silos. The Havens are ships meant for long-term space travel. They have a drive in them that's faster than anything ever built."

A light of revelation appeared in her eyes. "Cassandra was right. With that tech we can take over the entire solar system." Elise took his face in both hands. "You're sure?"

"Absolutely," Remy said.

Elise paced in front of the window. "We need to move quickly, Remy. We need to take one of those ships and get that drive for Cassandra. You need to go back. Get onboard, stall for time while we mount an attack."

"No." The words came out before he even thought about them. "I can't. I won't."

Elise pressed against him. He could smell her scent and his mind flashed to simpler times.

"But, Remy," she said. "This is our chance. With this tech Cassandra has everything she needs to—"

"To what?" he interrupted. He saw their reflection in the darkened window. She reached for his hand and he softened his voice. "I came back for *you*. Not to finish some stupid spy mission. I came back to save you."

Elise's laugh mocked his gentle tone. She turned away. "Save me? From what?"

He came up behind her, touching his fingers to the Neo tattoo on her slender nape. "You've changed—they've changed you. But I have a way for us to be together again. There's a woman on the Haven who's figured out how to set you free from this. We can be together again ... like it used to be at the beginning."

Elise spun around, sweeping his hand away. "Like in the beginning? Like when I was an invalid, a little girl who needed to be carried? Is that who you want me to be, someone you can take care of?" Her face clenched in anger.

"No, of course not." Remy had to take a step back from the intensity of her emotion. But Elise wasn't entirely wrong. He did want to take care of her, he did want her to need him.

"Why are you here?" she said again. The menace in her voice unnerved Remy.

"It's an implant, Elise, not a tattoo. This whole Cassandra thing is mind control—"

He stopped when Elise started laughing.

"What?" he said.

Elise moved closer, put her hand on his cheek. "God, I did love you, you know that? You were good for me back then. If it hadn't been for you, I probably wouldn't be here today. That's the truth." She slapped him gently on the cheek. "But that was a long time ago, Remy, and you have not kept up with me. In fact, you're an idiot."

Remy felt his face flush with heat.

"Sorry," Elise continued, her voice not unkind. The station's orbit entered another nighttime cycle. "That's not fair, I know. You mean well." She motioned the planet below. "But this is bigger than the both of us, bigger than humanity. This is the dawn of a new age, Remy. We're called the New Earth Order for a reason: to create a new Earth. We're reshaping a planet to meet the needs of a new age of man."

"For Cassandra, you mean," Remy said. "This is some sick power grab."

To his surprise, Elise laughed again, harder this time. "Cassandra? Cassandra is a tool like the rest of us. Like you, like me. Hell, Remy, Cassandra's not even real! She's a machine, an AI programmed to carry out a mission of taking control of the planet and remaking it into a more efficient growing operation."

"I—I don't understand. An AI?"

Elise's beautiful face twisted into a smirk. "No, you don't. I'm afraid you're not part of the long-term business plan, Remy."

From deep inside Remy's guts, anger flared. Rage, pain. This was not Elise talking, this was that thing inside of her. He gripped her wrists.

"No, Elise, that's not true—"

A Klaxon sounded. "Intruder alert. The station is under attack."

Outside in space, a boxy shape that looked like a mining dropship sped past the window. A low-pitched hum like the buzzing of a million bees sounded in his ears.

Elise pitched forward into his arms, unconscious.

# 21

## WILLIAM GRAVES • USS DAUNTLESS

Graves fidgeted in the command chair, his eyes glued to the viewscreen's tactical display.

"All MOABs report ready, sir," Ibekwe said, his voice tight.

"Very well." Graves's fingers dug into the armrest of his chair. "Stand by to deploy the Disruptor."

The suitcase he'd carried from Haven 6 was plugged into the comms suite. Ibekwe eyed the setup with disdain. Broadcasting their position would make the command ship an instant target for the space station.

"Launch the attack," Graves ordered.

Somewhere out there, the main engines of the six MOABs were coming to life. The big ships were on course to do a drive-by on the Neo station, deploying the dropships at their closest point of approach. The dropships, using the momentum from the MOAB launch and their own thrusters, would maneuver to connect with the station at predesignated points. Once attached, the combat engineers would spring into action, overriding the airlock or simply cutting into the hull to give the marines access.

A simple plan. The simpler the better. Graves imagined his small force as an army of bees overwhelming a much larger opponent.

"MOABs are on the move, sir."

"Acknowledged," Graves said, his mouth dry. "Deploy the Disruptor."

A burst of buzzing static went out over all frequencies. It lasted for a full ten seconds.

On the tactical display, Graves could make out the tracks of the MOABs converging as they began their approach run. Now was the critical time. They were coming into range of the station's point defenses, a killing zone for which the converted mining vessels had no defenses other than their thick hulls. Graves imagined the personnel packed into them being pressed back into their seats as their carriers accelerated to the attack.

Ibekwe twisted in his chair. "Sir, sensors are showing increased activity on the station. It looks like they've got some sort of automated early warning system." His screen flashed at him. "Rail gun emplacements are opening up. The MOABs are under attack."

"Go to external camera on MOAB 1," Graves said.

The Neo station loomed large on the viewscreen. The image vibrated, the sympathetic shaking of MOAB 1's camera as it initiated a hard burn. Tiny specks of light streaked past the camera like yellowjackets in space.

"All units report heavy fire from point defense rail guns," the comms officer reported.

There was a mushroom of color on the screen, quickly extinguished by the vacuum of space.

"MOAB 2 is down, sir," Ibekwe reported. Another burst of color. "MOAB 4 down."

Two MOABs gone in the first thirty seconds. Graves tried to keep his stomach stable. "What's the status of the Haven launch?"

"Haven 2 feed onscreen, sir."

The view shifted to an overhead of the Mojave Desert. Graves saw the familiar shape of the bluish-white dome and the security perimeter around the structure. If not for the brown landscape surrounding the dome, it could have been his own Haven 6. Even here, in the furnace heat of the desert, people camped outside the structure, hoping for a place inside.

The dome trembled, and a hundred yards inside the security perimeter, the ground crumbled away. The tiny dots surrounding the dome—people, his conscience reminded him—fled the sight. Inch by inch, Haven 2 pushed slowly out of the hole in the ground.

"Sir, you need to see this," Ibekwe said. He switched the viewscreen to the *Dauntless*'s external camera and replayed the last few seconds. Graves watched a bolt of energy lance out from the top of the Neo station and slice through a point in space. A puff of fire flared and was gone.

"That was MOAB 1," Ibekwe said.

Graves clenched his jaw. "Can that weapon hit a Haven in orbit?"

"Very probably," Ibekwe said.

"How many MOABs left?"

"Three," Ibekwe said. "MOAB 5 just deployed her dropships."

Graves came to a decision. "Get us as close to those dropships as possible. We'll cover them going in."

Ibekwe hesitated. He knew what that order meant. "Aye, sir."

Graves's head smacked back into the headrest as the *Dauntless* executed a hard burn, angling straight toward the source of the enemy fire. "Commence firing rail guns as soon as we're in range," Graves said.

Ten seconds later, he felt a steady, rapid thrum beneath his feet.

"Targeting the energy weapon," Ibekwe said, his voice like ice.

"Onscreen."

The rail gun projectiles streamed out from the *Dauntless*, their tracers painting a path to the enemy station.

"Fire-control radar is tracking us, Commander." The young man at the secondary weapons station was full of adrenaline, and his voice piped out of its register.

"Steady, Franklin," Ibekwe said. "Launch countermeasures on my mark. Helm, begin evasive maneuvers, pattern omega, on my mark." He hunched over his console. "Mark!"

The ship slewed hard starboard, pinning Graves against an armrest. A bolt of energy saturated the screen's filters like a sun exploding. The view cleared, and the *Dauntless* corrected her course, angling once again for the enemy station.

Ibekwe twisted in his chair. "My guess is they're using a capacitive source for that weapon, sir. Looks like they need at least ten seconds to recharge after each firing."

Graves nodded, still reining in his heart rate after they'd nearly been incinerated. As long as he lived, he would never make fun of the navy again.

"The dropships are taking fire from those point-defense cannons, sir!" the young weapons officer called.

"Let's do what we can to protect them, Commander," Graves said.

"On it, sir," Ibekwe said. "Helm, put us between the dropships and that cannon."

The ship made another hard turn, vectoring toward the nearest dropship. The shoulders of the young woman at the helm were racked with tension as she aimed the vessel straight at the projectiles. The *Dauntless* stuttered as the incoming rounds found their mark. Graves half expected to see a hole rip through their hull at any second followed by him being sucked into space.

"Return fire, Mr. Franklin," Ibekwe said, voice steady. "Target those cannons."

Graves felt the deck under his feet pulse again as the *Dauntless* returned fire. The bright burst attesting to their gunner's accuracy made him smile.

"Take us back to the dropships, Commander," Graves said. The ship slewed again and accelerated.

The squarish outline of one of the remaining MOABs filled the viewscreen. The sight reminded Graves just how desperate their attack was.

Using modified mining equipment to take on an armed space station. The emotional side of his brain wanted to beat the snot out of every UN negotiator who had decided it was a good idea to regulate space-based weapons. The rational part of his brain was thankful for the skill of Ibekwe and his crew.

Enemy fire sprayed across the length of the MOAB hull, and its engine flared and faded. Debris trailed from the ship as it hurtled past the station.

"Looks like we've got at least one dropship going for a hard seal, sir," Ibekwe said. "I'm putting up the external feed from that unit."

The camera switched to show the greenish tint of the Neo station's hull. The dropship's thrusters fired as it approached a maintenance airlock and executed an emergency seal procedure.

Ibekwe spun in his chair. "They made it, sir. It's up to them now—"

"Commander, we've got company," Franklin reported. He replaced the dropship's feed with the *Dauntless*'s own long-range camera. It showed a square of blinking lights around an opening bay door at the bottom of the station. Long black cylinders began to exit. Once they cleared the station, their engines burned hot. "Looks like ... armed drones? I thought they were illegal, sir."

Ibekwe bent over his console. "Confirmed, General. Drones."

"How many?" Graves demanded.

"A dozen," Franklin said. "MOAB 6 has deployed her dropships and is withdrawing. We've got five more shuttles aiming for the station."

All twelve of the enemy drones had begun maneuvering to intercept the attacking shuttles. The station's point defenses had ceased fire to avoid hitting the Neo drones.

"Can you get me on that dropship that's already docked, Commander?" Graves asked.

"You want to board it, sir?" He left his concerns unspoken.

Graves scowled. "How much time do we have until the Havens are in range of that laser?" he called to Franklin.

"Thirty minutes, sir." His voice still had not settled into a normal register.

Graves's gaze swiveled back to Ibekwe. "I'm not doing anything here that you can't handle, Commander. Maybe I can be useful over there."

Ibekwe nodded. "Helm, bring us about and position us over the dropship for a touch-and-go."

---

**Ming Qinlao • High Earth Orbit**

MoSCOW snapped Ming awake when the *Roadrunner* reached the preset distance from their target.

"I was just about to wake you," Lander said. MoSCOW reported the statement as a lie.

*"He's afraid of you."*

The voice inside her head was different since she'd slept. Less distant, more like her own thoughts.

She ignored him as she pawed through the supply bin for more fuel, squeezing three more gel packs into her mouth without bothering to taste them.

Ming caught a glimpse of herself in the darkened window. Her hair was plastered to her forehead in a sheen of fever sweat. Her complexion had a grayish hue, and her face was gaunt, ghostlike. MoSCOW's needle teeth had turned the skin around the eyepatch red and angry. She wiped a crust of dried blood from her nostrils.

He should be afraid. The sight scared even her.

"How long before we get there?" she asked Lander in a raw voice. Before she'd finished the question, MoSCOW answered.

*"Three minutes."*

"'Bout three minutes or so," Lander replied, his eyes on the panel. "I'll flip us in another thirty seconds."

Ming let the gel settle in her stomach, trying not to fidget. Half a minute was like an eternity to MoSCOW. Enough time to consume an entire library or plot a course to Mars.

The nap had done her good. Back at the Erkennen facility, the implant had seemed like a junkyard dog in her head, chained but out of control. Back there, the sheer volume of sensory input had made her nervous system raw, angry. She'd had to fight the voice in her head.

But now was different. Her relationship with MoSCOW felt more like a conversation, symbiotic, as if she could adjust the gain on MoSCOW's input at will. Ming shivered, wondering how far the earworm and MoSCOW's other connectors had burrowed into her human tissue. And if she were permanently changed, beyond whatever damage the radiation poisoning had wrought.

The vessel began to flip around. Ming just hoped she'd be able to maintain control of MoSCOW long enough to track down Elise Kisaan and take back the cryptokey. Then she'd have a real bargaining chip with Anthony Taulke.

"Heads up," Lander said.

Ming followed his visual cues to a series of small explosions from a distant space station. MoSCOW informed her the station was on her list of possible origin points for the mysterious UN shuttle. It appeared someone else had taken a keen interest in that station. Someone with lots of firepower.

"I'll drive," Ming said. She spun the nose of the shuttle and put them into a hard burn for the space station coming under attack. Lander grunted as the gees piled up.

"You know that's weapons fire, right?" Lander said. She didn't answer.

The shuttle sensor package was useless for long-range scanning, so Ming relied on her own visuals, continually updating as their destination grew closer. She waited until the last possible second to flip the shuttle and activate the decel burn. The station passed by the viewscreen as she continued to gather more observational information. Lander's head lolled as he succumbed to the g-force, while MoSCOW adjusted her bodysuit to accommodate the new stresses.

The analysis MoSCOW fed her made no sense. The debris from the attacking ships came from mining vessels mixed with military hardware, mostly US made. Someone was attacking a space station with mining units?

One of the MOABs opened its rear door and three smaller dropships launched. No sooner had they begun to burn away from their carrier than a bolt of energy lanced from the apex of the station, destroying the mother ship.

"Jesus," Lander said.

The slow-moving vessels used the momentum from their launch to race toward the space station, thrusters firing all the while. Point defense cannons opened up from the station, destroying two of the small craft. Another craft—this one MoSCOW identified as an actual navy ship, a sloop—accelerated toward the station, covering the lone remaining dropship. The sloop absorbed rail gun shells, then returned fire until the station's cannon erupted in a fiery burst.

A large bay in the center of the space station yawned open. Small, tubular spacecraft streamed out.

*"Twelve drones,"* MoSCOW reported. *"Armed and highly maneuverable."*

The navy vessel banked hard and raced toward a dropship that had attached itself to the station like a leech. The drones from the station fanned out into a search pattern.

"Looks like whoever runs this station doesn't believe in UN treaties," Lander said.

"This is the place we're looking for, Lander."

"Who are these guys?" Lander's tone sounded respectful. "They're willing to take serious losses to get on that station." He shook his head. "Suicide mission."

Ming spun the shuttle and started a burn directly at the station. "Don't know, don't care. The enemy of my enemy is my friend."

MoSCOW was already connected to the station's network, breaking through their firewalls. She went straight for the comms network and ran a facial rec protocol for Elise Kisaan.

*"Kisaan ... on the station ... observation deck."*

Ming banked the *Roadrunner* hard to avoid an incoming drone.

"Make yourself useful, Lander." She pointed to the rail gun controls. "Shoot something."

With difficulty he raised his hands to the gunner's pad on the main console, target-locked the drone now turning toward their port quarter, and fired. Its engine flared, then exploded in a short-lived cloud of orange dust. He targeted another and fired again.

*"Ingress point located,"* MoSCOW pulsed. The cargo bay where the drones had come from was still open. And it was only a few decks below where MoSCOW had located Kisaan.

"You're going in there?" Lander asked, his voice tight under the g-force. "Is that a good idea?"

Ming grinned as she felt the rage bubble up in her throat. She envisioned what she'd do to this Kisaan woman once she had her under her gun. "Not only is it a good idea, Lander. It's the only idea."

*"Bay door closing."*

"You're coming in too fast!" Lander warned.

*Not too fast.* The landing bay loomed large. *Just exactly fast enough.*

"Ming! Goddammit, the door is closing—"

She flipped the ship and performed an emergency decel burn. Ming smashed flat into her couch, the g-force too much even for the MoSCOW suit to compensate for.

Had the *Roadrunner* been bulkier, they'd have had no chance. But with its low, sleek design, MoSCOW calculated they would just make it.

"Ming!" Lander shouted.

The shuttle slipped through the gap engine first, and the bay doors closed like a toothy maw behind them. Ming killed the main engines and the ambient noise subsided until only Lander's heavy breathing remained.

"Repressurizing the bay," Ming said, directing MoSCOW to do so. Her own heart was racing. She'd never felt more alive.

"Never ... fucking *ever* ... do that with me in a ship again," Lander said.

She retrieved Lander's weapon from the locker and tossed it to him. She nodded at the bay doors separating them and open space. "This bay stays closed unless I get back. You can wait here or come with me. Your choice."

Ming felt Lander's eyes assessing her. She must look like quite a sight, she realized: sweating, eyes feverish, talking to herself in a clipped, freakish voice.

And above all, angry. Very, very angry.

Lander stood. "I'll stick with you."

## 22

WILLIAM GRAVES • USS DAUNTLESS

In Graves's opinion, the "touch-and-go" maneuver was not well named. The tech from the *Dauntless* positioned Graves's harnessed body over the emergency docking hatch and had just finished explaining about a two-meter chute that extended below the belly of the ship. To Graves's mind, the maneuver should be named something more like "get-close-and-throw-the-old-man-into-space." He reminded himself again that he'd ordered this against the captain's recommendation.

The young man—Yoakim, according to his name badge—had a worried look on his boyish face.

The ship banked hard, throwing Graves to the limits of his harness. "Where you from, son?" Graves asked.

The tech looked startled that a general was talking to him like a regular person. "Kansas, sir. Wichita." He fussed with the fasteners on Graves's chest.

"Twenty-five seconds to e-dock," the speaker said.

"You seem nervous. Ever done this before?"

The tech shook his head. "Honest to God, General, I thought this was just one of those textbook procedures we never really use in real life."

Graves forced a reassuring smile. "I'm sure Commander Ibekwe knows what he's doing."

From the speaker: "Fifteen seconds."

"The captain is the best pilot I've ever seen. If he can't do this, no one can."

The tech hugged his own chest. "Cross your arms, sir. Like this."

*Ten ... nine ... eight...*

"Now remember, sir: breathe out as hard as you can. That way your lungs won't burst if you're exposed for a few seconds in space."

*Two ... one...*

The *Dauntless* came to a hard stop, throwing Yoakim to the end of his safety tether, but Graves was held in place by his harness. He heard a whooshing sound under his feet and then he was being sucked downward, into the umbilical tunnel.

He saw a flash of light as he slid past the docking ring of the *Dauntless* and into the extension, then darkness again as he entered the dropship. His shoulder clipped the edge of the new hatch, and he felt his knee give way as his body landed hard on the new deck. The circle of light above his head snapped shut.

"Holy shit, it's the general," he heard someone say. A light in the eyes blinded him. "You okay, sir?"

He struggled to his feet, pawing at the light. His knee throbbed, but it held his weight. "I'm fine, goddammit. Fine. Who's in charge here?"

"Me, sir. Captain Quincy."

He faced the young woman with the stubby ponytail from the briefing. In the shadowy shuttle interior, her determined expression reminded him of Jansen. Six heavily armed marines ringed the two of them.

"Quincy? You were in command of the MOAB, not this strike team."

"Last-minute personnel change, sir," she said.

One of the marines snickered. "Yeah, the other guy crapped his pants when he found out the mission."

"Stow it, marine," Quincy snapped. "General, why are you here?"

"Last-minute personnel change," he said to Quincy. Out of the corner of his eye, Graves saw the marines exchange looks.

Quincy looked him over and shook her head. "Just so long as you don't slow us down, sir." She pushed through the marines and made her way to the next compartment.

Graves followed, closing the hatch behind him. Two combat engineers were busy cutting on the inner door of the station airlock with a plasma torch. They'd already jacked the first door open manually.

"This is a maintenance access port," Quincy said. "They probably don't know we're here yet. Once this lock is open, it stays open. If we need to get out of here fast, we'll vent this whole deck." Quincy leaned into Graves and lowered her voice. "How many dropships made it?"

"Two, so far."

She swore under her breath.

"How close are we to the reactor?" Graves asked.

Quincy pointed at the ceiling. "Two decks up." She jerked her head at the compartment behind them. "I hope those jarheads can fight as good as they talk. I'm one of three combat engineers—if one of us doesn't make it to the reactor in one piece, this will have been a complete waste of bodies."

The engineer running the plasma torch turned it off and stood. "We're ready, ma'am." He stepped aside to let a second man place the manual jack to pry the door open.

Quincy stepped to the back of the compartment and banged on the door. "Saddle up, marines. It's your turn."

The four men and two women filed into the tiny airlock compartment, three to a side. The joking air of the last few minutes was gone, replaced by stony faces and harder eyes. The marine who had spoken earlier pressed an M24 rifle into Graves's arms. "For luck, sir," he whispered, and flashed a brief smile.

They wore dark green battle armor and carried M24s and one heavy-caliber machine gun per fire team. A pair of grenades with selectable detonation settings were tucked into pockets at the smalls of their backs, and most carried a personal sidearm and a blade. Graves nodded to himself. This team would get them to the reactor. He could feel their confidence.

"Helmets on, marines," growled the sergeant leading the group on the right. The team detached the battle helmets from their belts and snapped them in place. A few seconds elapsed as they did comms checks, then the lead marine nodded at Quincy.

"Standing by, ma'am," he said, his voice amplified by the helmet speaker.

The combat engineer who'd set up the jack on the inner airlock showed the marine where to trigger the controlled detonation and stepped back to join Quincy and Graves.

Quincy put her fingers in her ears. "This is gonna be loud, sir." Graves followed suit.

When the blast erupted, the atmosphere in the compartment compressed, then released into the station in a rush of air. The marine team on the left moved forward, but the first man in line stopped short. His body stuttered, then collapsed. It took Graves a second to realize they were under attack.

He hit the deck along with Quincy as the marines regrouped behind the lip of the blown hatch. One of them tossed a grenade down the corridor.

"Fire in the hole!"

The blast rocked them harder than the breaching action had.

The heavy cal *thunk-thunk-thunked* for what seemed like a long time to Graves's ears. The two remaining marines in the first fire team rushed into the shattered, smoke-filled corridor. Small arms fire, then silence. The reek of gunpowder and hot metal drifted backward. The first fire team stood and signaled all clear.

Graves slipped a little as he stood, then tugged on Quincy's arm to help her up. When she resisted, he looked down. She held the limp body of the engineer who had manned the cutting torch. There was a red hole where his right eye had been, and the back of his head was a pulpy mess. Graves realized he'd slipped in the man's brains trying to get up.

Laying the body gently on the deck, Quincy stood and wiped her hands on her trousers. "So much for the element of surprise."

Both teams of marines advanced, each along one side of the blasted corridor. Quincy and the other combat engineer brought up the rear, carrying packs over their shoulders. They passed a pair of corpses in matching black uniforms, their bodies pocked and lacerated from the grenade's explosion.

"Up two decks, Sergeant," Quincy said. "I need to get to the reactor compartment."

The marine nodded. "Understood, ma'am. We'll clear the way."

### Ming Qinlao • Cargo Bay 2B

When Ming stepped from the *Roadrunner*, her right leg gave way. Lander reached down to help, but she shook him off with as much attitude as she could muster.

*"Your motor functions are unstable due to continued radiation exposure. Unpairing recommended."* MoSCOW's voice in her head was strangely comforting.

"You okay?" Lander asked.

"I'm fine. Just adjusting to the new artificial gravity here."

He frowned at the obvious lie. "Look," he said, "that thing is taking a toll on you. If you drop dead, how am I supposed to get out of here?"

Ming offered him a wolfish smile. "Guess you'd better make sure I get back here in one piece, right?"

While she traded barbs with Lander, MoSCOW projected the station's holographic security feed onto Ming's retinal display. Two dropships were attached to the hull. A pinpoint of red light showed an attack unit at the far end of the station, near the fusion reactor. Another boarding party was one deck below their present location. Ming could tell they were fighting their way down toward the comms array located near the observation deck. And Elise Kisaan.

A bright light flashed, overloading her display. The station feed disappeared.

*MoSCOW? Are you there?* Ming felt a rise of panic at the sudden emptiness in her head. She leaned against the hull of the shuttle.

*"I am here,"* came the reply after a few seconds. *"I was ejected from the space station network."*

"Ejected?"

*"Yes, by an extremely powerful synthetic entity with enough resources to dominate my attack."*

"What the hell is going on?" Lander demanded. "We're sitting ducks out here."

Ming's vision cleared. "We know where we're going," she said. "We'll just have to navigate the old-fashioned way."

The hallway outside the cargo bay was wide and strangely empty. Her footfalls made no sound on the thin carpet. It was too much to hope that the *Roadrunner* hadn't been detected slipping into the bay, but all the station's security seemed to be aimed at the intruders. Hugging the wall, Glock in hand, Ming reached the set of stairs leading to the next deck. Lander followed close behind, the big man surprisingly light on his feet.

The door to the stairwell opened with a sharp clack of metal. Deserted. Where were all the people on this station?

She led them upward, her suit adapting to offset her muscle fatigue. She paused at the door to the topmost level, the sound of her own ragged breathing filling the silence.

*"Caution."*

Ming closed her eyes to better focus on the sounds around her. The door was heavy, airtight, capable of sealing off the rest of the station in the event of catastrophe. She pressed her ear against the metal.

"What's the holdup?" Lander whispered.

She took his hand and placed it on the door so he could feel the percussive thump from the other side. Gunfire, heavy caliber.

"Is there another way in?" he asked.

Ming shook her head, staring at the downloaded map MoSCOW had secured before being kicked from the station's network. She used her hip to tap the crash bar on the door and crack it open. No longer muffled, the blare of a firefight echoed around the stairwell.

Ming did a quick visual survey of the scene. Two marines in battle armor occupied the right-hand corner, alternating fire down the long hallway. A mobile attack pod advanced on their position. According to her map, the observation deck was behind the pod.

"Fire in the hole!" one marine shouted, lobbing a grenade. The pod's shield deflected it, angling it back toward the marines. Ming slammed the door shut, and a loud concussion shook the stairwell.

When she opened it again, the pod had advanced closer. The marines continued their attack, but they were fighting a losing battle. It was only a matter of time before the marines would be forced to retreat. She could wait or act.

The back-and-forth firing entered a rhythm as the two teams battled for the last few meters of bullet-shattered hallway. She closed her eyes to assess the pattern of the gunfire, knowing in her heart she was applying logic to the actions of people under stress.

"Cover me." She kicked open the door, diving for the corner.

Lander used the surprise opening of the door to spray the assault pod with bullets, giving her a few precious beats to traverse the two meters to the nearest dark green uniform. Her carbon fiber knife was out as she grabbed the nearest marine and rolled him over on top of her for protection.

She laid the knife at his throat and barked in his ear, "I'm a friendly."

His partner was already swinging her weapon to bear.

"No one on this station is a friendly," the marine said. He was staring hard at the barrel of his partner's automatic weapon. "Shoot her!"

"We're the good guys!" Lander yelled from the stairwell.

The marine holding Ming in her sights glanced sideways, unsure what to do now.

"We could've shot you from cover if we wanted you dead," Ming breathed into her captive's ear. "I need to get past that thing. We can work together."

Through the haptics in her suit, she could feel the young marine's pulse hammering, feel his indecision. Then he made up his mind and nodded to his partner. "They're with us."

Ming let him go, and they scrambled together toward the firing line. In the few seconds that had elapsed, the pod had advanced another two meters.

"We've tried grenades and concentrated fire," said the female marine. "We were about to abandon this position and see if we could find a side hall, flank them somehow."

"I don't have that kind of time," Ming snapped back. "Do you want my help or not?"

The marine shrugged. "Sure."

"Here's what you do." Ming sketched out a plan of concentrated fire at a certain height for three seconds.

"That's it? What're you gonna do?"

"I'm going to run right over them," she said with a grin. "Try not to shoot me in the back, yeah?"

Ming backed down the hallway and assumed a sprinter's starting stance. Her suit began to tighten against her skin, embracing her muscles, gathering energy to support her. Her vision calculated the speed she needed to achieve by the time she reached the end of the hallway. Or MoSCOW did. It was getting hard to tell the difference. She nodded at the two marines, who swung their rifles out to provide cover fire.

Ming never heard the gunfire, or saw the cracked door with Lander's one eye spread with horror as he realized what she was about to do.

Her muscles released with an audible snap of energy. Arms pumping, knees driving, she bolted for the end of the hallway and leaped across the gap. She vaulted over the marines, their M24s firing what sounded like slow-motion rounds. Her right toe contacted the edge of the corner and she was running horizontally across the wall of the hallway, the covering fire from the marines shredding the air beneath her shoulder. Her stride devoured the distance between the end of the hall and the assault pod.

She felt the texture of the wall beneath the balls of her feet. One—two —three—four steps. The marines' covering fire ceased and Ming launched herself over the barrier of the assault pod. She rolled and skidded to a halt, already spinning, already drawing her Glock.

There were three black-uniformed soldiers behind the assault pod, one operating the pod, two manning the weapons. Their necks were craned back at her, the woman on the left already pawing for her sidearm. Ming fired, *crack-crack-crack*, and a neat red hole appeared in each of their foreheads as if by magic. MoSCOW's aim was perfect.

Unmanned, the pod dropped to the deck. Silence descended on the hallway.

Ming stood. "All clear."

The marines peered around the corner, then moved forward.

"What the hell was that?" one of them asked, amazement in his voice. "Some kind of advanced super soldier stuff?"

The door behind them crashed open and Lander stepped out, roaring, "What the hell was that?"

Another radiation warning appeared in Ming's display. She killed it.

Just a few more minutes, that's all she needed. Elise Kisaan should be just up the hallway.

"You're welcome," she said to the marines. Then, to Lander: "You and I aren't done yet."

It was a short walk to the locked doors of the observation deck. MoSCOW would be no help, since it had been forced out of the station's network.

"You sure this is it?" Lander asked.

Ming nodded. "Her last reported position." She just hoped Elise Kisaan was still in there. She wasn't sure if she had enough strength left to go chasing her around this ridiculously large station.

"You gonna do your voodoo thing to open the door?"

Ming found she was still gripping her Glock. She raised the weapon, aimed it at the door's control panel, and emptied the magazine.

"I guess not." Lander waited until she had lowered the muzzle to the floor before he said, "You have anger issues, you know that?"

Ming felt lightheaded, her mind drifting. "You have no idea."

She leaned against the bulkhead while Lander worked the blade of his knife into the narrow space between the door and jamb. He levered it open a crack and inserted his fingers into the slit.

"By the way, you're bleeding again," he said.

## 23

## REMY CADE • CASSANDRA STATION, OBSERVATION DECK

Through the windows of the observation lounge, Remy watched the space battle.

Not much of a battle, really. The attackers, whoever they were, were using some kind of industrial equipment to gain access to the station. He'd seen at least four of the attacking force turned into slag in the last thirty minutes.

Some of the attackers must have penetrated the station's defenses, because a firefight had started in the hallway outside. Remy considered his options: he was unarmed and Elise was unconscious. Staying put was his best play.

He checked on Elise again. Her limp body lay prone, the half face of Cassandra on her slender nape glaring up at him. Then her eyelids fluttered and Remy rolled her onto her back.

He ran his fingers along the delicate curve of her jaw and leaned close.

"Elise."

Her eyes popped open. Her gaze cut wildly from side to side until she focused on Remy.

"Easy," he said. "You fainted."

He didn't see the right hook coming. Or the leg that swept from behind and over his head, caught him on the sternum, and slammed him backwards into the deck. In a flash, she was on top of him. Her open palm flashed down. His cheek stung. Her forearm pressed into his windpipe.

No air. His vision started to tunnel in before Elise finally got off his chest.

She stood over him as he regained his breath. "You led them here," she said, framed against the observation windows. Behind her, orange flared, then was snuffed out. Remy felt the rapid-fire pulsing of the station's rail guns throbbing through the deck. "You betrayed us."

"No." Remy got to his knees. "I would never do that to you, Elise."

Elise turned to the battle raging beyond the window. "It's too late now. They're here."

The muffled gunfire that Remy had been hearing off and on for the last hour suddenly seemed closer. Right outside the door. The reinforced wall around the locked door of the room shuddered. The door cracked open. In its jaws was a knife blade, followed by fingers. A handgun pushed through.

"Everyone stay right where you are," a tall man said. His arm was through the door, his handgun pointed at them. He forced his body into the opening, then wedged it fully open with his hips.

A young woman followed him, staggering as if drunk. She was Chinese, clad in a skintight black suit, and had a device that looked like half a goggle consuming the right side of her face. Her complexion was waxy and her nose dripped blood. She came to a stop, swaying, her good eye focusing on Remy and Elise.

"Ming Qinlao," Elise said. "Welcome to the Temple of Cassandra."

Remy looked at Elise sharply. Who the hell was Ming Qinlao?

"Guard the door," the woman called Ming told the tall man. She stepped across the room, her stride uneven, almost like the movements of a marionette. She pointed the pistol at Elise.

"Give it to me." Her voice was thick. "The cryptokey. I want it."

"That's not possible, Ming," Elise said, her words like silk. "What you came here for was me, not the key. We think that's the best choice."

Ming's eyes shifted between Elise and Remy. The muzzle tracked with her gaze. "We? You and him? Why do I care what he thinks?"

Elise stepped forward, causing the man with Ming to tense. Remy assessed the room, looking for anything he could use as a weapon. Then Elise spoke, and her words stopped his thoughts cold.

"Not him," she said, the disdain dripping from her words. "Cassandra. I am her vessel. She is in me. I am what you came for."

With her left hand, Ming slipped a packet from her belt and tore the package open with her teeth. She sucked the package dry in two swallows. The food seemed to steady her. She wiped her nose with the back of her free hand. "Give me one good reason why I shouldn't waste you both right now and take what I want."

Elise smiled. In profile, Remy watched her lips thin and bend. The smile was cruel, manipulative. Same with the voice. This shell of a person was not the woman he loved. This was not his Elise.

"It is Her will that I come with you," Elise whispered.

Ming sniffed back a fresh flow of blood from her nose. "I don't have time for this shit," she said and pulled the trigger. Nothing happened.

"You need to reload, Ming," the man said. His weapon was out and covering the room.

"You see," Elise said. Remy knew that subtle tone, the one that made him putty in her grip. Now it made him sick. "I have been saved again. Cassandra provides for her true believers."

"One problem," Ming said, reholstering her Glock.

"Yes?" Elise was whispering now, sure of herself.

"I'm not a believer." In one smooth motion, she lifted an odd pistol with a square barrel from the holster on her left hip and pulled the trigger. It made a strange, compressive *punk* sound. Whatever the odd weapon fired, it impacted Elise. She staggered backward, stiffening suddenly, then collapsed.

Ming trained the weapon on Remy.

"Wait," he said, "you don't need to—"

He saw her pull the trigger, felt a shiver run over his skin like the room was filled with static electricity. Then a crushing force gripped his entire body.

Remy's mind went blank.

## William Graves • Cassandra Station, Reactor Deck

By the time they'd fought their way to the reactor deck, Graves's squad was down to four: Quincy, two marines, and Graves himself. Quincy carried one of the packs containing explosives. Graves carried the other, taken off the corpse of the other combat engineer.

"I guess it's just you and me left to set the charges, sir," Quincy said. The two remaining marines had set up interlocking fields of fire overlooking the long stretch of empty corridor between them and the reactor compartment. "How much of your explosives training do you remember?"

The idea of mission success depending on his atrophied engineering skills made Graves uncomfortable. It had been decades since he'd even touched explosives.

"Let's hope it doesn't come to that, Captain."

The door separating them from the reactor room was made of reinforced steel, double wide and over ten feet tall: large enough to allow equipment to be moved in and out. The access panel on the wall next to it flashed red.

Graves studied the twenty meters of intervening hallway. The corridor was extra wide and tall, with a sturdy gantry system overhead. Along the wall were pieces of machinery and structural supports—plenty of places for a man to hide—but the passageway looked empty.

"I'm sending in a recon drone," said Estes, the lead marine. Quincy nodded, her back still against the wall, her pack at her feet.

He pulled a disc the size of his fist out of a cargo pocket and activated it. The drone lit up, and Estes synced it to his combat monitor. The corporal flipped it in the air, and the drone rose to the ceiling, its red eyes mapping the walls and deck. Deliberately, it advanced down the long hallway.

Three tense minutes passed before Estes called out, "Looks all clear, ma'am." He got to his feet, helping his fellow marine upright as he did so.

Quincy shouldered her pack. "Let's go."

With Estes taking point, they approached the massive door. The other marine, Ortega, slapped his hand against the thick steel. He was the shorter of the two, his dark complexion suggesting an Aztec heritage. "How much boom-boom you got in that pack, Captain?"

Quincy inspected the door. "Not enough to open this baby without some help." She squatted to inspect the hinges that were thick as Graves's thigh. The door was designed to open toward them so that, in the event that the reactor compartment vented into space, the atmospheric pressure of the ship would help keep the hatch closed. She eyed the plasma cutter on the wall. "We could try to cut it open, but that would take at least an hour." Her gaze roved around the crowded hallway, then swept upward. "Unless..."

Within a few minutes, Quincy had formed a new plan. As Graves found the controls for the gantry and rolled the massive hook down the hallway to the door, Quincy and Ortega placed the shaped charges on the hinges and along the bottom of the door seal. Estes and his combat drone guarded their approach farther up the corridor.

When Graves had the gantry at its stops with the hook swinging above the door frame, Quincy pointed to a heavy steel eyelet welded to the top of the door.

"Gimme a boost," she said to the marines.

The two stood on either side of her and, making a cradle from their hands, lifted her to the height of their shoulders.

"That's good." Quincy directed Graves to lower the gantry, then slipped the point of the hook into the eyelet. "Raise it up, General ... take out the slack. Perfect." She hopped to the deck with a clang of boots on metal. "Let's pop this bitch open."

Gathering the remaining explosives and keeping the gantry remote in hand, Graves followed the team back down the hallway and around the corner until they got to the shelter of the stairwell. Quincy got out the remote detonator. "The door was designed to withstand pressure against the seals, but I'm betting it won't be able to take shear forces." She grinned at Graves. "Press the raise button on the gantry, General, and don't let up. If I'm right, we'll slice this thing right off the wall."

Graves held down the gantry button with his elbow and covered his ears.

Quincy laughed wickedly. "Cover your ears, gentlemen, this is gonna be a major fire in the fucking hole." She triggered the detonation.

Graves felt his eyeballs compress with the force of the blast. When he removed his hands from his ears, one of his palms was bloody.

Quincy got to her feet, shaky but grinning. "Let's see what that did," she shouted as if from very far away.

Graves knees were rubbery, and he accepted a hand up from one of the marines. The eyes of the marines were wide as they followed Quincy back down the hall and around the corner.

The end of the hallway was blackened and the deck plates bowed from the force of the blast. By some miracle, the massive reactor door was still attached to the gantry hook. Quincy hugged the wall as she spider-walked through the wreckage to the door. "It worked," she crowed, backing away from the structure. "General, drop the hook."

Graves realized he was still toting the gantry remote control. He pressed on the button to lower it, but nothing happened.

It took him and Quincy a few minutes to find the manual override. The young woman was operating on adrenaline. She laughed at the sight of the manual lever to drop the hook. "After you, sir," she said.

Graves threw the lever and the door crashed to the deck in a shower of soot, leaving the space station reactor compartment wide open.

"Yes!" Quincy scrambled over the door to the entrance. Beyond her, Graves could make out an enormous room filled with piping and racks of equipment in front of the massive fusion reactor. She spun on her heel to face them.

"Who's got the power now, eh?" Quincy said, her grin wide.

A single gunshot rang out, like the striking of a distant bell to Graves's deadened hearing. Quincy's left shoulder hitched and her champion's smile collapsed. She stared down at a growing red stain on her chest. She looked up at Graves, her face frowning in puzzlement at the sight of blood on her uniform.

The last combat engineer pitched forward on her face and lay still.

# 24

## MING QINLAO • CASSANDRA STATION

"What the hell is that thing?" Lander asked, eyeing the odd weapon in Ming's hand. He advanced on the bodies of Remy Cade and Elise Kisaan, his weapon at the ready. "Are they dead?"

"I hope not," Ming said. Although bulky, Erkennen's invention was well balanced and had zero recoil. "Viktor gave it to me. Some kind of modern Taser..."

Talking was becoming difficult again. With every exhale, another tiny bit of her life force seemed to drain away, as if she had a slow leak in her core. Without the suit, Ming doubted she'd even still be upright. She tugged another gel from her hip pocket and squeezed its contents into her mouth. When it hit her stomach, she experienced only a fraction of the energy boost she had before.

"They're not dead," Lander said. He knelt next to Elise, his index finger on her carotid artery. "Just knocked out, I guess."

"Lander ... I'm ... I'm crashing." Ming's knees went soft. Getting closer to the floor felt like a biological imperative. Her own voice sounded very far away.

Lander was next to her then, helping to steady her. "Don't flake out on me now, kid. I need you to get my ass off this death trap." He ripped open another gel pack and tipped her chin up. "C'mon, Ming. Eat this. Do not go to sleep on me."

She forced herself to swallow. With Lander's help, she was able to stand again.

"Get the cryptokey..."

He returned to Kisaan, rolled her over. "It's locked on her wrist."

"Then cut off her hand, for Christ's sake, Lander. Just get the damn key!"

Lander stood and drew his weapon again.

"Wait." Ming closed her eyes. Elise had talked about how she was Cassandra's emissary or some other bullshit. What if she was telling the truth? MoSCOW would have warned her if Elise was lying.

*"It is possible the cryptokey has somehow become part of this woman's biological identity,"* MoSCOW warned.

Ming pressed a shaking hand to her temple. "Bring her with us," she said. "Lander, carry her."

Lander hoisted the woman's stiff body under his left arm, leaving a free hand for his weapon. "That means you have to walk, Ming." He reached into the pouch at the small of his back and handed her another gel, his last. "I can't carry both of you."

Ming did her best to keep up with him as they retraced their steps back to the *Roadrunner*. In the stairwell, whenever Lander turned a corner, Ming was treated to a view of the frozen face of Elise Kisaan.

What the hell was she going to do with this woman when she woke up? Ming could barely keep her eyes open; how would she protect herself? She watched the armor on Lander's back flex under the weight of the woman. She had no choice. She would have to trust Lander, an ex-Taulke employee who'd been ordered to kill her.

"This place seems deserted all of a sudden," Lander said over his shoulder in a low voice. "Where is everyone?"

*"The intelligence that barred me from the system is no longer active,"* MoSCOW said. *"Neo personnel are massing near the reactor deck."*

Lander checked the hallway outside the cargo bay and they hustled to the safety of their shuttle. Ming collapsed into the copilot's couch. "Tie her up," she said to Lander. "I don't want to deal with her when she wakes up."

Lander complied, then booted up the flight computer. "Open the doors, Ming." His voice was even, but serious.

Ming stared at the cargo bay doors for what felt like only a second. But when she looked behind her, she saw Elise, still unconscious, restrained in her own seat. When had Lander done that? Maybe she'd blacked out for a minute...

"Ming." Lander's voice took on a tone of urgency. "I held up my end of the agreement. Open the doors."

Her skull was splitting, her vision distorting. Ming stared at Lander's square jaw jutting out like a bullfrog. She giggled.

"Ming, open the doors."

"Look at me," she said. It took all her willpower to stay focused on his face. "Promise to get me back to Mars safely, with Kisaan, in one piece?"

"I promise," Lander replied.

*"Truth."*

MoSCOW was still inside her head, but fading behind a curtain of crimson pain encircling her conscious mind. Ming reached forward to the controls and connected to the station's network. She found the network node for the cargo bay doors. Their ship rocked gently as the doors opened. The craft lifted under her as Lander applied power to the thrusters...

When Ming opened her eyes again, she saw the dark of space, the bright spread of the planet beneath them, the sight marred by floating wreckage. Lander's hands danced over the shuttle controls as he navigated around chunks of shattered spacecraft. A marine in full battle armor floated by, still clutching his rifle.

"Lander," Ming said. "I—I'm done." She reached behind her ear to trigger the MoSCOW release mechanism. There was a wet, sucking sound as the device separated from her flesh and fell into her lap. The air from the cabin touched her raw skin, making Ming whimper with fresh pain. She touched her eye and her fingers came back bloody.

Lander's hand was on her arm. "Easy," he whispered. "Just lie back."

She looked at Lander's face, heard his voice, but it all felt two-dimensional now. The extra layer of meaning MoSCOW had overlaid on every one of her senses was gone. She felt the loss like an ache, a hole in her perception.

As she laid back into the cushions, Ming caught a glimpse of her reflection in the window. The right side of her face was a blur of red, her eye milky white. Lander plucked the MoSCOW device from her lap, tossing it into the disposal chute. He put a bandage over the mottled skin, the analgesic in the cloth blessedly cool against her ravaged flesh.

"Radiation treatment," she whispered.

"Coming up." She felt a med collar being fitted around her neck, the device tightening, then a pinch as it tapped into her jugular to deliver drugs. Soft beeps as Lander programmed it. "I'm going to give you a sedative, Ming. To help you sleep."

Her mouth was dry, her voice hoarse. "I'm trusting you, Lander."

He may have replied, but she was already asleep.

***

### Remy Cade • Cassandra Station, Observation Deck

When Remy woke, the room around him was empty.

He forced his eyelids open, still unable to move his body, wishing in his heart of hearts he'd never woken up.

Elise was gone. Whether Ming and the soldier had taken her by force or she had gone of her own free will, it made no difference now. She was gone from his heart. He realized with great despair that she'd been gone a long time and he'd been a fool to think otherwise.

His muscle control came back slowly. A finger wiggled, the twitch of a wrist, the bending of his knee, but he remained on the floor.

His entire body felt thick, his brain fuzzy. The woman had electrocuted them with that weapon. And now they were gone. He remembered Elise had asked to go with them.

Had she ever really loved him? Or had he been just another link in the chain of events she'd used to pull herself into power?

He hauled himself up to a sitting position, every muscle screaming at him in protest.

Did it matter now? He was a dead man. When Brother Donald or one of the others realized he'd been the one to betray the location of the Temple station, Cassandra would tell them to skin him alive. Or push him out the nearest airlock. Or both.

*Cassandra.* He tried to work up enough moisture in his mouth to spit and failed. Remy hoisted himself to his feet and tottered to the window. The world lay at his feet. He sneered at his reflection in the glass.

Billions of followers of Cassandra were down there beneath the swirling clouds. How many of them knew they were worshipping a machine? He rested his forehead against the cool glass. There was some cosmic irony for you. Millions of people united in the cause for a new earth being led by a computer program.

This station, the Temple of Cassandra—this was Her house. She had taken Elise from him. Cassandra was to blame for all of this.

The answer came to Remy before he'd even worked out the question in his head.

She was a machine, a machine masquerading as a god.

Machines required power to function.

And power could be turned off.

His limbs responded easier now and his brain was focused with newfound purpose. Remy walked, each step becoming steadier, more determined.

A long time ago, he'd been part of another faith, an older religion, something his parents had tried to pass along to him and he'd ignored. He didn't remember much from those days, but one simple, balanced concept blazed in his memory.

*An eye for an eye.*

Cassandra had taken everything he cared about in life. He would return the favor.

The hallway outside was a war zone. Bullets had shredded the walls and ceiling, and the air was acrid with gunpowder and something heavier. He'd smelled a lot of blood in his time, too much. He'd shed blood, he'd spilled blood, and he'd seen those he loved cut down in body and in spirit. All in the service of someone else's cause.

No more.

Midway down the hall was the angular hull of a mobile assault pod.

Three dead Neos garbed in the black uniform of station security lay sprawled behind it. All had a small, neat hole in their foreheads.

There was a senior officer among the dead, a woman. Remy stripped her security token. At the end of the hall, he turned right. More devastation. The corner of the hallway was chewed away by bullets, as if it had been gnawed by an enormous rat. His footsteps crunched through the carpet of spent shells as he made his way to the lift.

No one tried to stop him. No one was anywhere to be seen.

Using the token, Remy put the lift into security override.

Maybe it wasn't too late to free the woman he loved.

"Reactor level," he said.

# 25

## WILLIAM GRAVES • CASSANDRA STATION, REACTOR DECK

"Get down, sir!" Estes shouted.

Graves stared at Quincy's body from his position crouched behind a hull stanchion. The young woman was looking right at him, sightless eyes open, mouth parted as if about to say something. One moment she'd been celebrating a feat of engineering genius, the next she was dead.

Fire from the M24s called his gaze to the marines' position, hunkered behind a control panel. They had absorbed Quincy's death with the stoic calmness of men who'd seen too much killing too often.

"Stay here, sir," Ortega called over his shoulder. "We'll be back in a few."

Estes peeked around the corner of the panel, flashed a hand sign to Ortega, then laid down a brace of cover fire as the smaller marine snaked deeper into the room.

Seconds later, there was the thick, broad eruption of a fragmentation grenade.

"Take it to 'em, Coyote!" Estes shouted.

The lights dimmed in a massive drawdown of power from the reactor.

*The laser,* thought Graves. *They're firing the laser.*

Estes stood, motioning to Graves. "C'mon, sir. Ortega's got them penned in the rear of engineering. You can set charges now."

*Set charges.*

He was the only trained combat engineer left alive. Graves pushed away his doubts. A lot of people under his command had laid down their lives today, and it was up to him to make their sacrifice worth it.

The fusion reactor was even more daunting up close. He climbed the ladder to the deck over the reactor body. The massive toroid was the size of a house, stretching three stories upwards with steel catwalks crisscrossing the open space overhead. The magnetic containment hub pierced the center of the donut-shaped reactor and flared out like an enormous mushroom head. He studied the design, looking for weak spots he could exploit.

His goal here wasn't to blow up the reactor, but to cause it to self-destruct. The resulting fire and heat would ignite the O2 tanks of the station's environmental system and the hydrazine that fueled its maneuvering thrusters. The explosion would tear the station apart.

A shot rang out, startling Graves. Estes smiled at him. "Don't sweat it, sir. That's just Ortega keeping 'em honest."

Graves nodded. He was acting like a greenhorn in front of this brave young man. *Think, dammit!* He forced his mind to analyze the system logically.

Best to combine the effect of all four charges on a single system element that couldn't be repaired. The fusion reaction was suspended inside the core by the magnetic hubs, one above the reactor, one below. Destroy either of them, and the reaction would cascade out of control ... but there would be an emergency backup somewhere to ensure containment.

Graves found the main magnetic generator panel, then followed the power source. The emergency backup would be a mechanical device, a fail-safe designed to safely shut down the reactor in case the high-tech redundancies failed.

The compartment was labeled *Emergency Magnetic Power*. Inside was a simple but elegant solution: a flywheel hub. He pressed his hand against the wall of the cylinder. Inside, the spinning wheel thrummed. Clever. In the event of a power outage, the wheel would provide enough energy to safely shut down the fusion reaction.

He threw the handle down. A Klaxon blared over the station comms.

*"Emergency magnetic power offline. Emergency magnetic power offline."*

Graves muscled the handle back and forth until it snapped off in his hand. That would slow any efforts to restore the backup. He found an operator panel and killed the audio alarm, leaving only a silent, blinking red light.

Hustling back to the main reactor, Graves knew what he had to do now, and he was filled with newfound energy. The magnetic hub. All he had to do was knock that magnetic containment device offline, and the laws of physics would do the rest.

Containment failure followed by a massive plasma breach of fire and radiation followed by highly volatile chemicals going boom.

Graves crawled out over the reactor body to the magnetic hub, feeling the hum of the massive machine under his knees. He ripped open the satchel. Four charges, with manual detonators and a timing device. He searched the bag again, looking for more remote detonators. The cold realization set in: Quincy must have used them all on the door. The best he could do was slave the charges to timing device—but if anyone came along during the countdown, they could deactivate the bomb.

Someone was going to have to stay behind.

"General!" Estes shouted over the roar of the engine room. "What's the holdup, sir?"

Graves flashed him a sign for five minutes. He used his knife to carve away the insulation and placed the charges equidistant around the base of the magnetic pole. He slaved them all to the handheld timer, then crawled back to the waiting marines. Ortega lay prone on a walkway, covering the barricaded doorway some fifty feet below. The back door to the reactor room.

Graves squatted next to the marines. The lights from the alarm cast alternating red and white tints across their features. They were so young, so goddamned young. He showed them the detonator and shouted over the din of the engine room.

"When I trigger this, you have fifteen minutes to get back to the dropship and get the hell off this station." He pointed at the blinking alarm. "I need to stay behind to make sure the charges go off." He reached for Ortega's rifle. "I'll need that, son."

Ortega pulled back. "No way, sir." He shot a glance at Estes. "We'll make sure this thing gets done together."

But the other marine wasn't listening. His head snapped to the side as if he was listening to something amid all the racket around them. He placed his hand flat on the catwalk and Graves followed his eyes toward the ladder they had climbed up to this level. The top of ladder was moving. Someone was climbing the ladder.

Ortega put a finger to his lips and crept back along the walkway, rifle at the ready. A hand appeared at the top of the railing, then another and a pause. Whoever it was seemed to be having difficulty with the climb.

The hands tightened, and a face appeared at the top of the ladder.

Remy Cade.

Ortega brought his M24 to his shoulder.

"No!" Graves shouted, crawling forward.

Remy's face registered surprise at seeing Graves and the marines, but he managed to hang on to the ladder. When he was satisfied the marine wasn't about to shoot him, he climbed the rest of the way up. He was unarmed, and Graves couldn't see any wounds on him, but he clutched at his right side and seemed to be dragging his left foot.

"General," he yelled, moving closer. His eyes were red and haunted, but he met Graves's gaze without hesitation. "You used me, General. You tracked me back here."

Graves could smell the sourness of his breath. "I did, son," Graves admitted. "It was the only way. These people, these Neos—"

"I hate them, sir. And I want to hurt them." Remy's voice cracked, but he didn't blink. "I want to destroy them."

Graves searched Remy's face. *When good men do bad things, they don't do them well,* he'd told Jansen. *Lying, for example.* Whatever Cade had come back to the station for, he'd been disappointed. No, more than that. Shattered. He was a man broken—or maybe brokenhearted—but that didn't mean he had to die.

He gripped Remy's shoulder. The muscles under the uniform trembled with energy. "We're on the same team then, Remy."

"For the first time in a long time, you're right, General. What can I do?"

"These men were just leaving. I want you to go with them. I'm staying."

Remy pointed to the detonator in Graves's hand. "I'll do it," he said.

Graves shook his head. "Remy, that's not a good idea. I can't let you—"

"You can trust me, sir. I won't let you down. They took everything from me. I want this. I need this, sir."

Graves searched every line of Remy's face. Every nervous flick of his eyes. "Why?"

"To end Cassandra. Slag the station, her programming dies with it. Maybe that'll be enough."

*I took everything from you,* Graves thought. This broken man was his responsibility. He'd been following Graves's orders at Vicksburg, and that miscalculation had changed Cade's life forever.

Ortega pulled the detonator from the general's hand and triggered the countdown.

*15:00 ... 14:59...*

"Let him, General," Ortega said. "It's his choice and we need to go." He handed the device to Remy.

Remy gripped the detonator. "I need this, sir. You can trust me."

Three more precious seconds evaporated as Graves weighed the choice.

"You're a good man, Remy Cade."

"Not yet, sir," Remy said. "But give me just under fifteen minutes."

They shared a grim smile, severe and final.

"Tick-tock, General," Ortega shouted. "We're literally on the clock, sir." The marine thrust his rifle at Remy and pointed him to the perch where he'd been guarding the rear entrance to the reactor room.

The three clambered down the ladder to the main deck. As he hurried to the shattered door, Graves looked back one last time. Remy Cade was a small figure atop the massive reactor chamber. He waved, the rapid hand flutter of someone who seemed happy.

Graves hurried past the body of Captain Quincy and after the fast-moving marines.

**Remy Cade • Cassandra Station, Reactor Deck**

Remy watched Graves and the two marines disappear through the hatch. Then he returned to his post watching over the back entrance to the reactor room.

13:00 ... 12:59...

He watched the last seconds of his life tick away.

Far overhead, the red alarm light blinked on and off, like the station was trying to hypnotize him.

He wondered if he would see his life flash before his eyes in his final moments. And what would those moments be? Graduating from basic training, the feel of a fresh army uniform against his skin, the shine of his boots, the flash of his belt buckle.

Or something less happy. His best friend's grin ... and his face shattered by a bullet at Vicksburg. The heavy, sticky feel of Jamie's blood on Remy's hands.

10:45

The first time he met Elise. She in her wheelchair, her beautiful face soured by her lot in life. The slow build of their relationship from cold enemies to warm friends to fiery lovers. The touch of her hand, the feel of her skin beneath his lips...

They were happy, they were in love, they were together. What would he give to freeze his life in that moment?

But the pressures of her family—her father—made that impossible. The price of those miraculous bionic legs was a life in the public eye, a life promoting Kisaan Ag to the world.

His Elise went from a shy, caring human being to an uncaring entity hungering for power. The elder Kisaan had set in motion a monster of consumption. The new Elise wanted more: the next promotion, the next politician in her debt. She surpassed any bar set for her by her father.

8:32

Remy fired off a round at the back of the reactor room just because, enjoying the kick of the rifle butt against his shoulder.

Somewhere in that span of time, the Neos had come for her. The kidnapping in Alaska had been a sham—how long had it taken him to realize that? How blind could one man be? His sole job was to protect Elise Kisaan and he'd let the seeds of her destruction into her life.

Remy saw Elise now with the cold precision of mental distance. He'd been too close. His job was safety, not happiness. He'd cared too much about her, and in doing so he'd been her downfall as a human being.

*The people are the problem, Remy.*

Her words chilled him even now. That was the moment he knew what his beloved Elise had become ... and even then he'd refused to believe he'd lost her for good.

Elise was a killer. He'd seen it and done nothing to stop her. That made him just as guilty.

5:27

*Cassandra* ... Remy's face contorted at the very whisper of her name. He'd lost Elise to a machine, a computer.

And that thought brought him to this moment. An icy rage consumed him, inuring him to his wounds, steeling his mind for the sacrifice to come. If Elise was unable to break free of Cassandra's influence, then he would end Cassandra.

He would free Elise. He would make her safe again.

Out of the corner of his eye, Remy detected a flash of movement near the reactor door. A pair of Neo soldiers in black battle armor stepped into the room. Remy fired a short burst from his M24, forcing them to withdraw.

3:19

He rolled to get a look at the other entrance. A concussion grenade clattered along the catwalk. He curled into a ball just as the grenade went off, the blast smashing Remy back against the handrail. With his hearing reduced to a ringing hum, he cracked his eyes to see a squad of Neo soldiers rush into the reactor room. He alternated fire between the front and back entrances until his magazine was empty, then rolled away as they returned fire.

Remy scooped up the timer and got on his hands and knees. The Neos were coming to take back their reactor.

1:56

Remy crawled farther down the catwalk, searching for a place to hide.

His hearing was coming back slowly, enough to hear a gunshot from below him and feel a searing sting in his side.

He flattened against the deck, the hot corrugated metal mashed against the side of his face. A comforting sensation. His fingers probed the wound in his side and came away heavy with blood.

Remy focused on the timer. *1:46.*

He wanted to laugh. Just when he needed a break, time was slowing down.

The catwalk trembled underneath his cheek. Footsteps. They were coming after him.

Remy slithered off the catwalk, and onto the body of the fusion reactor. He surfed down the slope of the toroid to the central magnetic hub, leaving a bloody trail in his wake. Worming his way to the far side of the structure, Remy forced himself into a sitting position. The face of the timer was bloody. His blood.

1:02

He peered around the edge of the hub. Brother Donald was on the catwalk, his eyes locked on the trail of blood. Remy wasn't fast enough to duck his head before Donald saw him.

"Remy!" Donald shouted.

Remy could feel his strength leaking away. He wrapped both hands around the timer and pressed it against his chest.

Donald was standing over him ... when did that happen?

He hugged the timer closer to his body, mashing the sharp corners into his breastbone. He tried to count seconds, but time seemed to have no meaning anymore.

Donald rolled him over and smashed his fist into Remy's face. Remy felt a boot crack his side and his automatic response was to curl his body more tightly.

"Where is it?" Donald screamed at him.

More blows rained down. Remy felt the bite of a knife on his neck. His strength was flowing away fast now. He felt his arms relaxing.

In the haze of his passing, a memory beckoned to him.

Elise at dawn, their favorite time together. He would carry her to the balcony off her bedroom and hold her as the eastern horizon lightened.

Dawn always came fast in that part of India. The horizon a pale etching, then a flash of sun so bright it made them close their eyes.

His strength was gone. Donald peeled Remy's arms from his chest, revealing the timer. The monk wiped the face of the device clean. His eyes grew round.

And the sun came up so brightly, it made Remy close his eyes forever.

## 26

WILLIAM GRAVES • EARTH ORBIT

The dropship jerked under his feet as they separated from the station, pushed away by the airlock's venting atmosphere.

Graves craned his neck to peer through the portside window. Bits of slag and dirt trailed behind them. Ortega applied max thrusters, and the acceleration pulled Graves away from the viewport.

"Best strap in, sir," Estes said.

Graves crawled to his seat and belted in. "Give us a view of the station, Corporal."

The aft camera came online. The station hung, slightly worse for wear with its pockmarked outer skin. The details of the station grew less distinct as they drew farther away.

"What's our time?" he asked.

"Three minutes and change, sir."

How far away did they have to be before they were safe from an exploding space station? Graves stared out the window, trying and failing to estimate the distance. Farther than they were right now, he was sure of that much.

"General, what the hell are those things?" Ortega called, pointing out the right window toward the far curve of the planet. A string of cylindrical shapes, seven of them, rose from the horizon. The Haven ships were colossal creations, each one larger than the Neo space station by an order of magnitude. The milky white domes gleamed in the sunlight.

As they drew closer, the Haven ships moved into a diamond formation.

"What are they?" Ortega asked.

"That's the future of humanity, son," Graves said. "That's why we're here. It's a chance for humanity to start o—"

A bolt of pure energy lanced out from the crown of the Neo station. It sliced across one of the cylindrical ships. The elongated structure began to separate like a great whale split in two in the seascape of space. The sections spiraled apart in slow motion.

Bits of spinning debris emptied from the broken vessel like confetti. Even at this distance, he knew what they were. Frozen bodies, limbs splayed in every direction, tumbled away from the craft, blown free by the atmosphere inside.

People, hundreds—thousands—of people.

Graves closed his eyes. His first thought wasn't the cost of that loss of life, or whether or not the six remaining ships were enough to accomplish their mission. He simply wished in the form of a prayer that Jansen's ship was safe.

"Ho-lee shit," breathed Estes. "How many...?"

"Three thousand," Graves whispered.

A blue glow appeared at the rear of the lead Haven. One by one, the same flare bloomed from the engine of the remaining ships, brightening the blackness of space.

"How much time?" Graves asked. His tongue dragged the roof of his mouth.

"Thirty seconds."

*C'mon, c'mon, get out of there.*

The blue glow intensified, and the Havens drew into a closer formation. Rickard had told him of the need for the ships to sync their nav systems down to the nanosecond to ensure they'd end up at the same destination.

"General, look." Estes was pointing at the station. The laser was booting up again, gathering energy into a pinpoint of light.

"No, no, no," Graves whispered. His fingers pressed against the glass. Jensen, Luca, Rickard, and eighteen thousand other souls were out there...

The explosion that destroyed the space station threw the dropship into a crazy spin until Ortega had the presence of mind to hit the autopilot. They used the last of their thruster reserves to regain control of the craft.

Graves had hit his head on the window. He swiped blood from his eye, peering into the blossom of wreckage from the shattered space station, looking for the Haven ships.

They were gone.

They made it, he told himself. They made it.

He unbelted from his seat, floating free. Ortega joined him at the window, passing him a bandage from the first aid kit.

After a few minutes, Ortega unbelted from the pilot's chair. "Well, sir, I've got good news and bad news."

"Good news first," Graves said. "For the love of God." He rested his head against the cool window. Debris from the explosion rained into the atmosphere, creating trails of fire in the sky. The view from the ground would be spectacular.

"We've got lots of food. Enough to last for weeks, I'm guessing."

"Bad news?"

"We have no thrusters left and our orbit is decaying. I'm no pilot, but the nav system tells me we've got about twelve hours until we burn up in the atmosphere."

Graves watched another piece of the space station meet a fiery death.

"But..." Ortega continued.

"There's more?"

"We'll run out of oxygen long before we burn up."

Graves took that in. He wasn't sure it mattered. The Havens had gotten away. The Neo station was gone. Mission accomplished. "Any booze in the supplies?" he said.

"Nope."

"Well..." Estes said. "Shit."

When the atmosphere in the dropship got thin, they donned pressure suits and floated free in the cabin. Like clockwork, every minute the emergency beacon would ping a distress call. Graves knew with all the debris and confusion around them, any chance of the distress call being heard, much less responded to, was slim. Worse than slim.

He closed his eyes. He dreamed about a lighthouse and a girl who had no fear. A girl who would stand on the railing far above the rocky shore and scream into the wind. Even now, he felt himself being pushed by the wind.

"General, wake up!" Ortega put his helmet against Graves's and screamed as he hauled at his arm. Graves floated to his feet. He heard a banging noise.

Ortega was tapping on his helmet. Graves blinked, trying to recall the hand signs used in space flight. His radio! His radio was off.

He chinned on the helmet receiver.

"Dropship, stand by for entry, this is *Dauntless*. I repeat, stand by for entry."

# 27

## MING QINLAO • TAULKE HEADQUARTERS AND HABITAT COMPLEX, MARS

When she woke up, the only voice in Ming's head was her own. MoSCOW was gone, and its absence left her with a sense of empty panic, a feeling of being less than whole.

Ming tried to shift her position and groaned. Her body felt like she'd been run through a meat grinder. She touched her face. Clean bandages covered her right eye, the smell of antiseptic underwrote all her senses, and her body felt clean. Her one good eye focused on the bank of monitors and she caught the Taulke logo on the corner of the screen.

Back on Mars. Lander had been as good as his word.

Lander rested in a chair, his big frame bent into an awkward curve, his unshaven jaw resting on a clenched fist. He was wearing the same clothes as when she'd last seen him.

"Lander," she whispered. It even hurt to speak.

Lander snapped awake. He looked as bad as she felt but offered her a tired smile anyway.

"She lives."

"Barely." Ming found the bed control and raised the bed. Sitting up made it easier to breathe. "How long?"

Lander shrugged. "I did a hard burn all the way back, so two days getting here. You've been here for about eighteen hours."

That explained the muscle pain. Hard-gee fatigue combined with immobility for almost a full day.

"How are you feeling?" he asked. "Doc Bishop says you might have some short-term memory loss." His eyebrows knitted together, and Ming realized he was actually worried about her.

"I remember you were supposed to kill me and you didn't," she replied. "How did that go over with the boss?"

Lander cleared his throat. "If by 'the boss' you mean Tony ... he doesn't much like it when things don't go his way. But Anthony told me to keep an eye on you. That's something, I guess."

Ming's head throbbed. Despite Tony's threat on her life, it was Anthony she had the biggest beef with. She just hoped Ruben was safe. He was Sying's problem now and probably safer for it.

"Ming! You're awake!" Viktor Erkennen bustled into the room, an ill-fitting white lab coat stretched over his shabby gray suit. The touch of his pudgy fingers on her brow was gentle. "You did not follow my directions about MoSCOW. I told you not to wear it for too long." Doctor Bishop followed but let Viktor take the lead.

Ming leaned her head back on the pillow. "I know, I know—radiation sickness. But you can treat me for that, right?"

Viktor shared a guarded look with Bishop.

"We've been treating you since you arrived, Dr. Qinlao," Bishop said. "Very aggressively. *Too* aggressively, if you ask—"

"Tut-tut," Viktor said, fussing with the monitor showing Ming's vital signs. "Everything will be fine in due course."

The silence that followed was uncomfortably loud. She didn't need MoSCOW to know Viktor was lying.

"There's more, though, isn't there, Viktor?"

Lander turned away from the bed. His body language screamed bad news.

"Viktor." Ming gritted her teeth from a flare of pain. "Tell me now."

"You didn't follow my directions," Viktor said again. This time his words carried less the tone of a disappointed professor, more that of a sorrowful friend. "I told you not to wear it any more than necessary, but you stayed integrated with MoSCOW for nearly an entire day."

"Which means what, Viktor?"

He wrung his hands. "I don't know, not exactly. I did a brain scan and the right side of your brain is enlarged."

"You mean swollen?"

"I mean ... changed." His eyes searched her face. "Do you feel different?"

Ming tried to take stock of her thoughts, but she was unable to focus. "I can't tell."

"We're not sure the damage is permanent," Bishop offered quickly.

"But it might be," Ming said. A tiny surge of panic flooded her mind, making thinking even harder.

"It is ... possible," Bishop said.

Viktor covered her hand with his own. "You will make a full recovery, Ming. Trust me."

"You should rest," Bishop said. Viktor nodded and gave her hand a final squeeze before he turned away. Lander resumed his seat next to the bed, studying her.

Ming pushed aside the panic, forcing herself to organize her thoughts. She ran back through the last minutes on the space station. MoSCOW had uncovered something—something important—and flagged it for her ... it was just beyond her grasp, a missing word on the tip of her tongue.

She closed her eyes, letting her mind relax, float from one idea to the next. Lander's hands on the controls, the debris field, the space station...

The space station!

Ming opened her eyes.

"My memory is coming back," she said to Lander. "I want to see Tony. Now."

---

**Anthony Taulke • Taulke Headquarters and Habitat Complex, Mars**

Anthony steepled his fingers and studied the woman across the desk. Elise Kisaan was tall and lithe, with straight dark hair that hid the New Earth Order tattoo on the back of her neck. Her face was relaxed, her dark eyes unreadable.

"Well?" she said, breaking the silence. Her voice was low and serenely confident.

"Well, what?"

"Am I crazy? What did your psyche doctors tell you?"

Anthony sat back in his chair to hide his discomfort. Her self-assuredness in a setting where he had the clear advantage was off-putting.

"What makes you think I have doctors evaluating you?"

She tapped an elegant fingertip to her temple. "It's what She said you would do."

"Cassandra?"

Elise nodded.

"But you've already told us Cassandra was a construct, not a real person. She—it—was a computer program."

"Artificial intelligence. There's a difference." She seemed to be enjoying the repartee.

"Yes, there is, but whatever you call it—Her," he corrected himself as she started to object. "Whatever you call Her, you still haven't told me the most important piece of information."

Elise raised an eyebrow.

"Who made Her?" Anthony said. "Someone created Cassandra. Who was it? Was it you, Elise?"

She shook her head gently. "I am Her vessel, not her creator."

He resisted the annoyance building up inside him. Someone was behind the Neos, someone with deep pockets and a willingness to play the long game against Anthony's interests. If Cassandra was nothing but a tool in this fight, then who was wielding the weapon?

He glanced at the digital report on his desktop. The psychiatrist who'd examined Elise Kisaan had concluded that she was not mentally ill. Fanatical, yes. Single-minded and cold-blooded in her actions, yes. But crazy? No.

And if she knew who was behind Cassandra, she wasn't about to tell him.

"Well?" she said again. Her wisp of a smile mocked his discomfort.

"Well, what?" This was his meeting, his office—why was he playing this ridiculous guessing game?

"My seat on the council? Have you decided?"

He swiped the desktop dark, stood, and paced to the window, buying time again. Tony's second dome was almost complete, ahead of schedule. Nighttime had fallen across Valles Marineris, hiding the deeper corners of the canyons in shadow. The view offered him no solace. He missed the reassuring glimmer of the Pacific Ocean. He missed Earth, if he was being honest with himself.

Elise was silent behind him, thankfully. He really had no choice but to come to an agreement, not if he wanted Earth as part of the equation. While the destruction of the Neo space station had stopped the weather war for now, Elise assured him the Lazarus nanites were still under her control. She'd simply made them dormant. A demonstration of her power to Anthony and the others on the council. Her leverage. Even Viktor could not guarantee that separating the key from Elise Kisaan would mean recovering control of Lazarus.

The weather crisis was solved—for now. Maybe that was enough —for now.

The council was in place and he was firmly in control again. Viktor and Adriana could be counted on to support him. Xi Qinlao had gotten what she wanted—Ruben, anyway—and had committed to supporting Anthony. He felt a twinge of regret for the way he'd treated Ming, but it had been necessary at the time.

He would find a way to make it up to her. Maybe a seat on the council for her as well. Now, wouldn't that be interesting? Xi and Ming on the same governing council.

"You need me, Anthony," Elise said in his ear, making him jump. He'd been so lost in his own dreams of what the council could accomplish, he hadn't heard her approach.

"Need you?" He tried to laugh like the king of CEOs that he was, but it sounded forced, even to his ears.

"Your council has expansion plans," Elise said, her breath moist against his skin. Anthony restrained a shiver. "Mars, the Moon, Titan, asteroid mining ... you might even launch a mission after those Haven ships. You need me, Anthony."

How the hell did she know all that? Fear walked on tiny feet up the back of his neck. It seemed to linger where a Neo tattoo would be.

"You've no doubt considered the size of the workforce you'll need to make that happen," she continued, still uncomfortably close. "I can reshape the Earth into the breadbasket of the solar system. Food for thought?"

Elise withdrew, chuckling quietly at the pun. She perched on the corner of his desk, her ankles crossed.

"What about the people?" he said.

Elise's confident smile slipped. "The people are the problem. It is Her will."

"And you have military forces in place to handle any, um, issues that come up with the Earth governments."

"She will provide." Confidence brimmed again in her gaze.

"And where is Cassandra now?" Anthony asked. "Was she destroyed in the explosion?"

"Cassandra is everywhere," Elise said. "Cassandra lives through me."

Anthony swallowed. If that wasn't crazy talk, he didn't know what else these shrinks needed to make a diagnosis. Still, whatever her mental state, she was right: if he was going to make the council work, he needed Earth firmly in his pocket, and that meant he needed her and her agricultural family ties.

"All right, I'll allocate a seat on the council to the Kisaan family."

"No," Elise said, her smile evaporating.

"No? I thought that's what you wanted."

She advanced again, less subtly this time. Anthony fought the impulse to take a step backward. When she leaned in, he could smell her perfume. "I have no family except Cassandra. The seat is mine and mine alone."

Anthony nodded, wanting more than anything for this creepy encounter to be over. "The seat is yours."

She held out a delicate hand. Her grip was cool and dry. "And I will give you the Earth," she said.

He watched her walk away, straight backed, her dark hair swaying gently with each step. No trace of the lurking menace that hid behind the elegant exterior. He didn't relax until the door closed behind her.

Anthony settled himself behind his desk and reopened the report from the team of doctors who'd examined Elise Kisaan. For all her self-confidence, he wondered why she hadn't brought up what she surely knew the doctors would report to Anthony.

Elise Kisaan was pregnant.

## 28

## MING QINLAO • TAULKE HEADQUARTERS AND HABITAT COMPLEX, MARS

The light rapping at the door stirred Ming from a fitful doze. She'd turned off the pain meds in an effort to be mentally sharp. That might have been a mistake.

"Come," she called in a harsh whisper.

Tony sauntered into the room, brandishing his smile like a shield.

"I hope you feel better than you look, Ming." His dark hair curled precisely over his left eye, and he grinned at her in a lopsided way he probably assumed was adorable. She ignored his greeting.

"I know about the station," she said.

His smile slipped a fraction, then returned.

"What station?"

"The one that went *boom*. The registration was hidden, of course, but I dug through the shell companies and aliases to the original founder. Taulke Industries."

The discovery had come from the mounds of data MoSCOW fed her when they'd first boarded the station. At the time, she was too focused on her mission to notice the detail. The days since had helped it float to the surface of her conscious mind.

Tony shrugged. "My father has his fingers in so many pies—"

"But it wasn't your father, was it? It was you."

The skin around his eyes hardened and he scowled. "There's no way you can know that."

"I know it." Her voice box was drying out again, and she desperately wanted a drink of water. "And I know about the arrangement with Lander, too."

Tony's demeanor took on a stony, piercing quality. "You didn't call me here for a confession. What do you want?"

"You owe me."

More at ease now that negotiations had begun, Tony found a friendly smile again. "You want a favor from Taulke Industries that you can keep in your hip pocket?"

"No, I want a favor from Tony Taulke when I need it."

He stared at her, then nodded. "In exchange—you keep what you know to yourself?"

"That's the deal," she said. "And one more thing, Tony. Lander works for me."

He blew out a breath. "You can have him, and good riddance. Anything else, Queen Ming?" He moved to the door, his back rigid. He'd been bested by a half-dead woman with only one good eye, and it stung.

Her self-satisfied smile came easy, but she was feeling the lack of morphine now, and there was still work to be done. Time-sensitive work. "Just leave. This is supposed to be a clean room."

As Tony retreated, Ming heard him offer snide congratulations to Lander.

Lander reentered, frowning. "I work for you now?"

"Consider it a gift for saving my life. Besides, when Tony and the old man clash, you don't want to be in the middle."

There was genuine relief in his face. "Thanks, Ming. I owe you one."

She pressed a button to jack up her pain meds. Bliss coursed through her system like cool water. Ming closed her eyes before she spoke again. "I need you to do one more thing before you go get the bath you so desperately need."

"Your wish is my command."

She cracked open her good eye. "Tell Anthony I need to see him as soon as possible."

After Lander left, Ming drifted off again. The sound of the door opening woke her, but she feigned sleep. Let him see what kind of damage he'd caused. If he had any sense of decency left, that might give her an edge.

She heard his breathing, knew he was close.

Ming opened her eye. His face was soft with worry, his eyes damp. Good.

"Why did you send Ruben back to my aunt?" she said in a small voice.

He startled when she spoke, then sat on the edge of her bed. "I'm sorry, Ming. I didn't have a choice. Your aunt demanded Ruben in return for helping us."

Ming forced herself to reach out and take his hand. "I understand."

"You do?" He gripped her fingers. Ming hoped her enjoyment of this moment didn't show. It was too easy. Anthony was as easy to manipulate as a child.

"She won't touch Ruben," Ming said. "Auntie Xi knows better. But I need your help."

He squeezed her hand. "Anything."

"I'm afraid, Anthony. Tony sent Lander to kill me."

Shock turned to anger on Anthony's face. "Tony did that? Why?"

"Isn't it obvious?" She waited a beat. "He sees me as competition."

"Competition?" Anthony seemed genuinely perplexed.

"For your affection."

The permutations of what that could mean played out on his face.

"Ming, that's absurd," Anthony insisted. "Tony wouldn't try to kill you just for—"

"Ask Lander."

Anthony took her hand in both of his. "How can I help?"

"I need your protection, Anthony. No one can touch me if I'm part of the council. My aunt won't dare make a move against me if I'm under your protection."

"Consider it done." He bent over her, and Ming closed her uninjured eye. She fought not to flinch as Anthony's cool, dry lips kissed her on the forehead. "You're like a daughter to me," he whispered. "Maybe Tony's not wrong about that."

"I feel the same way," she lied. "But ... I need sleep."

"Rest," he said, standing up. "Won't your aunt be surprised to see you at the next council meeting?"

Ming let herself smile. Genuinely, this time. The morphine was working.

"Yes. Won't she, though?"

---

Ming knew what to expect when she entered the newly minted boardroom.

Eyes. All on her.

She directed the maglev chair to enter the room at a modest speed, the better to let their gazes linger. They could have thought of her in so many ways—deposed CEO, kidnapper and fugitive, the mysterious badass who'd delivered Elise Kisaan to the Taulkes—but their eyes held only one emotion: pity.

Her face was still a horror show. She'd decided to shave her head for now, since all the hair on the right side of her scalp had fallen out. She could have worn a wig, but Viktor assured her that the hair loss was only a temporary condition. Her right eye was open and mostly functional, although the sclera was still crimson. That too would pass. The regrown skin on the right side of her face had a pinkish tone to it that made her look younger than her age. Who knows, maybe she'd start a new cosmetic treatment: burn off all the skin on your face and get new skin grafted on.

Let them see her as weak—she would turn it to her advantage.

Anthony nodded to her from his place at the head of the table. As he explained to the group how he'd designed the room especially for council meetings, Ming noticed Tony's impatience to get started. She scanned the wall behind Anthony's head. The corporate logos of the five family businesses—Taulke, Rabh, Erkennen, Kisaan, and Qinlao—were arrayed. A worm turned behind her breastbone when she saw that Xi had altered her father's design, adding what looked to Ming like a scar of jade across the center.

But today—today was about beginnings.

She sat next to Anthony, who wore a pseudo-military uniform with the Taulke logo on the left breast of a dark blue tunic that buttoned on the shoulder. Tony wore a stylish jumpsuit that emphasized his lean frame as he lounged in a chair to his father's right. He appraised Ming with a cool detachment, as if they'd never spoken of assassination attempts and suspicious ties to the New Earth Order.

Viktor chatted quietly with Adriana Rabh on Ming's left. The banking matron was attempting to school him in the subtle points of fine wine. Elise Kisaan openly stared at Ming from across the table. The cryptokey glittered on her wrist. According to Lander, Elise was the liaison between the Neos—considered friends now—and the council.

The holo pod in the chair next to Elise sprang to life. Auntie Xi was seated behind Ming's desk in her father's office in Qinlao headquarters, the Shanghai skyline behind her. The view caused a hard pang of nostalgia.

Xi's eyes flared when she saw Ming, then she nodded stiffly. "Niece," she said, her voice filtered through the speaker.

Ming stared at the image until her aunt broke eye contact.

Anthony rapped on the table with a piece of Martian rock. "This meeting of the Council of Corporations will come to order."

Ming half listened to the drone of the conversation as it unfolded on such mundane subjects as the assignment of roles at board meetings and the establishment of bylaws. She silently assessed the board members. The aloofness of Elise Kisaan, the businesslike authority of Anthony, the practiced insouciance of his son. Viktor's mad scientist enthusiasm next to the elegance of Adriana Rabh.

And Xi. She felt the icy glare of her aunt and met Xi's disdainful gaze without fear. But behind that scowl was an unease. Ming could see it even if no one else could.

*Let it fester in your soul, Auntie. I will be there soon.*

A vote on some triviality was required and she voted with Anthony. He favored her with a smile, which she returned. She would remain his faithful ally—until the time was right.

Her attention wandered. She was still weak, at least in body. Attending this council meeting was probably not the best idea, but her plans required gathering real-time data.

Without reflection, she formed a thought: *Record the meeting. Notify me of any required interactions.*

*"Yes, Ming,"* replied a familiar, comforting voice.

The response felt natural, like drawing a breath or blinking her eyes. It felt like she was whole again.

Ming Qinlao let her mind drift.

## HOSTILE TAKEOVER
### Book 3 of The SynCorp Saga

**The enemy of my enemy is my friend...until they're not.**

Cassandra Station is space dust. Anthony Taulke and the Council tighten their grip on Earth's resources to feed their ever-expanding empire. Inside the Council, jockeying to divide the spoils of corporate conquest has already begun—and so has the backstabbing.

Meanwhile, we the people make our peace with a new normal: nothing is within our control.

But new forces are on the horizon. An unlikely Neo leader emerges, rumors swirl of a rebel military alliance, and General Graves gets sucked into a new impossible mission.

**Experience SynCorp. Experience our future.**

**Get your copy today at**
**severnriverbooks.com/series/the-syncorp-saga**

# ABOUT THE AUTHORS

**David Bruns** is a former officer on a nuclear-powered submarine turned high-tech executive turned speculative-fiction writer. He mostly writes sci-fi/fantasy and military thrillers.

**Chris Pourteau** is a technical writer and editor by day, a writer of original fiction and editor of short story collections by night (or whenever else he can find the time).

Sign up for Bruns and Pourteau's newsletter at
severnriverbooks.com/series/the-syncorp-saga

Printed in the United States
by Baker & Taylor Publisher Services